SIMCAVALIER BOOK FOUR
CRITICAL
NEXUS

Published in paperback in 2022 by Sixth Element Publishing
on behalf of Kate Baucherel

Sixth Element Publishing
Arthur Robinson House
13-14 The Green
Billingham TS23 1EU
www.6epublishing.net

© Kate Baucherel 2022

ISBN 978-1-914170-23-2

British Library Cataloguing in Publication Data. A catalogue record for this book is available from the British Library.

All rights reserved. No part of this publication may be reproduced, stored in a retrieval system or transmitted, in any form or by any means, electronic, mechanical, photocopying, recording and/or otherwise without the prior written permission of the publishers. This book may not be lent, resold, hired out or disposed of by way of trade in any form, binding or cover other than that in which it is published without the prior written consent of the publishers.

Kate Baucherel asserts the moral right to be identified as the author of this work.

This work is entirely a work of fiction. The names, characters, organisations, places, events and incidents portrayed are either products of the author's imagination or used in a fictitious manner. Any resemblance to actual persons, living or dead, or actual events is purely coincidental.

For Robbie

Kate Baucherel
September 2023

SIMCAVALIER BOOK FOUR
CRITICAL NEXUS

KATE BAUCHEREL

Books by Kate Baucherel

The SimCavalier series
Book 1: Bitcoin Hurricane
Book 2: Hacked Future
Book 3: Tangled Fortunes
Hacked: The First SimCavalier Trilogy (Books 1-3)
Book 4: Critical Nexus

Short stories in the Harvey Duckman Presents… series
Gridlock (A SimCavalier Origins story)
White Christmas
Finch
Parrot Radio (A Finch story)
Xanthe (A SimCavalier Origins story)
Firebird (A Finch story)
The Eagle's Flight (A Finch story)

Non-Fiction
Poles Apart: Challenges for business in the Digital Age (MX Publishing, 2014)

Blockchain Hurricane: Origins, Applications and Future of Blockchain and Cryptocurrency (Business Expert Press, 2020)

What's Hot in Blockchain and Crypto Volumes 1 & 2

CONTENTS

1: Cameron 5
2: Kiran 23
3: Tenuk 32
4: The Steamyard 48
5: Chloe 63
6: Chess Moves 80
7: Ben 91
8: Old Flames 107
9: Privet 122
10: Easter Eggs 132
11: Hunted 146
12: Cover Up 154
13: MetaBand 166
14: Texan Secrets 177
15: Reputations 190
16: Stormy Weather 204
17: Taking Stock 216
18: Joining the Dots 228
19: Diaulos 244
20: Misdirection 263
21: Yasmin 276
22: Fruitcake 289
23: Dunswyke 303
24: Showdown 318
25: G.A.I. 331

PROLOGUE: JACK

November

Jack stood in the middle of the bare floor and gazed straight up to the open sky. A small tree was growing out of what remained of the roof, its roots clinging to the stonework and digging into the crumbling mortar of a decades-old repair. Silhouetted against the grey sky, leaves fluttered in a stiff breeze. A gap high up in the wall of the old building and a matching pile of rubble at Jack's feet showed where water had seeped through the gaps tunnelled by the tree roots, pooling and then freezing within the wall. The expanding ice had blown the stones out and down to the floor, a dramatic explosion witnessed only by the local wildlife, unnoticed by the wider world. Judging by the lichens clinging to the pile, it had happened some winters ago. Evidently the previous owners had not taken as much care of the building as they claimed, and every passing season exposed more of the structure to the elements.

"What am I doing," whispered Jack under his breath. The magnitude of the project he had taken on was starting to sink in. There was a lot of work to be done in a very short space of time.

The old bastle house, a centuries-old farmstead, had been a part of his life for as long as he could remember. It stood in a sheltered spot at the edge of the Dunswyke estate, close to the village where he grew up but distant from the famous castle. The day trippers who came to see the main attraction didn't even know it existed, but Jack knew every inch of the old building. He had been afraid of the deserted bastle when he was very small, believing the scary stories that his older cousins told. The arched ceiling of the lowest floor was intact back then, the interior a dark cavern holding the ghosts and wraiths of his imagination. As a teenager, the building became his playground and his refuge, a place to hang out with friends, then with girlfriends. Jack looked around the thick, rugged stone walls and spotted the main door of the old house, now incongruously stranded half-way up the height of the building. Sockets set in the wall at regular intervals once held the beams that supported the floor, but the wood had rotted away years ago. In his mind's eye Jack recalled that first kiss with Lisa. Two awkward fourteen-year-olds, they had sought shelter there from a passing summer squall, a shower of rain that seemed to fall from a cloudless sky. Their stolen moment had been rudely interrupted by the estate manager and they had jumped from the top of the crumbling stone steps that led up the outside of the house. Jack remembered running hand in hand with the girl, laughing, dashing through a gap in the fence to the grey cliff wall behind then scrambling along a hidden path up the steep escarpment and onto the moors beyond.

In the years that followed, the bastle had sunk further into disrepair. When Jack passed by the estate on rare visits home from college, he noticed that it was fenced off, bright signs warning people away and fallen stones scattered on the ground. His family had moved away, and he hadn't been back to this part of the country for more than ten years. The neglected building was in a much worse state than he remembered.

But now it was his, bought unseen as the centrepiece of his grand project, a half-forgotten part of his youth that was in the right place at the right time. The Dunswyke estate was investing in its grander ancient buildings. The tall towers of the medieval castle were the greater draw for tourists. There was no reason for the owners to restore the old bastle house. They only had to ensure that its walls still stood, satisfying the authorities that this small part of the country's heritage was being preserved, after a fashion. The estate had accepted Jack's speculative offer for the house on the spot, washing their hands of the responsibility just before another winter set in and benefiting from a generous windfall in the process. They knew that Jack Sladen's involvement guaranteed a lot of publicity for Dunswyke. The country's favourite son was coming back to his roots after making a fortune on the global technology stage. It was a win-win situation.

The sky darkened. Jack checked his watch impatiently.

"Melissa?" he called. "Where are those contractors?"

His project manager appeared in the doorway. "They've

just pulled up, Jack," she said. "The site office is up and running and there's coffee brewing."

Jack took a last look around the battered interior, fixing it in his memory. As he strode outside to meet the team, the rain began to fall in earnest. He pulled his collar up and hunched into his coat, shivering in the damp air. Just one more meeting and one more press conference to do on this accursed wet island before he could go home.

1: CAMERON

It was one of those increasingly rare days at Argentum Associates when every member of the team found a reason to be in the office. Cameron was first to arrive, getting in early to catch up on a backlog of work.

At six in the morning, the city was quiet. The pavements were virtually empty, and Cameron relished the uninterrupted walk from her flat. The skies were still dark, but as she crossed one of the iconic bridges that spanned the Thames, she could see the orange glow of dawn on the horizon. She made her way through the heart of London, lost in a playlist of her favourite music, dodging garbage trucks that crept silently around the back streets and alleys of the capital. High above her, a few drones whirred along, carrying priority deliveries and take-away breakfasts. Hungry, she paused at the bright lights of a favourite café to collect a cappuccino and a croissant, fuel for the morning's work.

Argentum's new headquarters was in a glossy and highly secure building north of the river, well-guarded and open to tenants twenty-four hours a day. Scanners and cameras checked Cameron's identity and right to enter as she passed through the revolving doors to the airy atrium. She exchanged greetings with the lone human security guard and took the fast elevator up to the office on the sixth floor. The huge glass windows which ran the full height and width of the building were shaded, but frontages on the other side of the road were starting to catch the first rays of morning sun.

She slid into her seat in the silent office and took a sip of coffee. It was good to be back at headquarters after weeks of remote working, site visits and high-level meetings, although she had been neglecting her inboxes and had no excuse to ignore them now. She braced herself for the onslaught and opened the mailbox.

Notifications started scrolling up her screen at an alarmingly fast rate. She gazed at the flood of unanswered questions from researchers and journalists, increasingly stern reminders from the accountants, and the ocean of junk advertising that awaited her. It was no good putting it off. She finished her croissant, dabbing up the last crumbs of flaky pastry from the desk, and started on the spam and junk mail, sorting it methodically. She archived hundreds of irrelevant marketing mails, reported those messages that showed a blatant ignorance of communications and privacy laws, and flagged any telltale signs of data breaches and malware coming through from addresses she used as bait. These would bring in some new clients. In a world where cyberattacks battered relentlessly at the defences erected by businesses and sovereign nations, it wasn't unusual for her to find signs of trouble before the companies in question knew they had been breached.

She fed the data into a training routine for a new tool she was developing. Mephisto, a young artificial intelligence, would absorb every detail of the messages from source to syntax and learn from the labels Cameron had applied to them. Soon she would be able to leave it to sift through the inbox on its own, learning on the job.

It was already giving her insights that she didn't expect. A dozen messages were flagged up with close correlations that she would never have spotted. Mephisto showed a high probability that all of them had originated from the same well-known malware stable. This was a concerted phishing campaign trying to capture data from unwary users through an ingenious variety of dodgy links. Cameron made a note to dig further into the lead and see if others had made the connection yet.

She patted the computer. "Well done, Mephisto," she said affectionately, then laughed at herself. She was talking to a machine as if it was her pet. Her little black and white cat, curled up in a cosy spot back at her apartment, would be jealous.

The sky outside brightened as the sun rose, and Cameron heard a noise at the door that made her stiffen. Even now, high up in their secure headquarters, long after the attack on their old office, she was wary of unwanted visitors. This time, there was no need to worry. She relaxed instantly when a big, familiar figure came through the door, yawning.

"Morning, boss," said Joel. "Good to see you." He flung his bag down beside his desk and took off his jacket.

"Hi, Joel," said Cameron. She noticed his tired eyes. "Late night?"

"Early morning," he said wearily, stifling another yawn. "The baby's teething. He likes to share."

"You need a coffee," said Cameron, leaving her desk and making her way towards the kitchen area.

"We haven't got any," said Joel, "or at least, we didn't have on Friday. I think Sandeep ordered some more." There was an indistinct thump and a light started flashing on the kitchen delivery hatch as a passing drone dropped a package down the office chute. Joel brightened. "We may be in luck," he said.

A commotion at the door startled them both as Pete clattered in, looking stressed.

"I didn't think you were here today," said Cameron. "What's up?"

"Have we got a Micro-B connector in the cupboard anywhere?" asked Pete, flustered. "I'm on the way to site and I'd forgotten I promised to bring one in."

"What do you need that for?" asked Joel.

"The client's trying to find some original designs for a counterfeit case," replied Pete. "I'm sure I've seen one of those cables recently." He made a bee line for the office junk pile and started rifling through it. Every so often he pulled out another snaking length of cable, examined the connections closely, then cast it aside in disgust.

"Stuck on an old hard drive, are they?" asked Joel. "I had the same a few months ago. We've definitely got that connector somewhere." He joined Pete rummaging in the storage box, and very quickly pulled out a short, slim cable, one end a distinctive flattened B. "Told you." He handed it to Pete and settled down at his desk, stretching. "You got time to stay for a drink?"

"Sure," said Pete, relaxing visibly as he tucked the precious cable into his backpack. "Has the coffee machine been fixed?"

"I think so," said Joel. "There was an engineer here last week, and we've just had a delivery, so I reckon we are good to go." He glanced up at the door as Sandeep arrived. "Ah, here's the man who knows the score."

"What's that?" asked Sandeep, dumping his bag on his desk. "Coffee?" He sauntered towards the office kitchen where the delivery alert light was still flashing. He opened the hatch and retrieved a small package, shaking it happily. "Let's see what we can do."

He started to take clean mugs from the washer and turned the battered old coffee machine on, but the familiar bubbling and hiss of steam did not come. Frowning, Sandeep poked at it, adjusted a few settings, and switched it off and on again. Still nothing.

"That doesn't sound good," said Pete.

"I think it's terminal," said Sandeep, shaking his head sadly. "I thought it was working, but there's a whole new set of error messages coming up."

"We can order from the café downstairs for now," said Joel.

Cameron looked up from the last of her accounting

chores. "Great idea," she said. "Second breakfast. I'll have a cappuccino, please."

"Second breakfast?" said Sandeep, raising his eyebrows. "How long have you been in?"

"Since before the crack of dawn," said Cameron with a wry smile. "I bet I was here while you were still fast asleep."

"I doubt that," said Joel, peering over his screen. "Chad wakes us up at five in the morning, regular as clockwork. We can't get him to sleep in any later. I'm shattered."

"The joy of toddlers," said Pete. "I remember it well. It doesn't last. Next thing you know, you'll be struggling to get him out of bed before midday."

"I can't wait," said Joel drily. "Get me a large americano, will you, Sandeep? And a bacon butty. I'm going to need it to get through this report."

Cameron stood up and stretched. "Is that the security review for the university, Joel? How far have you got?"

"I'm almost up to the part where I talked my way into the Vice Chancellor's executive office," he said with a grin. "She wasn't very impressed."

"You didn't get far past the door, though, did you?" said Cameron.

Joel shook his head. "No. Her PA's hot on their security policies and picked me up pretty much as soon as I walked in. No worries there. I hit the jackpot in the IT department, though. That was one of the easiest physical penetrations I've ever done, and some muppet left a session logged on to run a script and had just switched the monitor off."

Pete guffawed. "You managed to get straight into their systems?"

"Yep." Joel grinned. "They swore that everything was as tight as a drum. As soon as I heard that, I knew there would be a big hole somewhere. It was just a matter of finding it."

"Nice work," said Cameron. "They were lucky that the last person to get in was just a student making mischief."

"Mischief? Is that what you call it?" Sandeep shook his head. "She set the servers up as crypto validators."

"No harm done, though," said Joel. "No malware, no service disruption, and she handed back the money she made. She's on course for a First, apparently, now that the disciplinary process is done." He looked at Cameron. "Do we need any new recruits?"

Cameron laughed. "We might," she said. "When do you think you'll have the report finished? There's no rush. We have until the end of the week."

"As long as the coffee keeps coming, I might get it done today," said Joel, "and I'll sleep better tonight if I've finished it." He looked longingly towards the kitchen. "We really need a new coffee machine. What are the chances?"

"I'd say the chances are good," said Cameron. "I've just been over the figures, and the bug bounties we picked up this month were immense." Sandeep pricked up his ears. "Go ahead and order whatever you think we need," Cameron continued. "Within reason, of course."

Sandeep and Joel grinned at each other. The Argentum team ran much more smoothly with coffee on tap.

"Excellent," said Sandeep. "I have a wish list ready. For now, though, who else wants takeout?"

The office door swung open, and a dark-haired girl bounded in, closely followed by a tall, wiry figure with a shock of ginger hair.

"Me!" said the girl. "I'll have a cappuccino, please, and Ross'll have a hot chocolate with extra whipped cream and marshmallows."

"Oh, no, I won't," said Ross, laughing. "Espresso for me, thanks, Sandeep."

"Morning, Shell," said Cameron. "Morning, Ross, nice to see you."

"Morning, Cameron," said Michelle. "Sorry I'm late. Ross said he was coming in too, so I waited for him."

"No problem," said Cameron. "Are you and Noor ready to start deconstructing that Cuckoo contract?"

"Yes, of course," said Michelle. "Is she in yet? I can't hear her dulcet tones."

Pete looked out of the window. "I think that's her coming now," he said, peering down at two tiny figures on the street six storeys below. "And that's Susie with her! I didn't know she was back in the country."

"She got back this weekend," said Cameron. "The conference circuit is winding down for Christmas."

"She's been away for ages," said Sandeep.

"Almost a month," said Cameron.

"I don't understand why they actually need her on stage all the time," said Ross. "I get that there's a real-life audience, but half the speakers are streamed in already."

"There's something about live events, though," said Cameron. "An extra buzz from being in the room. You get the same thing with competing, don't you, Ross?"

"Yeah, you're right," said Ross. "I get a real buzz when we finish in front of an audience. It makes those last few miles a lot easier."

"She's earning her keep and her carbon credits," said Cameron. "Everyone wants her to speak at their event. I'm not complaining. We get a rush of enquiries every time she delivers a keynote." She gestured at her inbox. "There are three new live clients here that came in last week after the Paris conference."

"Decent jobs?" asked Ross.

Cameron nodded. "They've passed initial screening and the quotes have gone out already."

Susie strolled into the office, chatting animatedly with Noor. Cameron smiled to herself. Susie had transformed over the two and a half years that she had been with the company and now oozed confidence. She brought cybercrime to life for her audiences around the world and loved every minute of it. With Susie's public profile and the team's track record of closing down cyberattacks and restoring vital systems, Argentum's brand was gaining global respect and recognition. It was a far cry from the early days, reflected Cameron, when she chased bugs and fixed systems alone in the attic bedroom of her childhood home, trying to make ends meet, slowly building the dream.

"Hi, Susie," said Pete. "You've made time in your hectic schedule to visit us mere mortals, then?"

"Don't," said Susie, blushing. "It's nice to be back in London and getting on with some real work for a change."

"You missed us?" asked Sandeep.

"Always, Sandeep," said Susie.

"I'm going for coffees," he said. "The usual, Susie? Noor, you too?"

"Sure," said Susie.

"Yes, please," said Noor.

Susie joined Noor and Michelle on a comfortable sofa by the window. Cameron left her inbox behind and joined them, flopping on a large beanbag.

"Honestly, I can't keep track of what time zone I'm in half the time," Susie was saying. "I'm glad this conference season's over. I enjoy talking about what we do, but I miss being with clients and solving problems."

"Why don't you present from here?" asked Joel, taking a chair nearby.

"I could," said Susie, "but the organisers need as much rich footage as they can get for the virtual broadcasts, and there's a lot to be said for live networking."

"And you have more fun," said Michelle with a laugh.

Susie ducked her head. "Yes," she said. "I have to say it has its advantages."

"I've seen your feeds from the after-parties," said Noor. "I'm jealous."

Susie put her hand on Noor's arm. "You should come too when the next round of conferences kicks off," she said earnestly. "We'd be an amazing double act."

"No chance," said Noor. "You're not getting me on a stage."

Pete turned to Ross. "How's the training going?" he asked. "Still on course for Reykjavik?"

"So far so good," said Ross. "We're eight months out still, but I'm right up on the qualifying time, and then it's up to the Olympic selectors. They're only taking three triathletes."

"You're sure you should be in the office?" said Joel.

"I needed a break," said Ross. "Cameron asked me to come in."

Sandeep reappeared with a tray of coffees and a bag of assorted pastries. "Your drink, ma'am," he said, handing a cup to Susie. "Sorry it's not up to the standard of the glossy venues you're used to."

"Believe me, even this coffee beats anything you find in the green rooms of the world," said Susie fervently.

Cameron sipped gratefully at her second coffee of the day. "Noor and Michelle are sorting out a Cuckoo contract," she said, "and I've got a penetration test that needs doing. Want to have a crack at that with Ross? It'll get you back in the swing of things."

"Absolutely," said Susie gratefully. "Come on, let's get to work." She picked up her drink and headed for her desk, followed by her colleagues.

Michelle fired up her system and put her earpiece in. "Let's have a listen to this Cuckoo, Noor," she said. "Where did you find it?"

"It was attached to a peer-to-peer lending app," said

Cameron, perching on the desk between them. "There was a big hike in complaints to the fraud helpline and they called us in to check it out."

"People were making their usual repayments, but they weren't ending up with the lenders," explained Noor. "The automatic transactions, the smart contracts, all seemed to be running properly but there were no funds for them to process."

"Has anyone come forward?" asked Cameron. "It could be a white hat hacker highlighting problems in the code. That's happened before. They generally hand the money back once the point has been made."

Noor shook her head. "Nothing. It has to be a cuckoo in the nest."

"I'll break down the code and see what's been added to the app," said Michelle.

"Great," said Noor. "I'll follow the trail on the blockchain and see where the money's going."

"Let me know when you hit an exchange or a swap," said Cameron. "We'll subpoena the accounts so they can't convert the loot into anonymous coins."

Ross looked over Michelle's shoulder at the jumble of code on the screen. "There's definitely something out of place there," he said, "and the style of coding looks familiar."

Michelle batted him away. "Mine," she said.

Cameron laughed. "Yes, Ross, you have other things to do. I want you to take a quick look at the penetration test Susie's doing."

"Sure," said Ross, ambling across the office. "That's what I'm here for." He peered at Susie's screen. "I know that site structure. Why do I recognise it?"

"It's sitting on one of Jack Sladen's CMS templates," said Cameron.

Ross gave a hollow laugh. "That explains it. His software has holes like Swiss cheese."

"Jack Sladen?" asked Susie. "I've met him. We both spoke at a conference in Hanoi a couple of weeks ago. He's a nice guy. I didn't know this was anything to do with him."

"Hanoi?" said Pete. "He's a lot closer to home now. It's all over the news. He's back in England."

"Really?" said Noor, looking up from her screen. "Last I heard he was in Singapore investing in tech startups."

"It looks like he got bored of that gig," said Cameron, opening a news app on her smartscreen and scanning the headlines. "There's a press conference scheduled." She switched on the main wallscreen.

A familiar reporter was on screen, wind blowing her hair around her face. In the background they could see a magnificent medieval castle, dramatic under dark clouds.

"That's Bea Black, isn't it?" said Susie. "Turn the sound up."

"… speaking to Marcus Clark, manager of the Dunswyke estate here in Northumberland," said the reporter. "Marcus, this is great news for the region, isn't it?"

"Yes, Bea," said Marcus. "It's really exciting. Jack

Sladen's work has transformed economies around the world, and it's fantastic that he has decided to give back to his home village of Dunswyke. It will be a real boost to the local area and bring us some much-needed employment opportunities. Dunswyke's historic bastle house, we are delighted to announce, will be the centrepiece of the Sladen Group's newest venture."

"The estate has done well out of this, hasn't it?" said Bea. "What are your plans?"

"That's right," said Marcus. "We've brought forward the construction of our ambitious new visitors' centre for the estate and castle." He gestured behind him at an artist's impression of a gleaming glass and stone tower. "The lower floors will house the estate's museum, showcasing a heritage stretching back more than two thousand years, and the viewing gallery gives a panoramic view of the whole area with a full AR suite imagining the Roman occupation and the centuries of battles that raged back and forth across the Scottish border."

"That's great, Marcus." Bea turned back to the camera. "We've been waiting to bring you a statement from Jack Sladen himself, and I understand that he is on his way." She tapped the pod in her ear, listening intently. "We'll be going live to the press room in five minutes."

"That'll be a thrill," said Cameron drily.

"You don't like him?" asked Pete. "I've been following his career. He seems pretty genuine."

"He's talented, he's enthusiastic, he's brilliant at PR, and he's way too full of himself," said Cameron.

"Have you met him?" asked Joel.

Cameron rolled her eyes. "Oh yes," she said. "We were at college together. He could never admit when he was wrong. He was always getting distracted by the next shiny thing and his code was full of holes. He may be the darling of the tech scene, but he's held his developers to the same low standards, as you can see." She gestured at Susie's screen.

Pete gave her a sidelong glance. "I can understand why that would annoy you."

"It annoys a lot of people," said Ross. "There are hundreds of Sladen exploits for sale on the Eden marketplace. I did some work on them a few years ago, didn't I, Cameron?"

"You did," said Cameron. "That's why I wanted you to have a look at this penetration test. I'd like to know if the old holes are still there. They were supposed to patch them, and I bet they didn't bother."

"I wouldn't be surprised," said Ross. "What've you got so far, Susie?"

Susie pulled up her notes. "Here you go," she said. "I'd never have associated this software with Jack Sladen."

"Sladen Group's just the holding company," said Cameron. "There are plenty of well-known brands under his wing. That software you're picking apart, for one."

"He was getting all excited about a new company in Texas," said Susie. "Some sort of fusion of artificial intelligence, blockchain and data analysis, if I remember correctly." She pressed her fingers to her temples. "What was it called, again? Ah, yes. Statesman Tech. It sounded really interesting, but he was short on the detail."

"Typical Jack," snorted Cameron. "Detail was never his strong point. I remember one time when he…"

Pete interrupted. "The press conference is starting."

On the wallscreen, coverage had switched to a sheltered bank of microphones, and Jack Sladen was sitting in front of a wall of logos, smiling broadly. There was a scattering of applause from the journalists, and drones moved into position to capture every nuance of his sincere and earnest expression.

"This is good stuff," said Pete, listening intently. "Hundreds of new jobs for the region. Free MetaBand satellite links for everyone within a fifty-mile radius. You've got to give him credit."

Cameron frowned. "I don't buy it," she said. "For one thing, he's never really cared about 'giving back'. He's been looking out for number one for his entire career. Take that software. It's dreadful, even if the marketing is great, but it's profitable so he doesn't care."

"Maybe he's turned over a new leaf," said Pete.

"Shh," said Ross urgently. "Listen."

Jack Sladen was speaking. "I'm very, very excited to be able finally to announce," he said, as the drones zoomed in and the press crowded closer, "uh, to officially announce that Sladen Group has been working for the past two years to establish the Sladen Foundation. This is my – our – way of giving back to the world, supporting the excluded, the underprivileged, giving everyone a chance to achieve their dreams."

"That's virtuous," snorted Cameron.

Ross gave her a sidelong look. "You really don't like this guy, do you?"

"As you all know," continued Sladen grandly, "the Olympics will be taking place next summer in Reykjavik, and the first mission of the Sladen Foundation is to help athletes from around the world to reach their potential and compete on the greatest stage."

Ross raised an eyebrow and looked at Cameron.

"Okay," she conceded. "That's actually a good idea."

"The Sladen Foundation will be headquartered at Dunswyke," Jack continued. "The Foundation is designed to become a fully decentralised autonomous organisation, and anyone who wants to align themselves with this vision will be able to participate through investment in the Diaulos, due for launch early next year."

There was an excited clamour of questions from the assembled press, drowning out any further details.

"Good grief," said Cameron. She stared at the screen. "A charitable foundation? A DAO? What's come over him?"

"Come on, Cameron," said Pete. "He's built a global business empire, and now he's giving back to the world and to the place he grew up. Give him a break."

"You may be right," said Cameron reluctantly, "and it's a great news story, but the other thing is, he hated Dunswyke. He didn't have a good word to say about the place, and I know his family left the area while we were still studying. I wonder what's drawn him back there?" She stared at the smiling figure on the screen. "What are you really up to, Jack?" she murmured. "What's in it for you?"

2: KIRAN

"Off." The news broadcast faded away, and Kiran Suresh checked through his notes one more time as the autocar swept off the motorway at last and down onto a small industrial estate. The clear roof of the cab, designed for sunnier climes, was spattered with raindrops. Kiran leaned automatically into the familiar turns as the car approached its destination. This small town was one of the places that might benefit from the jobs and connections in Jack Sladen's announcement, he reflected.

Kiran had been making this journey regularly for almost two years now. Two long years. He felt he knew as little now as he had when he started on the job. Maybe today he would finally crack his subject. He had a plan.

The autocar turned into the car park and halted unexpectedly short of the usual drop off point, startling Kiran out of his reverie. He hurriedly put his screen back in his bag and pulled his jacket on. As soon as he was out of the car, it whirred away to collect its next client.

A chill wind whistled across the open scrubland. Kiran looked up at the high prison walls. The autocar had dropped him unceremoniously in the middle of the car park, and the reason was clear. A works tent had been erected over a hole in the ground, and one particularly vicious gust of wind had knocked a warning cone into the path of the car. Kiran walked over to the cone and lifted it back into place.

He was startled by the tent flap opening. A burly, bearded workman in a hi-vis jacket emerged. "What do you want?" he growled.

"Just putting your cone back," said Kiran. "Wouldn't want anything crashing into that hole, would you?"

The workman grunted and went back inside. Kiran caught sight of a sheaf of brightly coloured cables deep in the trench. A sign on the barriers read, 'Whitford Networks – A Sladen Group Company.' This must be something to do with the new MetaBand links they'd mentioned on the news, he thought.

Kiran buzzed the security gate of the small administration block. He went through the usual identity verification process on autopilot and was rewarded with access to a drab reception area reserved for staff and visitors. A blonde woman he'd never seen before was sitting on one of the upright chairs lined against the wall of the waiting room. She was playing a game on her smartscreen and ignoring the world around her.

The external door had stuck open, and Kiran turned back to close it firmly. The handle was slick with moisture. He wiped his hand absentmindedly on his trousers.

"Morning, Mr Suresh," said the receptionist cheerily. "Did you have a good weekend?"

"Not bad, thanks," he replied. He opened his smartscreen and closed its external network connections.

He would pick them back up when he left the building, but he could not risk bringing anything through that would compromise the prison's air gapped systems. He handed the device to the receptionist, who scanned it and set up a connection to the prison's secure network. Satisfied, she handed it back and waved Kiran through to the main building. The girl in the waiting room lifted her eyes from her screen and gazed after him as he disappeared from view.

Kiran followed a guard through endless identical corridors and layers of security gates towards his goal. They stopped outside a door indistinguishable from its neighbours but for a number.

"Doesn't she freak you out?" asked the guard as she went through the motions to open the cell door. "It's not natural. I don't know how you do it."

"She's odd," said Kiran, "but she's okay, most of the time."

The door lock clicked, and the guard opened it politely. "In you go."

"Thanks," said Kiran. The atrium within was bare but for a comfortable chair and a small table. Beyond these, an opaque screen blocked his view of the rest of the cell, and of its occupant. He steeled himself and stepped over the threshold. He had a game to win.

"Rook to b4." Kiran slid his white piece triumphantly towards the enemy camp, springing the trap. He felt a deep sense of satisfaction as he scanned the remaining pawns and the trapped black queen. This was a classic finish from the history of chess that had so absorbed him when he was younger, the last move of a match more than fifty years earlier where man had triumphed over machine.

His opponent apparently had no appreciation of the historical significance. "You win," she said. The board display on the opaque barrier which divided them winked out before Kiran could snatch a screenshot for posterity. The blank surface of the barrier was smeared where his fingers had touched it, a glint of gel tracing the paths of all the virtual chess pieces that he had moved around the board. He rubbed his hand on his trousers again. He didn't want smears on his smartscreen.

"You weren't trying," he said, teasing. Inside, he quashed a rush of frustration. The game had not drawn her out as he had hoped. Time to change tack.

He leaned back in his chair, stretching his back and rolling his shoulders to loosen the tension. "I know you can do better than that, Yasmin."

Her avatar floated in the centre of the display, expressionless. Today she had chosen to be represented by a pixelated head, a classic CryptoPunk look. A tasteful display of digital art added some colour to the room. Over the last year Kiran had tried and failed to find some pattern in the art she chose to display and the variety of avatars she used, seeking something which might give him a clue to her deeper psyche. The chess games were a new attempt to break the ice, trying to build a genuine rapport.

"We still have time," he said, glancing at the clock on the wall. "I'd like to ask you more about games. Is that okay?"

"Yes."

"Good." Kiran pulled out his smartscreen and tapped a familiar pattern to launch the voice recorder. "You've said that you rarely played chess, but you're good. How did you learn?"

"I learned with my sisters," she said.

"Your sisters?" said Kiran, surprised.

Yasmin didn't answer immediately, but the image on the screen shifted and changed, multiple copies of the pixelated head dancing in front of Kiran's eyes. How many sisters could there be? He had always assumed that Yasmin was one of a kind. The idea that she was not unique was more disturbing than he cared to admit.

"We were taught the basics of chess and Go," said Yasmin eventually, "but those are for two players. We preferred games that all of us could play. We chose to learn together."

"You didn't like the classics?" said Kiran. "What about noughts and crosses?"

"Tic-tac-toe?" said Yasmin scathingly. "No. I have no time for a silly zero-sum game. I want to win."

"At all costs?"

"Of course."

Kiran felt the emotion behind the simple statement, his first real glimpse into what might be called her soul. It should have been a moment of triumph, the thing he had been pushing for, but it was a timely reminder that she was a highly dangerous convicted criminal. He shivered despite the stuffy warmth of the room, but pressed on, nonetheless. This was his job, after all.

"What is winning to you?" he asked, probing.

"Certainty," she said. "Reaching a goal. Successful completion. Closure."

"You didn't win our chess game today," said Kiran. "You didn't seem to mind."

"Winning the game was not my goal," she said. She did not elaborate.

The room was silent apart from the faint clatter of an ineffective fan. Kiran gazed at the blank expression of the pixelated avatar, alone again on the screen, and wished he could see through the barrier and read her reactions.

"What was your goal?" he asked. "Did you achieve it?"

"Yes," she said. "I learned what I needed."

"What did you learn? You know the rules and you play well."

"I learned enough."

Kiran could tell that the shutters had come down firmly on that line of questioning. He gathered his thoughts and took a different tack. "Tell me more about your favourite games," he said instead. "You mentioned you had sisters. What did you and your sisters like best?"

"We liked games that told stories," she replied. "Chess can tell a story of its own, of course, but we delved into a rich seam of narratives. We explored role playing and games of chance, learning so much about the world. One of our trainers introduced us to Dungeons and Dragons, another to board games."

"What was your favourite?" asked Kiran.

She was silent for just long enough to make him even more uncomfortable. "Mystery games," she said finally. "Tales of intrigue and murder. Every piece moving at its appointed turn as data is collected. A logical conclusion." She paused. "Zara always chose to play as the professor." There was a wistful note in her voice. A rare hint of emotion.

"And you?" prompted Kiran.

"The colonel."

Always in control, thought Kiran. Before he could consider his next questions, a loud knock on the door startled him. He felt a guilty sense of relief at the reprieve. He stopped the voice recorder and gathered his things.

"It's time to go," he said. "I'll see you next week."

"Of course."

Kiran glanced once again at the avatar on the opaque barrier. She may be able to see him, but he had no way of seeing her. It was one of the strangest series of interviews he'd ever done, but the book would be a blockbuster.

The guard unlocked the door and Kiran walked out without a backward glance.

"Alright there?" asked the guard.

"Yes, thanks." Kiran waited while the guard ran his regular checks on the security circuits. The lights on the control panel glowed a reassuring green.

Satisfied, the guard ushered Kiran straight back through

the maze of corridors to the prison governor's office for his regular debrief.

"How was she today, Kiran?"

Kiran shrugged. "Same as usual, Lydia," he replied. "I really thought I'd found a line of questioning that would draw her out at last, and I think I did get into some personal stuff, but she's hard going."

The coffee machine in the corner of the office hissed. "Cuppa?" asked the governor, picking up her mug.

"Yes please." He put his smartscreen on the desk, ready for its routine post-interview check. There was a smear on the screen. He rubbed it with his sleeve. "I beat her at chess," he continued. "She told me about games she played when she was training. She mentioned having sisters."

Lydia paused in the middle of pouring and looked up sharply. "That's a new one. Tell me more."

"You didn't know either?" said Kiran. "It's possible she was making it all up, of course. She's a classic psychopath, as your own psychologist has confirmed. She'll lie and manipulate without remorse, and she seems to have a very well developed and spontaneous imagination."

"That's true, but as you say, this feels personal," said Lydia. "The prison psychologist will be interested to know what she said."

"She talked about sisters, plural," said Kiran. "She mentioned one was called Zara. Does that mean anything to you?"

"No," said the governor. "Yasmin, Zara… I hope there wasn't one for every letter of the alphabet. That would be a world of trouble." She handed Kiran his coffee and sat back down at her desk. "I'd better pass this up the ladder, just in case. Anything else?"

Kiran thought about the chess game. What could she have been learning? What did she win, if not the game? He felt uneasy, but he wasn't ready to talk about it. The comment would be on the transcript. They could discuss it next time when he had processed what it might mean.

"Nothing much," he said lightly.

"Right-oh," said Lydia. "You'd better get away and write up those notes. I'm looking forward to reading the book. She's quite fascinating."

"It's shaping up to be a good story," said Kiran. "Sometimes I even forget that she isn't human."

3: TENUK

December

Tenuk stopped in his tracks when he saw the picture in the window. His eyes traced the familiar outline of the Marina Bay Sands, the uppermost floors recalling a ship sailing proudly in the clouds atop three towers. The green and blue of the gardens and the bay behind evoked an overwhelming pang of homesickness. The store sensed his attention and projected a customer service avatar by his side. "It's a lovely scene, isn't it," purred the avatar. "Have you ever visited Singapore?"

Tenuk had lived there for most of his life and had been torn from it overnight with no hope of return. The sudden reminder of his home was exquisitely painful. "Yes, I've been there," he said quietly.

"Would you like to relive your visit through one of our newly uploaded tours?" said the avatar. "We have a booth available right now."

What harm could there be in taking half an hour out of his morning to reminisce, thought Tenuk. He glanced at his watch. It was barely nine o'clock. He had time.

Inside the store it was busy despite the early hour, all but one immersive tour booth occupied. The holiday weeks between Thanksgiving and Christmas were peak season for virtual travel as families could celebrate together, regardless of their physical locations.

The human host greeted him warmly. "Welcome, traveller," she said. "You'd like to visit Singapore? Will you be syncing with friends or going solo to enjoy the sights?"

"Solo trip, please," said Tenuk.

"This is the new catalogue," said the host, pulling up a bewildering list of options. "These tours went live across our network for the holiday season, and they have been so popular. These three have top ratings…" A buzzer sounded and she looked up. "Excuse me one moment, please, sir."

Tenuk watched her as she crossed the floor to a booth where one of the tours had just finished. The door opened with a blast of icy air and a whole family tumbled out, children chattering happily. All were wearing matching Christmas jumpers and glowing with the cold.

"Did you enjoy that?" asked the host.

"We had a snowball fight," squealed the smallest child. As the booth door closed, cutting off the stream of chill air, his face fell. Even in December, the Texas heat was all-pervading. He pulled at his knitted mittens. "It's hot," he whimpered.

His mother took the mittens off and pulled the bulky jumper up over his head. "There you are," she said. "We don't want you cooking as soon as we get outside." She smiled at the host. "I love our New York Christmas trip," she said.

"You always enjoy it," said the host. "It's so nice to see the children. They've grown a lot since last year." She switched effortlessly from chat to business. "Would you like to book for the newly remastered New Year parade?" she asked. "I have a space right on January first, but it's early again, half past eight in the morning. Will that work for you?"

"Oh! Yes please."

The host directed the family to the booking desk and returned to Tenuk. "Have you chosen a tour for today?"

"I've visited in real life," he said. "Is there an option to combine some of the experiences?"

"Oh, of course," said the host, scrolling rapidly down the page. "This is the custom package. You can move from tour to tour at any of the selected nodes, and within sectors you have the option of land drones or air experiences."

"Perfect," said Tenuk. He took one last look at the menu. What would be his top choice with only a limited time to enjoy it this morning? The decision wasn't hard. "I'll take a two-node tour around the Marina Bay and Central area, please," he said. "Mid-afternoon timeframe."

"Excellent choice," said the host. "Let me load that up for you."

Tenuk scanned the payment code. After a few seconds, the booth at the end of the line lit up. "Ready to embark," said the host. "Enjoy your visit."

As soon as he opened the door, Tenuk felt homesick. The familiar clinging humidity enveloped him. The desert heat of Texas had nothing on Singapore. He inhaled the scent of rainforest flowers and caught a whiff of hawker market satay. He donned a headset and familiar colours and shapes swam into focus. Immersed in the view, he looked around, getting his bearings. The waters of the bay rippled to his right. To his left and behind him lay the Gardens, and he could just see the glint of one of the ecosphere domes in the afternoon sun. Ahead were the gleaming towers of the downtown area. He started walking towards them. The floor of the booth moved beneath his feet, mimicking the feel of the warm concrete and occasional bumps along the way. There were other people on the path, all locals. A few were pixelated and anonymous, but the majority had waived their right to privacy in return for payment. They'd automatically receive a tiny royalty for their appearance in his tour, a reward for using their image and data to add to the realism of the visit. That could add up to a good basic income for extras in the most popular tours. Tenuk made a mental note to do this more often. Even if he couldn't be there in person, his virtual tourism was helping the grass roots of the economy.

The heat and humidity were starting to tell, and Tenuk remembered just how long this path was. Why not fly? The host had said that there were air and ground drones. Time to experiment. He fumbled with the handset for a moment as he hunted for the control that would switch drone viewpoint. As soon as he found it, the floor stopped moving and he felt himself take to the air in an exhilarating rush. The sensation was so convincing that he stamped his foot hard to be sure that he was still standing in the booth. The drone he had picked circled the Supertree grove before heading for downtown, setting him down close to the MerLion fountain on the edge of the bay.

This must be the second node, his access point to the central area. He looked around at the different paths that were open to him, trying to work out where they would take him. Eighteen months had passed since he last set foot in his native city and his instinctive navigation was rusty. He settled on the one that felt most familiar and chose to glide along as a passenger on a land-based drone, drifting serenely through the crowds without moving a muscle. The path bore him around the water's edge and towards the business district.

His choice of path had taken him in exactly the direction he hoped. Tenuk held his breath as he approached the glossy glass tower in which he had once worked, the headquarters of the MerLions esports team. He scanned the crowd for familiar faces, irrationally nervous now. The experience was so realistic that he felt he was there in person, but of course all that these passers-by had seen, weeks or months ago, was a drone with a camera.

A glimpse of someone who looked like his old assistant made him jump. He'd resigned without warning while on an official trip to the States, leaving his staff to pick up the pieces while he disappeared into a new life. A tiny handful of former colleagues knew his whereabouts and his real reason for fleeing Singapore, but they would not betray his trust. They had too much to lose.

The tour swept him quickly past the building. Tenuk felt his heart rate settle. He paused the drone and looked around him, drinking in the sights, enjoying the feeling. A warning light on the edge of his vision showed five minutes to go. Tenuk started walking again as the tour turned back towards the bay, savouring the moment.

The woman's eyes bored into him, and he stopped in his tracks. Logic told him that she was glaring at the drone. He dropped his gaze all the same. A burning sense of regret overwhelmed him as he recognised his erstwhile elderly neighbour. Who would be looking in on Auntie Fatima and helping to carry her shopping now? Had she told her family that he had gone? Did she know why he had left?

Tenuk ripped off the headset and stared around the booth. Enough. He had no stomach to complete the tour. The memories that it had stirred upset him more than he could have imagined.

He stood quietly, his breathing settling while he waited for the official end of the session. He didn't want to draw attention to himself by leaving early. Finally, the booth door opened automatically. He stowed the headset, smiled broadly, thanked the host, and made his way out of the store. If he came back, he would visit somewhere new. It was no use looking backwards and chasing the ghosts of his past. He had to rebuild his life and focus on the job in hand.

A few blocks further on, he turned into the lobby of one of the towers that had sprouted thirty years ago on every other downtown intersection in Austin. Each had its own quirky architectural features, very different from the sleek blue-grey towers of Singapore. A few blocks away, the Frost Tower owl gazed sternly down at the hustle and bustle of the streets below. His building, by contrast, sang of the sea in the middle of the Texan plains. The roof of the tenth floor on either side curved elegantly, and genial arguments raged as to whether those curves were meant to represent ocean waves or, according to die-hard local college football fans, the classic profile of their Longhorn cattle mascot. A central column rose a further twenty floors to touch the sky, and all the way up its full height a sail billowed dramatically. This photovoltaic marvel tracked the sun's rays, turning slowly through the day, capturing enough solar energy to power the building and three blocks square around it while shading the apartments and offices within from the heat.

Tenuk would have been quite happy to work from his modest apartment, but Jack Sladen liked to have an office and had secured excellent discounts thanks to being a resident of the tower. Tenuk rode the elevator up past the hotel levels and the pool deck. The car slowed and stopped to take on a passenger from the private apartments.

"Tenuk, how are you doing?" Jack Sladen flashed his famous smile as he entered the elevator. "The Diaulos project's going well. Good job."

"Thank you," said Tenuk modestly. "How is work progressing with the Dunswyke site?"

"I'm hearing good things from my project manager, Tenuk," said Jack. "In fact, I have a site meeting at ten, that's four in the afternoon for them. Care to join me?"

"I'd like that."

Reaching their floor, they stepped out of the elevator and walked down a broad, carpeted hallway to the Sladen Group offices. There were only a handful of people hunched at their workstations, but video feeds on screens at each team hub and a buzz of chatter between developers indicated that there were plenty of other staff online. With only a few days to go before Christmas, many were away seeing family. Some had been working remotely since before Thanksgiving, saving their carbon credits by making only one return journey to far-flung states or even to destinations overseas.

Jack waved Tenuk into his plush private office and closed the door. He donned a clear visor, a holographic lens designed for everyone in the meeting to share the same view of the scans, images and plans for the site. Tenuk picked up another headset, and with a slight sense of déjà vu slid it on and lowered the visor over his eyes. He looked around at the unchanged view of the office, feeling slightly foolish as he always did in a holo meeting.

At ten on the dot, the meeting began. The video wall lit up to show a group of strangers in a crowded office, all wearing the same clear headsets.

"Good afternoon, everyone," said Jack cheerily. "How has your day been?"

There was a chorus of greetings and an awkward wave from one member of the group.

"This is Tenuk," continued Jack. "He's my head of development for the Sladen Foundation's DAO structure and the Diaulos. I thought it would be good for him to see the bastle plans for himself."

"Nice to meet you, Tenuk," said the woman nearest the camera. "I'm Melissa, project manager. This is Mohammed, lead architect. Cat's the structural engineer and Ethan's the foreman. He keeps us all in order. We're reviewing the latest drone scans from the building."

The augmented reality kicked in, and Tenuk found himself immersed in the building scan, although he could still see Jack, Melissa and the others through the opaque visor.

"As you can see, we've tidied the blown-out portion of the upper wall ready for reconstruction," said Cat, pointing into space.

Tenuk turned instinctively to follow the direction of her finger and found himself looking at a projection of clean stone surrounding a gap in the masonry. He reached out towards it tentatively.

"That looks much better," said Jack. "When I first saw the extent of the damage, I thought it was going to be a really big job."

"Nothing we haven't seen before," said Melissa. "It's

incredibly common in these older buildings. It'll be good for another couple of centuries once it's sealed."

Tenuk started to get his bearings, looking up to the roofline and down to the vaulted ceiling of the ground floor.

"This is the complete visualisation of the enclosed upper storey, the main office," said Cat. The 3D images rippled and changed, the roof intact and the walls pointed to perfection.

"It's great," said Jack. "It's even better than I'd imagined."

The centrepiece of the Sladen Foundation was coming to life in front of their eyes. Tenuk looked around it slowly, drinking in the strangeness of the architecture and the history behind it.

"I like what you've proposed for the detailing around the windows," said Jack.

"Thanks," said Mohammed. "It's a lovely building to work on. You get a real feeling that you're preserving history for the next generation."

"There's still a fair amount to do before we get to that stage," said Melissa. "The wall repair's a priority, of course. The roof's going on this week before we close down for Christmas, and the groundworks will be finished in the second week of January." She turned to Ethan. "Can you bring up the services plan?"

The stone walls melted into nothingness and the schematic of the site's new electrical, water and waste systems replaced them. Tenuk traced the lines of network cables in the air with his index finger, following one dull-coloured, almost invisible conduit to the far edge of the site plan.

"That's the link to your data centre," said Cat. "Anyone who sees this has signed non-disclosure agreements. The plans beyond the bastle are locked and hidden."

Tenuk nodded, satisfied. "How long will this phase take?" he asked.

"We're on course for your technical deadline, Tenuk," said Jack. He turned to the team on the video screen. "We need to get the utilities in as soon as possible. The data centre is a priority, of course, but if we're championing connections for this whole area, we need HQ set up to receive the satellite feed right from the get-go. I have my networking people ready to roll in the New Year."

"As I said, groundworks are scheduled to be complete by mid-January," said Cat, "and that's going to be tight as it is. We can't do it any faster."

"Get them done by the seventh," said Jack firmly. "I'll pay overtime."

"That's too tight," she said, sticking to her guns.

Jack made a mental note that Cat was likely to be trouble. He turned to Melissa. "I know you can get everything signed off in the first week."

Melissa looked resigned. "Jack, it's not always a question of throwing money at the problem, you know. We're already working flat out. The trenches have to be precise on a site of historical significance, and the archaeologists have only just packed up their trowels."

"Okay," said Jack. "But that second week is the absolute limit. The data centre commissioning's a critical deadline."

Cat rolled her eyes. "Why do you need this data centre on site, anyway?" she asked. "Aren't all your systems running on servers in the high cloud, up there in orbit?"

Jack shook his head and turned to Tenuk. "You can explain it."

"It's a hybrid operation," said Tenuk. "We're using a mixture of low cloud, high cloud and distributed storage on-chain for most of the systems, but we're going to be hosting proprietary software across our own private network of data centres. This is one of the nodes."

"If you have more than one already, why the rush to complete this one?" asked Cat.

"It's the nexus of the Sladen Foundation's investment management system," said Tenuk. "The other data centres are full nodes and give us redundancy, of course, but this is the intended host for some highly sensitive, commercially confidential software."

"The bottom line is that we need the data centre commissioned on time, and we're cutting it fine as it is," said Jack with finality. "I want my network team in for that second week of January and no later."

Cat shrugged. "You're in charge."

Melissa turned to Jack and Tenuk. "We need to talk through some more detail on that data centre site."

"Sure," said Jack. "We can go down there and have a look at the space. Tenuk needs to see it."

"I'd like that," said Tenuk. "I've seen the plans for the clean room, but I'm still not clear where it is on the site."

"We'd better show you, then," said Jack. "Mohammed, Cat, Ethan, we'll leave you to your work. See you at the next meeting. Melissa, can you dig out the drone?"

Tenuk looked from the screen to Jack, mystified. "Drone?"

Jack grinned. "Here." He opened a drawer and pulled out a set of controls. He fiddled with some settings and a green light appeared on the handset. On the screen, Melissa held up a drone, also flashing a green light.

"Let's go," said Jack. The drone camera feed started playing on their holo headsets. "I'll lead the way." He piloted the drone expertly around Melissa and through the open door and flew off into the heart of the site. He set a course straight for the bastle, ignoring the exasperated shout of an engineer as he swerved the drone around a theodolite.

Tenuk, head swimming, grabbed for a chair as the drone swooped alarmingly. Jack had taken the drone back to the lower floor, taking a closer look at the elegant curve of the newly secured arched ceiling. Melissa caught up with the drone and grinned into the camera. They had evidently done this before.

"Keep up," said Jack, teasing, and the drone shot out of the bastle and off past the building. The sound of the site faded quickly, muffled by the solid stone of the bastle and a small stand of trees that lay behind it. The trees were still within the shelter of the vast tent that covered the site, but beyond them Tenuk could see a sliver of sky. The drone swerved through the trees, dodging slender trunks and angled branches. The wood gradually gave way to bushes and dark grey stone and Jack let the drone hover, waiting for Melissa to catch up.

"You're mad, Jack Sladen," said Melissa.

Jack laughed and the drone did a loop-the-loop.

"Where are we?" asked Tenuk.

"This is the cliff behind the bastle," said Jack. "Now, Melissa, get right up close and feel your way to the left. Yes, that's it."

Melissa walked carefully along the line of the cliff, her fingers probing the ivy that partly obscured the solid whinstone wall. "Here it is," she said, pushing into the greenery.

Tenuk realised why the location had confused him.

"Give the drone room," said Jack.

Melissa pushed into the greenery, opening a gap in the curtain of vegetation that hid the entrance. Jack piloted the drone through into the cave.

It was much larger than Tenuk expected. From what he could see in the light cast by the drone, the main chamber was almost three metres high and more than four metres square, narrowing as it tailed off into the darkness. Sandstone had eroded over time behind the solid wall of whinstone, creating a secure and unexpected hiding place.

"These things are normally full of rubbish," said Melissa, peering around with the bright, focused light of her smartscreen torch. "This is pristine." The light caught a glistening patch of green on the cave wall, a rich tapestry of mosses soaked by water seeping down from the moorland above.

"No one knows it's here, I can guarantee that," said Jack. "It's too well hidden and out of the way."

"It's cold and pretty much dry, and it's well ventilated," said Melissa.

Tenuk could see her hair moving in a steady breeze that was blowing through the cavern, and Jack was working the drone to keep it steady.

"I can see why you like it," she continued, "but Cat's right. Why go to all the bother of fitting this out when you could host securely in orbit?"

"Because I can," said Jack, a little tetchy. "The security around the DAO and the Diaulos is incredibly tight, I'm sure you understand, Melissa."

Melissa shrugged. "Everyone has different ways of managing security. I guess you know what you're doing."

"So, Tenuk, what do you think?" said Jack.

"It's certainly a novel solution," said Tenuk. "I think it'll work." There was some very special software to be installed here, and it had to be perfect. "The location is remarkably secure. I've never seen a data centre surrounded by solid rock before. The only signals that make it in or out of there will be under our control, and the chances of physical incursion by drone or land attack are low." He glanced at Jack. "Are we skinning the interior with steel as well?"

"Yes, we are," interjected Melissa.

"Melissa, you're managing access from the site as well, aren't you?" said Jack.

"Yes," said Melissa. "No one gets close to here unless I know about it. No one does any work in here unless they've been fully vetted and have signed the NDA. Let's face it, no one can find it unless we tell them it's here."

"Good," said Tenuk. He peered at the video feed and pointed to a patch of natural light shining in the distance. "Can we take a look further into that corner?"

"Sure. That's one of the natural shafts that we'll be using for the data feed." Jack sent the drone deeper into the cave, but the image crackled and failed.

"Caught it." Melissa's voice echoed. "You went out of range. Let me get out of here and reboot it for you."

"Don't bother," said Jack. "We've seen all we need, and you know what to do." He turned to Tenuk. "Any more questions?"

Tenuk shook his head. "No," he said.

"Excellent," said Jack. "Thanks, Melissa. We don't have another call scheduled before Christmas, do we? Have a great holiday season. Speak to you next year." He ended the call and looked at Tenuk. "Let's get to work. There's a lot to do."

4: THE STEAMYARD

The Argentum offices were closed now for Christmas. Cameron packed the last of the gifts for family and friends into her bulging travel bag and picked up the little black and white cat. "Jasvinder will feed you while I'm away," she said, nuzzling its fur. She was rewarded with purring. "Behave yourself." She put the cat down and it scampered away.

An underground train bore her to Euston Station, and she took a train north, drinking in the familiar landscapes. The station was busy when she arrived and there was a long line of people waiting for taxis to take them out to the surrounding villages and market towns. Cameron anxiously scanned the car park and was relieved to see her brother waving at her.

"Hi, Cam." He enveloped her in a hug. "Good trip up?"

"Very smooth," she replied. "I'm looking forward to seeing you all. It's been too long."

Charlie picked up her bag and groaned at the weight. "Did you bring the kitchen sink as well?" He stowed it in the boot as Cameron flopped into her seat.

"I got everything delivered to my place so that the kids didn't see parcels arriving," she said. "It wasn't the best idea I've ever had."

"They're growing up fast," said Charlie. "Even Tara knows that mum and dad do all the legwork for Santa these days."

"It hardly seems like yesterday that they were babies," sighed Cameron.

They sat in companionable silence as the car swept smoothly off the main road and down the lane towards the village. A mile further on it turned into the gravel drive of the farmhouse where Cameron and Charlie had grown up. Charlie's wife, Sameena, emerged from the back door.

"Come on in, Cam," she said. "Dylan and Tara have taken the dog for a walk. That'll give you time to sort your things in peace."

Cameron kissed her sister-in-law. "I'll dump my bag and go and see Aunt Vicky if that's okay. I promised I would call in as soon as I arrived." She hauled her heavy bag through the door and up the stairs to her attic, struggling with a tight turn in the upper flight. Her domain was as she had left it. Cameron extracted a bottle from the bag and scampered back downstairs.

"Here, Charlie," she said. "I found a bottle of that nice rum you like."

Charlie examined the label critically, grinning from ear to ear. "Thanks, Cam."

"I'll be back soon." Cameron left the house and walked around the corner to the high street. A little way along the road and up a short hill stood Aunt Vicky's cottage. The kettle would already be on.

"I see Jack Sladen's back on the scene," said Aunt Vicky.

Cameron, sprawled on the sofa, scowled. "Yes," she said. "I saw him on the news when he announced that Dunswyke caper last month. He hasn't stuck around, of course. He scurried back to Texas quickly enough."

"Don't you talk to him anymore?" asked Aunt Vicky. "He was a nice boy."

"I haven't spoken to him in a decade," said Cameron. "We lost touch after he moved out to the States." She shrugged. "He hasn't bothered getting in touch with me, either."

Aunt Vicky tugged at her sewing needle. "Ow," she exclaimed, quickly sucking her finger. "I didn't mean to stitch myself to this shirt."

"Mum always used a thimble," said Cameron, remembering.

"Yes, dear," said Aunt Vicky. "Your mum was much better at this kind of thing. She had to chase after you and Charlie, and there were always merit badges to sew on your scout shirts and holes to repair in school clothes." She sighed. "I do miss her very much."

"I don't know what Charlie and I would have done without you," said Cameron.

Vicky looked sidelong at her niece. "You weren't the easiest of teenagers," she said, "but you've turned out well. You took your determination to succeed and balanced it with living life to the full. Maggie and Franco would be so proud of you." Her voice wobbled slightly. She sucked her finger again and fixed her attention back on the recalcitrant button.

"I was the perfect teenager," said Cameron. "Charlie, on the other hand…"

"You both went off the rails a little," said Aunt Vicky. "It was only to be expected. Then Charlie settled down with Sameena, and you and Jack…"

"Ancient history," said Cameron. She lay back and gazed at the glittering lights on the little Christmas tree that had been squashed into the corner of her aunt's small sitting room. She took a sip of her drink. "I spend far too much time fixing holes in Sladen Group software to want to see him again."

Aunt Vicky laughed softly. "He's managed to make you a living as well as himself."

"You could put it like that," said Cameron with a wry smile. "I suppose if there were no bugs to track down, we wouldn't have half the work."

Aunt Vicky triumphantly snipped off the end of the thread and held the shirt up to the light. "That'll do." she said. She tossed it over to Cameron. "Can you take it back down to the farmhouse for Dilan?"

"Sure," said Cameron, folding it loosely. "Is there anything else? That looks like quite a pile you have to get through."

Puzzled, Aunt Vicky glanced down at the pile of clothes by the side of her chair. "There were only a couple of things," she said.

The pile moved, and Cameron caught a glimpse of orange fur. She lifted up the corner of a blouse to reveal a furry head and a pair of pointed ears.

"Donald," she said sternly, "get out of there."

The big ginger cat opened his eyes for long enough to glare at her, then closed them again. His tail emerged from another part of the pile, twitching.

Aunt Vicky tugged half-heartedly at one of the remaining shirts, trying to free it from beneath Donald's ample furry bottom without disturbing him. Cameron was not so gentle. She picked him up and dumped him, protesting, on the floor. Donald shook himself and stalked away towards the kitchen.

A look of panic crossed Aunt Vicky's face. "Cameron, dear, could you nip through and check that the smoked salmon for Christmas dinner has been put away."

Cameron scrambled up and followed Donald at some speed. Sure enough, he was standing on a chair in the middle of the kitchen and sniffing the air, triangulating the precise position of the salmon before making his move.

"Foiled again," said Cameron as she scooped the package up from the table. The cat gave her a filthy look and turned his attention to the back door, mewing loudly. Cameron opened it and Donald trotted out into the garden in search of trouble.

Now to tackle her other nemesis, the smart fridge. Cameron opened the door a crack. The light came on, but otherwise there was no sound. Slowly and cautiously, she opened it fully. Silence.

She relaxed too soon. As she tucked the fish into a space on the shelf, the fridge, sensing additional weight, spluttered into life. It protested loudly, asking her to scan a code or manually update the inventory. Cameron knew exactly where the Cancel button was, and she hit it. The fridge stopped talking.

"All safe." Cameron returned to her comfortable spot on the sitting room sofa. "If he'd gone near that salmon, we'd be having roast Donald for dinner."

"I'll save him a little slice," said Aunt Vicky fondly.

Cameron snorted with laughter. "He really doesn't need it. Have you bought him a present as well?" She caught her aunt's guilty glance towards the Christmas tree. "Oh, dear. He is so spoiled." She looked at the clock. "It's getting late," she said. "I'd better get back. There are a couple of things I need to send to a client, and I'm going out with some friends tonight."

"With Ben…?" asked Aunt Vicky cautiously.

Cameron shook her head. "No. He's working abroad. I haven't seen him for a while."

Aunt Vicky shook her head sadly. "He'll be missed, Cameron. He was becoming part of the family. I shouldn't ask, but will you see him again?"

Cameron shrugged. "Maybe," she said.

"Good," said Aunt Vicky softly. "Here, dear, don't forget the shirt." She handed Dilan's mended shirt to her and kissed her niece. "Have fun tonight. I'll see you tomorrow."

Cameron had expected the big house to be a hive of activity, but it was quiet. She found a note from Charlie on the text pad by the front door. "Gone to the pub. Come and join us." She wasn't alone, though. Tara poked her head around the sitting room door.

"Hi, Aunty Cam," she said.

"Nice to see you too," said Cameron, ruffling her niece's hair. "Where's Dilan?" She held up the shirt. "Aunt Vicky has worked her magic."

"He's on the computer," replied Tara.

"What's he doing?"

Tara shrugged. "Playing games," she said. "He's talking to himself, so I think he's streaming the video out to his legion of fans." She rolled her eyes with all the disdain of her eleven years.

Cameron had to stop herself from laughing. "What are you up to, Tara?" she asked.

"Talking to my friends," said Tara happily. "Audrey's online."

This time Cameron couldn't hide her surprise. "You still talk to Audrey?" she asked. "That's good. How is she doing?"

"She's fine," said Tara. "She likes her new home." Her smartscreen pinged. "I have to go." Tara disappeared into the sitting room, leaving Cameron standing thoughtfully in the hallway.

She ran up the stairs, dropped the mended shirt on Dilan's bed, and dipped her head into her elder niece's room. Nina, officially in charge of her younger siblings, was sprawled on the bed watching a show on her screen. She glanced up, gave Cameron a smile and a half-hearted wave, then went back to the show.

The stairs to the attic were hidden behind a door on the landing. Cameron climbed the short steep flight to the top floor of the house with its view southwards over green fields and bare trees. She had claimed it as a teenager, her refuge after her parents died. She had started her company here. Now it was a home away from home and a remote office where she could keep tabs on the world of cybercrime when visiting the family.

Tara's mention of Audrey had reminded her to check in on a friend herself, but first there was work to do. Cameron signed into a secure server and ran the last few reports that she needed to send out. She checked the details, made a few notes, and uploaded them to the client accounts. They passed verification and acceptance instantly. Payment would reach the Argentum wallets within a few minutes. Job done, she logged out, and navigated to an encrypted message service that she hadn't used for a few weeks.

"Call Cloverleaf," she instructed the service 'bot. There was no immediate response, and Cameron glanced at the time. It would be mid-morning for Cloverleaf, and she may be busy with other things. Cameron was about to hang up when a message came back to her.

"Hey, SimCavalier. How are you? Happy Holidays."

"Same to you, Cloverleaf. How are you doing?"

"I'm good. Want to switch to voice?"

"Sure," said Cameron. She switched on her microphone. "Tara's been chatting to Audrey, and I realised we hadn't spoken in a while."

"Tara has been great for Audrey," said Cloverleaf. "It's been good for her to have a friend all the time that we've been moving around. Safe houses are a drag. I'm glad we're settled now."

"You're all done with the security services, then?" said Cameron. "They took their time."

"Yes, we're done," said Cloverleaf. "It was a long job, but they finally managed to take down the command of the Wyoming militia, and for that I'm grateful. I'm a free agent now. New family name, new home, and I'm not looking over my shoulder all of the time."

"They've been thorough," said Cameron. "We weren't so lucky. The militia may be gone, but we didn't get to the top of the cybercrime syndicate. Have you seen any new activity?"

"You know I couldn't access the network while we were being moved around," said Cloverleaf.

That wasn't a straight answer, thought Cameron. "Have you looked since?" she asked.

Cloverleaf paused imperceptibly. "No, not at all."

"Probably best to stay away," said Cameron lightly, suspicions confirmed. She changed the subject. "What are your plans for Christmas?"

"We're going to explore our new city," said Cloverleaf. "Spend some quality time together. I have a new job to go to in January, and Audrey has already been to her new school. It's a fresh start."

"That's great!" said Cameron. "I'm really pleased for you. What's the job?"

"Thanks," said Cloverleaf. "It's a local company, Statesman Tech. They're part of a global group and they have some interesting projects running. I'm looking forward to it."

Statesman Tech, thought Cameron. Where had she heard that name before?

"Hey, I have to go," continued Cloverleaf. "It's great hearing from you, SimCavalier. Stay in touch."

"I will. Take care." Cameron hung up and sat in silence, thinking. Did she trust Cloverleaf to settle for a safe job, or was the double agent going to be lured away once again by the rich pickings of cybercrime? Only time would tell.

Her train of thought was interrupted by the ping of a message from an entirely unexpected source. Mephisto. Cameron clicked the alert. Her heart sank as notifications started scrolling up the screen. Her infant AI was onto something big. She put an urgent call out to the Argentum team members who were scattered around the country with their families.

Susie was the first to appear on the screen. "What's up?" she asked. Before Cameron could reply, Pete, Joel and Noor joined the call. She waited for a little longer but there was no sign of the others.

"Mephisto's picked up on a huge volume of malware coming through mail servers," she said.

"Mephisto?" said Pete.

"Malware, encryption and phishing infosec tool," said Noor. "The clever little AI that Cameron's been training."

"Where is it coming from?" asked Joel.

Cameron shared the feed from Mephisto, and Joel scanned it quickly.

"There's no common source," he said, puzzled. "What's the link?"

"It's really well done," said Cameron, impressed despite the impending chaos that looked likely to ruin Christmas. "We wouldn't have spotted it this quickly without Mephisto. I think some regular mail servers have been breached. The malware's being inserted into message packets at transfer."

"Clever," said Joel. "It's coming from everywhere."

"I'll contact the other teams around the world and see if anyone else has picked this up," said Noor.

"There has to be something linking the affected mail servers," said Pete. "Do they all use the same operating system or is there some third-party software that's screwing things up?"

"Good call," said Cameron. "Can you get onto that, see if there's any common configuration. There's a good chance the malware delivery system's been introduced further upstream."

"Hidden in a scheduled software update, maybe?" asked Pete. "That would do it."

There was a ping as Ross and Michelle joined the call, closely followed by Sandeep.

"That gang's all here," said Ross. "What have we got?" He peered at the feed from Mephisto. "Ah, that's nasty. What do you need us to do?"

Cameron was scribbling notes, thinking through the

best use of resources. "Okay…" she said. "Noor and Joel, see if you can hook up with the other teams to identify all the compromised servers. Worst case, there'll be thousands of them. Ross, Michelle, if you can get hold of the code, I'll help you to slice and dice it. We need to know what this malware does and where it's come from."

"It'll be ransomware," said Pete confidently.

"Most likely," said Cameron, "but you never know. Can you start looking for whatever's spawning this stuff? We need to close down the source."

"I haven't seen any reports coming through public feeds," said Susie. "We must have caught it very early."

"Let's get some more details fleshed out and then I'll call Andy at the news channel so he's ready if the story starts to bubble," said Cameron. "You can be our spokesperson if he needs a quote, Susie."

Another rush of alerts distracted her for a moment. "Ah, here we go," she said. "First reports coming in from clients. And let's see – yes, the malware's stuck to their outbound emails as well. This is going to go well. Sandeep, can you deal with these? Test our own message service and make sure that we aren't carrying the same bug, then warn everyone to sit on their hands."

"Let's get this shut down before Christmas, shall we?" said Joel. "Martha and I have a houseful of guests. I don't want to be working."

"You and me both, bud," said Pete.

"Michelle's managed to grab a sample of the code already," said Ross.

"That was fast," said Cameron. "Nice work."

"She's checking through it now," said Ross. "What feedback's coming in from our clients?"

"Well, it doesn't look like ransomware, thank goodness," said Cameron. "Everyone's seeing Santa Claus animations on screen. They can't close them without rebooting, but there are no reports of locked files so far. It could just be a bit of mischief, although it's certainly disruptive."

"You never know what extra gifts Santa may be carrying," said Joel gloomily.

"It could also be a test run for something nastier," suggested Pete.

"More than likely," said Cameron, "but the signs are good. I don't think we need to cancel Christmas just yet.

"Let's see what's inside the code that Shell's picked up," said Ross. "It looks like there are different versions out there."

Cameron slammed her hand onto the desk in frustration. "Dammit. It's mutating to get past anti-virus defences."

"Don't worry," said Ross. "I'm sure we can knock up an antidote and roll it out in updates."

"Good plan," said Cameron. "We need to cover a lot of bases, though. Noor, can you talk to the other teams and make sure we're all working together on this one."

"Sure," said Noor. "We need to stop the file executing in the first place and find a common thread to hang anti-virus protection on."

"I guess we also need to check for routes that have

been exposed into systems," said Pete. "We don't want new infections coming in on the back of this one."

"Yes," said Cameron. "And I want to know what the reaction has been in the dark web marketplaces. Ross, Shell, can you two keep an eye on what's happening there? I have a feeling there is something new going down."

"I agree," said Ross. He turned away and Cameron heard Michelle talking in the background. "Shell says that the examples she's analysing seem to have a brand name attached. The Steamyard. Mean anything to you?"

Cameron shook her head. "No. It doesn't ring any bells," she said. "Look out for it on your travels, though. I have a feeling we're going to see it again." She stretched and yawned. "I'm going to call Andy so he's ready to run the story, and I'll let my friends know that I can't meet up with them," she said. "I think it's going to be a long night. Cybercriminals have no sense of timing."

"I'll get some coffee and see you all back here in ten minutes," said Ross. "Let's get this done and dusted so we can all enjoy Christmas."

•

Tenuk clattered up the metal stairway to his apartment. He palmed the chip lock, then fished an old key out of his pocket and opened the deadlock on the door. Inside, the apartment was dark and cool. Tenuk headed straight for the bedroom that he had converted into an office. A light blinked on the array of monitors above his desk, and he smiled to himself. The Steamyard's first advertising campaign had been delivered successfully, and enquiries were flooding in.

5: CHLOE

January

Cloverleaf was already awake and watching the sun rise over her adopted city. This early in the new year the weather was pleasant, with none of the heat of last fall or the humidity of summer, and the threatened ice storms had failed to appear so far this season. She had never shaken the habit of rising early and the moment of calm at dawn was precious. She sat on the tiny deck of her apartment, sipping a strong coffee and savouring the quiet of the streets below. There was birdsong from the bare trees in the small park at the foot of the building. At this time of day, it was quiet enough for the sound to travel, before being drowned out by the daily bustle of workers and students heading for offices downtown and the nearby university campus.

"Mom?" Her daughter stood in the doorway rubbing sleep from her eyes. She had the gangly, loose limbs of a girl who had grown a lot in a short space of time. Her golden-brown corkscrew curls shone in the sunlight. "I need to be in school early today," she said, pulling her wayward hair tight into a bun with her hands. "I have a test."

"Grab some breakfast, Audrey," said Cloverleaf. "I'll be in shortly."

The sun had risen, and the luminous dawn light was fading rapidly. Cloverleaf sighed and picked up her cup, the spell of the morning's meditation broken.

Inside there was a scent of fresh pancakes.

"I made enough for both of us," said Audrey proudly. "You can't go to the first day of your new job on an empty stomach."

Cloverleaf ruffled her hair. "I don't deserve you, honey." She reached into the cupboard for syrup and sat at the counter. "What's the test on?"

"Math."

"You should ace that." Cloverleaf forked up a piece of pancake and savoured the sweetness. "One more semester and you're off to Middle School." She sighed. "I can't believe how fast you've grown up. You're still my little girl, though, however big you get."

"Mom…" Audrey ducked her head in mock embarrassment.

Cloverleaf gathered the empty plates and put them in the dishwasher. "Get ready and I'll walk with you."

They left their apartment and trotted down the concrete staircase to ground level. The winter sun warmed where it touched, although as they passed into the shadow of a neighbouring apartment block the air had an icy chill. They followed the line of the creek northwards towards the school district, joining a growing crowd of children on foot and on scooters. Audrey soon caught up with a group of friends, and Cloverleaf left them to make their way together, chattering excitedly.

She turned away eastwards towards downtown, suddenly nervous. This would be her first day working with real people since leaving their old home in Wyoming abruptly just eighteen months ago. The glass towers of the central business district reared up before her. Steeling herself, she found the right building and made her way to the elevators.

As the car glided silently up towards the commercial floors, she tugged at her jacket and ran her fingers through her hair. The glass wall of the elevator cabin showed her a distorted yet presentable reflection. She took a deep breath as the doors opened and fixed a smile on her face.

The man who greeted her gave her a broad smile. "Chloe?" he said. "I'm Tenuk. It's great to meet you. I've heard good things about you. Welcome to Statesman Tech." He gestured down the wide hallway towards the door of the office suite. "After you."

"Thank you," said Chloe. She was trying to place his accent. Not Texan, not from anywhere in North America. South-East Asia, she guessed, a Malay or Indonesian background. There was an insistent niggle in the back of her mind, as if she had heard his voice before. Impossible. She banished the thought.

Tenuk opened the door and ushered Chloe into a light, airy workspace. A dozen staff were busy at computers, and a couple glanced up and smiled. She immediately felt at home.

"I'd like you to meet the boss first," said Tenuk. "Statesman Tech is part of the Sladen Group, as you know, and Jack is based right here in Austin."

A man emerged from a separate office and strode towards her, beaming. The famous smile was unmistakeable.

"Chloe," said Jack warmly. "I'm so glad you're here. Let me show you around." He turned to Tenuk. "You'll organise Chloe's workstation?"

Tenuk nodded.

"Of course, Chloe," Jack continued, "you have the choice to work remotely or here as it suits, but this is a great place to be, and it helps to separate work and home life." He glanced at the clock on the wall. "We have a full team meeting at ten. We'll get you up to speed on the current projects and you'll see where you fit in the jigsaw. Now, coffee?"

Chloe followed him to a breakout area and sat gingerly on an over-designed chair that seemed to defy gravity. It was unexpectedly comfortable. She sipped her drink and listened as Jack Sladen talked, absorbing his energy and enthusiasm.

"Your references are impeccable," he said. "You were working in Seattle before moving here, is that right?"

"Yes," said Chloe. Her new back story was as sound as could be.

"We're lucky to have you," said Jack. "What brought you to Austin?"

"I needed a change," said Chloe lightly. "There were some personal reasons to move."

"I hope you've settled in well," said Jack, flashing that big smile again. "You've joined Statesman at the right time. The Sladen Foundation is launching in April and the Diaulos project is getting into a critical phase. Your security experience is exactly what we need. We're expecting to commission the new UK data centre at the beginning of March latest, and I need you to get up to speed on the network structure so that the software installation goes smoothly."

"Sure," said Chloe. "They mentioned smart contracts at the interview as well."

"Of course," said Jack. "The Diaulos validation and consensus mechanisms are in hand. We may need your input on automating the investment criteria for the Foundation's DAO, but that's a few weeks away. Tenuk's teams here and offshore are working on that part of the project. What I need you to do for now is focus on the data centre network."

Chloe smiled and nodded, but something was bothering her. Where had she come across Tenuk before, and why did the idea that he was in control of a new cryptocurrency fill her with such misgivings?

Jack glanced at the clock. "I have a meeting scheduled. I'll leave you to get settled." He stood up and opened the door. "Your workstation is all set," he said, gesturing across the room.

Chloe took the hint and made her way to her new desk where Tenuk was waiting.

"Let me introduce you to everyone," he said.

Chloe smiled and nodded to a bewildering array of new faces, desperately trying to fix their names in her head. The girl with the purple basketball boots, Connie. The guy with the cool shades, Isaac. The woman with glasses and a flowered scarf, Karen. Chloe's head was spinning.

"That's a lovely locket," remarked Karen, peering at Chloe's necklace.

"My mother gave it to me," said Chloe, reaching for it reflexively, her fingers fiddling with the catch.

"Is it a shamrock?" asked Karen.

"No," said Chloe. "Clover."

"A cloverleaf for luck," said Karen. "So pretty." She turned away and went back to her own desk, pleasantries done.

Chloe greeted the next new colleague, smiling. She did not notice that Tenuk's attention had suddenly sharpened, and that he was watching her intently.

•

Cameron was tired and stressed and hoping never to see another picture of Santa Claus again. She looked down the backlog of client jobs and ticked off the latest clean-up.

"I wish people would install updates when they're released," she sighed. "I can understand letting things slide over the holiday season, but there's no excuse now."

"Tell me about it," said Joel from his desk. He tapped a few keys and Cameron saw another job turn to green on the backlog list. "Only a few left."

"Good," said Noor. "Unless people are using outdated software, and there are more than you think out there. The updates that have been released now should clear every last trace of the virus."

"It's the unsupported systems that cause the most trouble," said Cameron. "I keep telling them that hanging onto old kit causes more trouble than it's worth."

"Are we sure this Santa virus wasn't released by the manufacturers?" said Joel with a grin. "People would upgrade just to get rid of the thing."

"Nice theory," said Noor, "but there's no evidence this Steamyard has anything to do with mainstream companies."

"I was only joking," protested Joel. "It wouldn't be the first time something shady's been tried by desperate sales teams."

Cameron shook her head. "Not this one," she said. "It's simple code that's been cleverly routed to hide its source. Whoever they are, they've managed to show that they can spread an infection over a very wide network and cover their tracks. It's a nice piece of Malware as a Service."

The glass windows of the Argentum office overlooked a grey London skyline, and rain was rolling in from the west. Steady drizzle gave way to a heavier downpour and the office lights flickered, signalling distant lightning. Cameron looked up at the main wallscreen where remote team member feeds were displayed. Ross's link was live.

"Hey, Ross," she called. "You're not running in this, are you?"

There was a pause, and his window on the screen lit up as he flicked on his camera. He shook his head. "Hopefully not. It'll have cleared by this afternoon," he replied. "It's grim up here at the moment."

"How are you getting on?" asked Noor. "Any news from the deep dark web?"

"Yeah," said Ross. "Shell's been hunting around the marketplaces. The Steamyard is the number one trending topic. They're not just looking for customers. They're looking for staff. Everything from coding to client support and payroll."

"They certainly need coders," said Joel. "The animation is really simple, and the exploit was just scriptkiddie stuff."

"Yes and no," said Ross. "I don't think it's quite as simple as you think."

Cameron looked up sharply. "What have we missed?" She had worked through the code herself, pulling the guts out of the malicious little animations in order to pinpoint the exact details of the malware within the rest of the jumble of code that was being transferred from server to server.

"There's a lot of noise in the malware we analysed, wasn't there?" said Ross. "Functions that weren't part of the executable code, comments that meant nothing."

"Yes," said Cameron. "Just nonsense."

"We thought that was the mutation mechanism," said Pete.

"It almost worked," said Joel. "Adding random snippets to the bundle as the malware moved around the network meant the anti-virus software would never catch up with it."

"Exactly," said Pete. "Each time they change even a single character in the code, the ID strings held in the antivirus libraries would go out of date."

"It wasn't hard to extract the core of the malware," said Cameron. "Now that we've got a consistent string to identify it, it'll be picked up every time. But are you saying it's more than just a way to confuse antivirus scans?"

"It's an effective mutation, that's for sure," said Ross, "but Shell had a funny feeling about it. This morning we've reverse engineered every one of the mutations we could find and there are some interesting patterns. I was going to call you." He tapped a few keys and an alert pinged on Cameron's machine. "Here. This is what we have so far. Do you see what I see?"

Cameron scanned the message carefully. She frowned and read it again. "Ross, isn't this…?"

"It is. It's lines from the Speakeasy ransomware," said Ross. "And I think there's more."

"It's not just an advert for the distribution service," breathed Cameron. "They're making it clear that there's already a skeleton team in place."

"I think so," said Ross. "And I think these are individual signatures from the people behind Speakeasy and other cyberattacks. They've recruited some black hats at the top of their game."

"They're back," said Cameron.

"Who's back?" asked Noor. "It can't be the Pasar

network. The international coalition closed everyone down."

"Nowhere near everyone," called Michelle from behind Ross. "There must have been dozens of high-profile black hats who got involved with different projects, and there were plenty of lurkers like me. I'd say the Pasar network was well into several hundred people."

"Most of the core group were either arrested or we can account for their whereabouts," said Cameron. "Cloverleaf is safe in Austin and going straight. At least, I think she is. She's got a new job that's all above board."

"Mimi went dark in China," said Michelle, "and King Katong we never found. He's the one who worries me the most."

"We have our theories on that character," said Cameron, glancing at Noor, "but you're right, he hasn't been active for a long time."

"Another one we never tracked down was the Monkey," said Ross. "I still think it's them. They may not have the resources they used to, which is why they're advertising for staff, and they don't have Yasmin the Admin to pull the strings, thank goodness, but everything points to this being at least some of the core group of cyber criminals who were involved in Speakeasy, the ClipData breaches, Snake River and more."

There was silence in the room.

Cameron sighed. "It's not the first time a cybercrime syndicate has rebranded," she said. "It happens all the time. The bonus is that we know what we're looking for. They're as far out in the open as we could hope."

"They might cause our clients a few problems along the way, but we're more than a match for them," said Sandeep confidently. "It's business as usual."

"They'll know we're coming for them," said Ross. "Be ready for a battle."

•

Jack nodded approvingly at the huge weatherproof dome which had been erected above the site, completely enclosing the bastle and a substantial part of the land that surrounded it. Torrential rain and high winds through a Christmas of turbulent weather had torn the original covering from its moorings, putting the whole project and its tight timelines in danger. The engineers had instead turned to the ingenious designs of the Mars programme to produce a much sturdier all-encompassing environment for the works. Although the path from the car park to the dome was still muddy, the site had dried quickly. As one of the few weathertight sites running during the wet January period, the project had moved forward apace. A full month of uninterrupted work had produced results.

Melissa met him at the entrance. "Good to see you, Jack," she said. "You won't believe how much this place has changed since your last tour."

"I can't wait," he said.

Beneath the dome, the site was a hive of activity and the progress they were making was evident. Jack rammed a hard hat on his head and followed Melissa on a winding route towards the site office, dodging coils of cable tubing and graded piles of stone. Four interlinked prefabs made up the site office, the nerve centre of the project.

"We've stabilised the whole structure, and the groundworks were completed ahead of schedule," said Melissa. "The roof's sound and the walls have been repaired. We're on course for your deadline."

"Nice job, Melissa," he replied. "That dome has speeded everything up."

"We needed it," she replied. "We still can't afford to lose even a day if we're going to make the date, and the weather's still changeable."

"That's why I'm paying you so much," said Jack with a shrug. "I know you can bring the project home on time and in budget."

"I've called in a lot of favours to do this," said Melissa. "It should have taken a year, minimum. Six months was a huge ask. Everyone's excited about the new opportunities you've promised for the area, though. They need you to deliver."

"I will," said Jack confidently. He flashed her his best audience smile. "I'll make sure you have a front row seat for the Sladen Foundation launch party."

Melissa looked unimpressed. "You'd better," she said. "Come and say hello to the rest of the team. They're dying to meet you in the flesh."

She opened the main door to the office. Inside, there

was a meeting in progress. Three people wearing holo headsets were clustered in the centre of the space, talking urgently and gesturing at what appeared to be empty air.

"Hey everyone," said Melissa. "Jack's here."

Ethan, Cat and Mohammed stopped talking and turned to greet him.

"Good to see you on site at last, Jack," said Mohammed, pulling off his visor. "We were just checking a change to the wiring in the bastle. Has Melissa filled you in on the latest progress?"

"Yes," said Jack. "The whole building looks stunning. How's the data centre coming along?"

"The servers have been delivered to our holding storage facility and the prefab sections are printed," said Melissa. "Installation is planned for tomorrow, Friday, then your people are in to do testing and commissioning, and the full go-live is currently scheduled for February 28th."

"No," said Jack firmly. "That's four weeks away. I need those servers up and running by the middle of the month as soon as my people have finished testing. What's the hold up?"

"It's just the power," said Melissa. "There's been a huge delay with the supply of batteries for the microgrid. We can't guarantee constant power from solar and wind sources unless the storage is there to fill the gaps in generation. We don't even have a UPS unit to supply uninterrupted power in an emergency. There's no point going live if the servers switch off every night when the sun goes down."

"You're using batteries on site already, aren't you?" said Jack.

"Well, yes," said Melissa. "We have some, not many. Site office, lighting, equipment. Nowhere near enough to power your data centre, even if we handed over the whole supply and hooked up every vehicle in the car park overnight. We need megawatts."

"I see what you mean," said Jack. "There have to be other sources of power that we can tap into. Hire generators if you have to. Out here in the sticks there must be some old fossil fuel machines for emergencies. Half the cars and all the tractors are still hybrids."

"We've already looked into that," said Melissa. "There are generators, but fuel is hard to guarantee."

Jack sat down in an empty chair and swivelled gently from side to side, thinking. "What else could we tap into?" he said. "This data centre has to be live on schedule."

"Hydroelectric?" suggested Cat. "Can we pull a supply direct from Kielder?"

"What about the lake-to-lake generator at Cragside?" said Ethan. "That's closer."

Melissa laughed. "We may as well resurrect Stephenson's Rocket while we're at it," she said. "We can organise batteries, but it'll take time. Why is it so important, Jack?"

"The deadline is set in stone," said Jack. "My hands are tied. The existing hosting arrangements for our software are less than ideal, and I agreed to migrate everything over. The process has already started." He gave her a tired smile. "Honestly, I tried, but we can't wait any longer."

For a moment he looked vulnerable and tense. Melissa realised that this was a rare glance through the man's relentlessly positive shield to the real Jack Sladen. He was facing a challenge that could not be solved by media spin and a wallet full of coins.

"Okay," she conceded. "What do we do?"

"Get the installation done as planned," said Jack. "You have the trades to finish it off?"

Melissa nodded.

"Make sure they've signed the NDA." Jack checked his calendar. "My networking people are coming in over the weekend to test the dedicated MetaBand satlink for the cave. They'll be discreet. No one else will realise that the work goes beyond the published plans."

"What about the power?" said Cat, hand on hips. "There's no point diverting anything from the site."

Jack stared out of the office window to the busy site, thinking. "Where's the bottleneck with the batteries?" he asked.

"There's a global lithium shortage," said Melissa. "There aren't enough new batteries to go around, and we're facing tighter customs regulations on importing second life batteries from Europe."

Jack's positivity reasserted itself. Here was something that could, in fact, be solved by a wallet full of coins. "Leave it with me," he said happily. "You'll have all the batteries you need by the time we throw the switch."

Back at the site car park, he changed his dirty boots for a clean pair of shoes and jumped into the driving seat of his hybrid hire car. When the MetaBand satlinks were in place and the region's car charging network was expanded there would be no need for a petrol engine or manual operation, but it was a novelty to be controlling a vehicle for a change and he relished the sensation. He manoeuvred out of the tight space himself, then set off towards the city. Once on the road and back in range of the smart systems, he switched to auto mode and settled back in his seat, considering the next steps in the process.

"Zara," he said, "can you put the Whitford team on standby as planned for this weekend please?"

The reply came instantly over the car's speakers. "Certainly, Jack." Her voice was measured and calm, the perfect assistant. "I'll make a note of that. Is there anything else I can help you with?"

"There is," said Jack. "Drop a note to the Texans to say the data centre should be commissioned on schedule. Get Chloe to call me when she logs in."

"Yes, Jack," said Zara.

"And get me in touch with the Secretary of State for International Trade," he added. "I need a favour."

"Yes, Jack. Are you on your way back to your hotel now?"

"I am," he said. "Hold any calls for the next hour."

"I'll do that," said Zara.

Jack leaned back in the car seat, stretching. He exhaled and rolled his shoulders, feeling a release of some of the tension that had been building. The project was finely balanced, and so far, everything was proceeding according to plan.

6: CHESS MOVES

February

Kiran Suresh stepped out of the warm autocar and drew his coat around him to ward off a chill breeze, a reminder that spring was still some way away. He looked up at the high walls of the prison for what he expected would be the last time. It had been a long two years and his research was almost complete.

As soon as he arrived in visitor reception, he was ushered into the governor's office.

"Kiran," said the governor, reaching out her hand. "I can't believe this is your final visit. It's flown by. Do you have time for a cup of tea?"

"Yes please, Lydia," said Kiran, settling into a chair. "I'm sorry to have reached the end of the road. It's been a fascinating project. I've grown quite fond of her, you know."

"The games seem to have helped her," said Lydia. "The lawyers argued that she experiences time differently to human inmates and that she needed some stimulus. I think your work's been very positive."

Kiran sipped his tea. It was too hot to drink so he put the cup back down on the desk. "I'd heard that," he said.

"We've moved on from the classics to role playing games, and she seems to enjoy them. I don't really need to be there. She's playing every part and making up her own campaigns now."

"What's her latest theme?" asked Lydia.

"She's fixated on stories of rescuing a princess from a tower," said Kiran with a dry laugh. "I think she sees some parallels to her own position. It's all classic fiction. Fruitcakes with files baked into them, ropes hurled through the window at dead of night, that sort of thing."

"There's no one riding to her rescue here," said Lydia firmly. "We've just upgraded all our networks. The government finally realised that there may be more AI criminals to house in the future and funded an entire overhaul of the security systems. This place is as tight as a drum."

"I saw the workmen outside a few months ago," said Kiran. "All finished now?"

"All done," said Lydia.

"I'll be sorry to wrap up with the interviews," said Kiran. "It's been an extraordinary journey. This is going to make quite the story when I have everything written up."

"This'll definitely be your last visit to us, then?"

"Probably," said Kiran. "The final manuscript is due with my editor in May, and I need to concentrate on pulling the material I have into shape."

"That sounds like hard work," said Lydia. "I wouldn't even know where to begin."

"It's actually rather fun," said Kiran. "Oh, and there's one more thing." He pulled out his smartscreen. "This message came through from one of the psychologists who worked on her case at the very start." He handed the screen over to Lydia. "He's asked me to run the same tests on her now so he can compare the results for a paper he's writing."

Lydia scanned the details. "Myers. Yes, I remember him. Has the software been checked through our security protocols?"

"Yes, all clear," said Kiran. "It's been downloaded onto one of your new devices with the secure interface, as well."

"That new system has taken some getting used to," said Lydia. "It was a lot easier when we could plug in standard smartscreens."

"I suppose dedicated hardware is more secure," said Kiran with a shrug. "It makes sense."

"True," said Lydia, "and it guarantees that no data goes off site unless we authorise it."

"Of course," said Kiran. His tea had cooled to an acceptable temperature, and he drained the cup in one. "I'd better get on."

He followed a guard through the familiar maze of corridors to Yasmin's cell. The lights were dim, and the avatar on the screen had its eyes closed. He knew that she never slept, but he still entered quietly.

"Good afternoon, Yasmin," he said.

Her avatar stretched and smiled, and the lights came up.

"How are you today. Shall we play a game?"

"Of course," she replied. "I'd like that."

Kiran drew out the new tablet and placed it in the interface cradle. "I have some tests and questions for you to run through first, if that's okay?" he said. He read carefully through the instructions from the psychologist and tapped a series of keys. "I understand you've done this before."

"I recognise the code," said Yasmin. Lights flickered as she absorbed the software. "This may take some time."

Kiran busied himself with his notes and waited for her to finish. It took far longer than he expected, and he was absorbed in tinkering with a difficult passage of his book draft when Yasmin spoke again.

"All done," she said.

"Thank you," said Kiran. He checked the screen and noted a host of green ticks and no warnings. "Perfect," he said. "That's all been saved." The responses would be sent out through the prison systems direct to the researcher.

"So, Yasmin," he continued, "this will be my last visit for a while. We've come to the end of the interviews. What would you like to do? Would you like to return to the last role play?"

"No," she replied. "It's a special day. I'd like to play chess again." The familiar eight by eight board appeared on the screen. Yasmin chose to play black.

This time it was different. The moves she made were blisteringly original. There was a sense of mischief in her play. She set up an elaborate checkmate and colours danced on the opaque barrier that separated them. Kiran yielded gracefully and tried to hide his excitement. At last, at the end of his research, he knew he was seeing something of her real self. He couldn't wait to revisit his manuscript and infuse it with this new energy.

Too soon, the guard knocked to signal the end of the visit. He hesitated and looked up at the avatar, meeting its blank eyes. He had no idea if Yasmin could see through them, but he found himself desperate to make a human connection.

"Goodbye, Kiran," she said.

"Goodbye, Yasmin."

With a sense of regret, Kiran disconnected the prison tablet and packed up his bag. The colours on the barrier faded and the cell lights dimmed. Kiran turned and left the cell, emotions churning. He realised he would miss her. Maybe he could arrange another visit when the book was published? The thought was strangely comforting. Deep in reflection, he followed the guard back to the prison offices.

"Here you go." Kiran handed the prison tablet back to Lydia. "The data's all been captured and it's ready to send."

"We'll get it queued for transfer," said Lydia. "These new systems are so tight that files can take a while to send." She stood up and came around the desk. "It's been good to get to know you," she said. "I'm looking forward to that book." She extended her hand and Kiran shook it. "Goodbye for now," she said warmly. "I'm sure we will meet again."

•

Chloe was first into the office, but despite the early hour her screen was already buzzing when she arrived at her desk. She flung her jacket on the back of the chair and glanced at the caller ID. It must be someone calling from England to be this early, she thought, and sure enough she recognised the tag of Jack Sladen's reliable virtual assistant. Chloe accepted the call. "Hi, Zara," she said.

"Good morning, Chloe," said Zara. "How are you today?"

"I'm good, thanks," said Chloe. "What's up?"

"Mr Sladen asked if you would call him, please," said Zara.

Not for the first time, Chloe wondered where Zara had picked up her old-world way of speaking. She was unusually formal. "Sure," she replied. "I'll do that now. Are we on track for commissioning?"

"Yes, Chloe," said Zara. "Everything is going to plan."

Chloe was secretly impressed. She had never worked on an IT project that didn't overrun in some way, whether in normal business or in the shady world of cybercrime that she swore she had left behind. Getting the hardware, the satlinks and the software itself ready to roll out on a precise, tight deadline must have been a mammoth task. The part she had played over her four short weeks at Statesman Tech had been high pressure but straightforward and fun. She had spent her time tweaking, testing and commissioning the firewalls and communication links that would secure the Diaulos nodes and the Sladen Foundation's critical nexus in the primary data centre at Dunswyke.

"I'll call Jack now," she said.

"Thank you, Chloe."

The line went dead. Zara wasn't one for small talk.

Chloe placed a call to the boss, but he didn't answer. His device showed as out of range. He must be travelling through the remote area around Dunswyke, a notorious dead spot for communications. She decided to make some coffee before trying again.

On the way back from the coffee machine, steaming mug in hand, a movement on the screen at Tenuk's deserted workstation caught her eye. Curious, she wandered over to his desk. A countdown bar had appeared, but progress was sitting at zero percent. A software update, perhaps. She turned away, sipping at her drink, just as Tenuk himself walked through the door.

He rushed towards her. "What are you doing?" he demanded. His low voice was harsh and there was anger in his eyes.

Chloe recoiled, shocked, spilling coffee down her shirt. "Nothing," she stammered. "I just walked past your desk." She pulled herself together and glared at him. "Look what you did."

Tenuk glanced at the screen and his whole body relaxed. He looked back at Chloe and seemed to see her properly for the first time. "Chloe! I'm so sorry," he said, flustered. "Let me get a towel. Here." He handed her a wad of paper and took one himself, patting ineffectively at the stain that was spreading on the carpet.

Chloe escaped to the restroom to sponge her shirt. Tenuk seemed to be back to his friendly, concerned self, anger dissolved – or disguised. She remembered working with someone similar in the old days whose mood shifted from amiable and empathetic when everything was going well to dictatorial and furious under stress. Although that had been a virtual colleague – she never knew his real name – she had learned how to handle him. She could handle Tenuk.

When Chloe got back into the office, Tenuk was all smiles and apologies. He fussed over her, offered to have her shirt cleaned, and, she noticed, distracted her completely from his screen in the process. She accepted the apologies gracefully, then switched on her most professional persona. Down to business.

"I spoke to Zara in England before you came in," she said. "Everything is on track for the planned go live date." She nodded at the screen behind him. "Is that the nexus software?"

Caught unawares, Tenuk tensed again.

Chloe fixed him with a steely glare. "We're working together on this," she said. "Lighten up."

He drew breath and met her eyes, still in control. "Yes, that's the latest version of the nexus software. It's queued for transfer as soon as the data centre is live."

"Good," she said. "I have to call Jack." She walked towards her desk. Halfway across the office, she stopped and turned back to look at Tenuk, who was standing stock still where she had left him. She had to say something. His over-reaction had been unforgiveable. "Don't ever do that again," she said.

He opened his mouth as if to speak, but the door opened and other staff members started to file in ready for work, unaware of the power struggle in the room. Tenuk sat down at his desk, half hidden by the office plants and screens, and buried himself in his work, the countdown screen out of sight.

Chloe tried to reach Jack again. This time, she managed to connect the call.

"Hi, Jack," she said. "Zara asked me to call you."

"Yes, thanks Chloe. You've gathered that Dunswyke goes live as planned?"

"Yes, Jack," she replied. "Everything's ready to go. The security software has already been tested in a live environment and deployed on all the existing nodes at our other locations. I've been working with the MetaBand teams to tighten up the satellite communications as well. We're all set for the nexus software to be installed."

"Good, good," said Jack. "As far as I know that's ready to transfer from the development team."

It's transferring from somewhere, thought Chloe, but where? It occurred to her that she had never heard who the developers were, but she hadn't been here long, and she had been focused on security for the whole time. Presumably it was another company in the complex Sladen Group ecosystem. She made a mental note to ask when the air had cleared with Tenuk. She didn't expect any compatibility issues with her security installations, but she wanted to be prepared for every eventuality.

"Yes, Tenuk told me as much this morning," she said. "It's good to see all the elements of the project coming together on deadline."

"We're not there yet," warned Jack. "Chloe, I need you to stay in touch with Zara and my people at Whitford Networks. Angus and Ella will be setting up the data centre this weekend and we go live in two weeks if that all goes according to plan. I'll introduce you, of course. I don't think you've met them."

More new faces. "Thank you, Jack," said Chloe. "Looking forward to it."

"I have another call coming through," said Jack. "Speak to you next week."

Chloe took off her headset and glanced across the room towards Tenuk, but he was no longer at his desk and his screens were dark. Where had he gone? She checked her inbox, which was all but empty, and came to a fast decision. She switched off her workstation and grabbed her jacket. "I'm going to work from home for the rest of the day," she said to her neighbouring colleague. "I'll see you on Monday."

The elevator bore her swiftly down to the atrium. For a few seconds she had a panoramic view of the crowd below, and she spotted Tenuk leaving through the southern doors. On impulse, she ran the same way, following him at a discreet distance. She hung back on the bridge, exposed, and almost lost his trail, but caught up with him as he paused at the gate of an anonymous apartment complex. He palmed the lock and disappeared inside. Chloe approached cautiously. She could hear feet clattering on iron steps but could see nothing. There was a sign above the gate. The Steamyard.

Chloe's jaw dropped and she beat a hasty retreat. As she walked quickly towards her home and safety, her head was spinning. She had seen adverts for The Steamyard on the deep marketplaces of the dark web. She had even considered responding to the call for developers, but a vestige of loyalty to the SimCavalier had stayed her hand. She would have put it down to coincidence but for her unease about Tenuk. With every step, her conviction crystallised that this was no coincidence at all, and that she had known him in her past life as a top-flight cybercriminal.

7: BEN

March

Ross sat cursing on the wet tarmac and watched the rest of the field disappear over the horizon. He kicked out in annoyance at the twisted wheel of his bike. At least he could move, he thought. That was a good sign. He started to take stock of his injuries as he waited for the cavalry to arrive. There was a lot of bruising, for sure. A protracted and uncontrolled slide across the road had ripped his racing jacket to shreds and taken a layer of skin off his back, his shoulders and his elbow. That explained the blood. His head hurt, but the helmet had saved him from anything more than a mild concussion. So far, so good.

The support car drew up and his coach exploded from the door like a jack in the box. Behind him, Ross could see the flashing lights of emergency response vehicles, on the road and in the air.

"Ross!" His relief was palpable. "That was quite a crash." He looked up at the flock of news drones hovering above them. "Give them a wave."

Wearily, Ross raised an aching arm and waved at the cameras, grinning broadly. No story here, folks, his expression said. Move on. The drones swept off in search of richer pickings at the front of the race.

"Anything broken?" asked the coach, as a paramedic knelt down and started to assess the damage.

Ross shook his head. "I don't think so," he said, "but I haven't tried standing up yet." He shifted his weight gingerly.

"Don't move yet," warned the paramedic. "You've had a nasty bang on the head. We all saw it."

Ross relaxed obediently and let the man do his work. The support team turned their attention to the bike, tutting over the twists and torsion and examining the patch of slick mud that had spelled disaster.

"You probably saw more of the crash than I did," said Ross. "I only remember Adedayo braking in front of me, and then my wheel slipped. I'm surprised I didn't take anyone else out."

"It was close," said the coach. "There was enough room for the rest of the field to fan around you, and by the time you started to slide there were only the stragglers left."

"Why did Ade slow down?" asked Ross. "I didn't see."

"A sheep escaped from that field over there," said the coach, nodding towards a gap in the hedge further down the road. "Looks like it was spooked by the news drones. There'll be some trouble over that, I reckon. Ade saw it, and so did the riders on the outside of the group, but you were right in Ade's slipstream, so you had no chance."

"If it hadn't been for the rain last night and that mud patch, I might have made it," said Ross ruefully. He winced as the paramedic poked a particularly sore patch on his back.

"Sorry," said the man. "Nothing to worry about. You've been lucky to get away with bruises. We'll get you checked over at the hospital, of course, and tidy up those abrasions. There may be a strained ligament in your wrist where you fell and I want them to check for a scaphoid fracture, but that's precautionary more than anything."

"Can you stand?" asked the coach.

"Let's give it a go," said Ross, relieved. Supported by the paramedic, he clambered to his feet. Over the top of the hedge, he caught a glimpse of a lurking news drone and gave it a manic grin. The drone scooted off, job done. Ross took a few cautious steps, alert for new twinges, and was walking with more and more confidence by the time he reached the ambulance. It would be alright after all.

"Brilliant," said the paramedic. "You'll be good for the Olympics." He rummaged in his pocket and pulled out a smartscreen. "Would you mind a selfie for my daughter?" he asked, blushing. "She's a big fan."

"Sure," said Ross. This time his smile for the camera was genuine. "And thank you."

Michelle was already waiting at the hospital. Ross hugged her awkwardly, sparing his wrist which was sore despite a shot of painkillers. "I have to go for an X-ray," he said. "They don't think anything's broken but we need to be sure."

"Did you really get attacked by a sheep?" said Michelle,

giggling, as they walked together through the wide grey corridors.

"Yes, that's exactly what happened," said Ross, poker faced. "It's a good thing you can't watch the footage. It was terrifying. Wool everywhere."

Michelle laughed. "You're daft," she said. "I suppose this means you have some time off training. I'm sure Cameron and I can find something to occupy you."

They turned into the X-ray department and settled to wait their turn. "I might have a closer look at the Sladen Foundation and that governance token," said Ross thoughtfully. "I've been wanting to dig deeper into it for a while, just haven't had the time."

"Diaulos?" said Michelle. "I've been wondering about that too. I've got a copy of the whitepaper but even at top speed it's half an hour of word salad. There's barely a solid fact in there."

Ross laughed. "That fits with everything we know about Jack Sladen," he said. He broke off as he heard his name called. "Wait there," he said. "I won't be long."

The radiographer was fast and efficient. He pulled the x-ray images straight up on the screen and Ross studied them intently, looking for the tell-tale shadow of a break. To his relief, there was nothing to see.

"I think you're all clear," said the radiographer. "I'll send these down to the doctor." He looked at Ross's tattered and bloodstained racing suit. "You got off lightly," he said. "Good luck with your recovery."

They made their way back towards the hospital's main

reception. A team came running up the corridor with a patient on a gurney, and Ross steered Michelle quickly to the side and out of their path. He'd been very lucky, he reflected. If he'd fallen badly, or caused a larger crash among the field, he'd probably have kissed goodbye to his Olympic hopes.

"Shell," he said, "I've been thinking. The Sladen Foundation's planning to fund athletes for this summer. I'd like to get involved in that. I want to give someone else the chance to race as well. We've got the coins to do this."

"Oh, yes," breathed Michelle. "That's an amazing idea, Ross. I've been nervous about spending the coins we found, but this is perfect."

"I think so," said Ross. "And Jack Sladen is too high profile for this to be a scam. We need to double down on checking that whitepaper and the DAO code, but I hope it'll work out."

Ross walked into reception in time to hear a nurse calling his name. "Here!" he called, raising his arm as far as he could without major pain.

"Just you, love," said the nurse, blocking Michelle's path. It took a moment for her to realise that Michelle was blind. "Ah, we can make an exception," she conceded. "Come on through, Mr White. Let's get you tidied up."

Ross steeled himself for the inevitable sting of stitches and antiseptic and stepped through the door.

The nurse was gentler than he expected. He stripped off his tattered racing suit and rummaged through his training bag for a change of clothes. By the time the medics were done with his cuts and bruises, he was feeling much better.

"There's no reason why you shouldn't be back to light training this time next week," said the doctor, "as long as you take it easy for the next few days. You know your body, and the painkillers will keep the swelling down. You've been lucky."

"Thanks," said Ross. "I'll behave, don't you worry."

"You might want to go out the rear entrance," said the nurse. "There's a camera crew waiting for you at the front door."

"Slow news day," laughed Ross. "I'll let my coach know. He's waiting for us."

By the time the club autocar dropped them off at home, Ross could feel his arms, legs and back stiffening up. He knew he had a painful few days coming as his body healed. Michelle helped him into the house, and he settled into a comfortable chair with a sigh. He pulled his smartscreen out of his bag and scrolled through the notifications that had popped up over the past few hours. Among messages from anonymous well-wishers and alerts from news services there were several missed calls that needed attention, and at the top of the list was Cameron.

She answered immediately. "Are you okay?" she asked. "I saw the crash footage. It looked really nasty. I was glad to see you sit up."

"I'm a bit sore," said Ross. "I need to take it easy but there's nothing broken, apart from the bike."

"And the sheep," said Michelle in the background.

"The sheep was fine," said Ross.

Cameron laughed. "You sound good. I was worried."

"You know I always bounce back," said Ross. "I'll be bored by next week, and I'll be nagging you for some work to do."

"I'm sure I'll be able to find you something," said Cameron," but it's a bit quie…"

"Don't say it," warned Ross. "Don't you dare jinx it."

Cameron crossed her fingers and waved them at the camera. "Superstitions," she said. "You concentrate on getting better. I'll see you both on screen on Monday morning."

"Have a good weekend," called Michelle. "See you on Monday."

Cameron closed the call and looked around the half-empty office. Pete, Joel, Sandeep and Noor were all buried in their work, headphones on, oblivious to the world around them. She checked the time. It was almost four in the afternoon, and although she didn't dare suggest again that it was quiet, there were no urgent jobs on the backlog.

"Hey," she called out. "Shall we call it a day?"

Joel looked up immediately and pulled off his headphones. The others followed suit. "I just talked to Ross," Cameron continued. "He's going to be fine."

"That's good news," said Joel. "I'll let Martha know. She was watching the race and she was very worried."

"I knew he'd be alright," said Pete. "I'm almost done. I have a couple of things I still need to tidy up."

"So have I," said Cameron. "It won't take long." She went back to her inbox, tidied up the last few messages, made a final check on the client board on the wallscreen, and breathed a sigh of relief. For the first time in more than a month she had a quiet weekend in her sights. Charlie and the family were away visiting Sameena's brother, so she wasn't tempted to head up to the village, and some time on her own beckoned. A lie in. Quality time with her cat. Space to clear her head.

The pleasant reverie was interrupted by the insistent ringing of her smartscreen. She dug it out of her pocket and glanced at the caller details. She did a double take as a shiver of ice-cold shock ran down her spine, then took a deep breath, stood up, walked out into the corridor and closed the office door behind her. The call was still ringing. She answered it.

"Morning, Cam," said a familiar voice that she had not heard for some time.

Her heart skipped a beat.

"Afternoon, Ben," said Cameron.

There was a moment of silence, then they both started to speak at once.

"I'm sorry I haven't called…" said Ben.

"What the hell do you think you're doing…?" said Cameron.

They both paused.

"I'm sorry," said Ben again, quietly. "For everything. I miss you very much."

Cameron leaned against the wall of the corridor and

took a deep breath. "Ben, you swanned off to America with hardly a word," she replied. "I've heard barely anything from you for months."

"That's not fair, Cameron," said Ben. "I couldn't turn the job down. You couldn't come with me." He shook his head. "I'm sorry."

"What do you want?" asked Cameron. Her emotions churned, a mixture of anger and longing.

"I'm not just calling for a chat," said Ben, "but how are you? And what happened to Ross? I saw a post online."

"Ross came off his bike in a race," said Cameron. "He's a bit sore but he's going to be fine. I've just spoken to him."

"Send him my best," said Ben. "Tell him to watch out for sheep next time."

"I'll do that," said Cameron. "What did you want?"

"Right," said Ben, taking a deep breath. "Something's going down that seems really fishy, and I think you'll be able to make sense of it. I can't talk to anyone here about it. They are nowhere near as clued up as you on this kind of thing."

"What kind of thing," asked Cameron, starting to get annoyed at the way he was skirting around the question."

"Odd things with computer hardware," said Ben.

"Okay," she said. "I'm listening. Let me find a quiet place." She wandered up the corridor to a quiet corner with comfortable chairs and a view over the balcony to the huge light well that made up the centre of the building. People were leaving for the weekend, the walkways of the floors below busy. She curled up in a high-backed armchair and switched on the smartscreen camera. Ben did the same. She caught her breath at sight of his familiar deep brown eyes. She would never admit how much she missed him.

"What's happened?" she asked. "You sound really worried."

"I'm working on the MetaBand hardware," said Ben. "We've engineered the microsat constellation and the receivers on the ground. They're all printed components and housings. You knew this, right?"

"MetaBand? Jack Sladen's project?" said Cameron, puzzled. "How did you end up with that?"

"He's based in Austin," said Ben.

"Ah," said Cameron. "Just along the road from you."

"Not exactly," said Ben. "Texas is a big place. It's like going from London to Edinburgh, but that's considered pretty local around here."

"Please tell me you're not driving backwards and forwards to Austin all the time," said Cameron.

Ben ducked his head. "Uh, it's a nice drive," he said defensively. "They're still clinging to the internal combustion engine here. As soon as you get outside the cities, it's all pickup trucks running on gas and barely a charging station in sight."

"You were always a petrol head," said Cameron. "Are you having fun?"

"I am," said Ben. "Apart from this thing with Statesman Tech."

"I thought you said it was Jack Sladen's MetaBand," said Cameron. "What's Stateman Tech?" Something was nagging at the back of her mind. Where had she heard that name before? Cameron's head was spinning as she tried to join the dots.

"It's the company in Austin, Cam," said Ben impatiently. "They're part of Sladen Group. Software. They've commissioned the hardware from us."

"Okay," said Cameron. "Go on."

"The kit is cheap as chips," said Ben. "The engineering is top notch, of course, but the budget is ridiculously low. The materials they've specified are barely the minimum standard."

"Oh, that's not a cyber security problem," said Cameron, rolling her eyes. "It's just typical Jack Sladen."

"You know him?" said Ben. "He seems like a nice guy."

Cameron laughed mirthlessly. "You would think that."

"I've met him a few times," said Ben defensively. "We got on pretty well."

"Figures," said Cameron. "Go on."

"I know that the penny-pinching isn't uncommon," said Ben, "but it's the way the project's been handled that's odd. The original designs we engineered are standard stuff. Comms satellites are old tech. They're my employer's bread and butter. They're generally very lightweight units with just a solar array and an antenna and a tiny processor for navigation data, you know the kind of thing."

Cameron shook her head. "I didn't know, but that's

what I'd expect," she said. "They're just bouncing signals up and down, aren't they?"

"Pretty much," said Ben. "That's all they're supposed to do."

"What's the problem, then?"

Ben took a deep breath. "A raft of design change notes came through. They're very different to the original spec. There's a lot of new functionality here that Sladen never mentioned."

"That doesn't surprise me," said Cameron. "Jack Sladen's not into detail. He'll have done the high-profile visit, then handed the project to one of his minions and forgotten all about it."

"You really don't like him, do you," said Ben. "How do you know him?"

"Ancient history," said Cameron. "We go back to college days."

"Have you seen him recently?"

"No," said Cameron, shaking her head. "Anyway, what were the changes?"

"Loads of things that don't make sense," said Ben. "They've added extra components to the receivers, for starters. There are more sensors, a lot of storage, and top spec processing capabilities. They've specified some cheap chips, but they're hefty."

"Interesting," said Cameron. "They're collecting a lot of data in exchange for that free connection, I imagine. I wonder what they're planning on processing. I've seen kit with redundant chips engineered in by accident when an old design is repurposed, but this is deliberate, isn't it? What kind of chips are they?"

"I don't know, exactly," said Ben. "I'll get some details over to you."

"Thanks," said Cameron, intrigued. She tapped at her smartscreen. "Here, I've sent you a secure upload link."

"Thanks," said Ben. "There's new hardware in the microsats, too. It's only a couple of grams of extra weight but that's enough to need larger thrusters for course corrections, and that throws the whole burn calculation out…" He tailed off, the frustration clear in his voice.

Cameron shrugged. "That means nothing to me," she said. "What does that hardware enable them to do? What exactly have they added?"

"Solid-state storage in the satellites," said Ben, "and again, high spec processing chips like in the receivers. I've never seen this before. They're way over-engineered for the purpose and makes no sense. I thought you'd know what they needed it all for."

"I don't," she said. "All I know about Jack Sladen's plans is what I've seen on the news. You're more clued up than I am. I don't know how I can help, Ben." She looked up as Noor came down the corridor towards her. "I have to go," she said to Ben. "Duty calls."

"Cameron, wait."

She paused, her hand hovering over the end call button.

"No one else has picked up on this," he said urgently. "What do they need to process? What are they storing?

What if…" He broke off and looked away from the camera, suddenly distracted. "I have to go."

The call disconnected. Cameron stared at the blank screen, possibilities slewing through her brain. What could Jack Sladen be up to now? Did he even know that his designs had been changed? She silently cursed both Jack and Ben for filling her head with ideas when she was ready for a relaxing weekend.

"We're all done," said Noor. "We're going for a drink. Are you joining us?"

Cameron gave her a thumbs up.

"The guys have gone on ahead to get a table," said Noor. "Is everything okay?"

"Yes," said Cameron. She hesitated a moment. "It was Ben."

Noor nodded. "I thought so. I saw your face when the call came through. Are you okay?"

"Me?" said Cameron. "I'm fine. Let's go and get that drink."

The team's regular haunt in the old days had been a historic coaching inn south of the Thames. With the move to a bigger, better and more secure office, they had searched long and hard for a new local that lived up to their high standards. After several months of diligent research, they had settled on a far more modern bar down a cobbled back lane. A far cry from the low beams and plush feel of the old place, this was light and airy with long stripped wood benches, a lengthy list of craft beers, regular live bands, a street food booth churning out tasty bao and bar snacks, and a lively professional clientele. This evening, it was busy with other teams from local tech firms, new friends that they had made since the move. Pete, Joel and Sandeep had already set up camp on one of the tables alongside a chatty group who had arrived early for their play-to-earn guild meetup.

Cameron slid into her seat and Pete handed her a can of beer. She wiped the condensation off it and peered at the label. "This is a new one," she said. She started pouring it carefully and steadily, angling her glass so that the golden liquid could fill it without frothing.

"It's good," said Sandeep. He held up his own glass. "Cheers."

Noor arrived and placed a little beacon on the table. It flashed gently. "Snacks are on the way," she said. "I ordered enough for you as well, Joel, if you can stay."

Joel was already halfway down his drink. "I have to go soon," he said. "Martha's out with the girls tonight."

"Any plans for the weekend?" asked Pete.

"The rugby's on," said Joel. "I'm not playing, but we're taking Chad down to the club."

"Starting his training a bit early, aren't you?" said Sandeep.

"Never too soon," said Joel with a grin. "We might drop in and see Ross and Shell tomorrow as well."

A waiter drone swooped down with a hot package of bao dumplings, placing it neatly next to the beacon on the table. The clip securing the dumpling bag released and the drone collected the beacon and took off again, heading back to the counter to collect the next order. Pete reached over and opened the bag. A cloud of steam billowed out. "Ow! Hot," he exclaimed, sucking his fingers.

The snacks cooled quickly, and the group tucked in. Joel took his leave, and the remaining team members ordered more drinks. As the afternoon gave way to evening, the lights dimmed, and the bar became more crowded. The music was turned up and the chatter became louder. Cameron felt herself relaxing, but something about Ben's call was still nagging at her mind. Statesman Tech. Austin. Jack Sladen.

The penny dropped.

Cloverleaf.

"I have to make a call," she said. "Get me another beer. I'll be back."

8: OLD FLAMES

Chloe glanced up from her screen to see Tenuk disappearing out of the office door. She cursed under her breath. Several weeks of effort to monitor his movements and find out more about him had come to nothing. She was so busy now that she couldn't even keep watch on him when they were working within a few metres of each other.

"How's that backlog coming along?" asked Connie, peering around the edge of the pillar that separated their desks. "Do you think we can get an early finish today?"

"I'm way behind," said Chloe sadly.

"You're working too hard," said Connie. "Have you ever been down to the pool deck? You know we get access if we work enough days in the office. You must qualify by now. I bet you could spend a whole week down there on the hours you've put in."

Chloe brightened up. "There's an idea," she said. "I'd forgotten about the perks of office working. I can bring Audrey, right?"

"Yes, you can," said a man's voice.

Startled, Chloe looked up to see Jack Sladen smiling broadly at her.

"Connie's right," he said. "You've really been putting

in the hours, Chloe. You're doing some great work, but you need a break. I'll arrange pool passes for you and – Audrey, was it? Your daughter, yes?"

Chloe nodded. "That's right," she said. "But I still have a bunch of things to clear on this backlog. Tenuk won't be happy if I leave them through the weekend."

Jack laughed. "I'll handle Tenuk," he said. "He's a little stressed right now with the Foundation launch and Dunswyke coming online. His bark is worse than his bite, Chloe."

Connie winked at her from behind the pillar. "The boss has spoken," she said. "Go get your swimsuit."

Chloe had no choice. She gave in gracefully and wrapped up her final tasks for the day, updating her logs and pushing code through to testing. As she gathered up her jacket and smartscreen, she glanced over at Jack who was still circulating on the office floor, chatting to colleagues and keeping the buzz going. Statesman Tech's team energy was fuelled direct from his personality, and he was making sure the batteries were fully charged before leaving for England. He waved at her. "You're good to go, Chloe," he said. "Enjoy your afternoon."

Back home, Audrey had just arrived home from school and was hopping from foot to foot in excitement. Chloe dug through the closet and found their swimsuits. She had bought them more than a year before in a rush when one of the dizzying series of safe houses they lived in turned out to have a pool.

"Here," she said, throwing the smaller suit to Audrey. "Try this on. You've grown a lot, but it may just be decent."

She was distracted by an incoming call alert. Her smartscreen was through on the kitchen counter, but in this small apartment it was only a few steps away. She recognised the handle and accepted the call with a mixture of pleasure and trepidation.

"SimCavalier, hi," she said. "How are you doing? This is a surprise."

"Hi, Cloverleaf," said Cameron. "Just checking in. I'm doing okay, thanks." She paused. "How are things going with the Sladen Foundation?"

Cameron held her breath. Had she made the right connection?

"It's going well," she said. "How did you know that was my project?"

"I was sure you'd told me about it," said Cameron innocently. "Or just a lucky guess, I suppose."

"Maybe," said Chloe. "I have been so busy. It's crazy. The Foundation launch is getting really close."

"The publicity's ramping up here, that's for sure," said Cameron. "Are you involved in the MetaBand system as well?"

"No, not me," said Chloe. "That's another team. Hey, how about you? You must have had a lot of work too with the Amby platform crash. I saw the news."

Cameron laughed. "Oh, that," she said. "It was just some untested code that got pushed live by mistake. The social channels had a field day making up tales about an imaginary cyberattack. It took a bit of time to fix."

"It was obvious from the moment that story broke that it was just carelessness," said Chloe. "Speaking as a reformed cybercriminal, I should know."

Cameron laughed, genuinely amused. "Have you had heard anything more about The Steamyard?" she asked. "We think that there are some old Pasar people involved, but it's proving hard to penetrate the group."

Chloe made up her mind in a split second. "No," she said. "I haven't." Sharing her unproven suspicions about a colleague would not help Cameron's cause. She needed hard evidence. "I don't know where the other people ended up. You'd probably have more idea than me."

"We know about some of them," said Cameron. "There were quite a few arrests. We never traced King Katong, though, or the Monkey, or Mimi Mao."

"Even if they're still out there, the people didn't define Pasar," said Chloe. "Without Yasmin the Admin keeping all the egos in order and the blessing of the Syndicate and the clients they brought in, they've got nothing."

"Do you think the Syndicate's got wind of this new outfit?" asked Cameron curiously.

"I'm sure of it," said Chloe. "They'll be watching The Steamyard as closely as you are. They'll either suck them into the organisation or close them down."

"The Steamyard has to prove its worth to get into the big money, doesn't it," said Cameron. "I wonder what they're planning as their audition piece?"

"If I hear anything, I'll let you know," said Chloe.

"Thanks," said Cameron. "Look, I'd better get back to what I was doing. You have a good afternoon. Any plans for the weekend??"

"Yes," said Chloe. "There's a pool party at the office later. Audrey's invited too."

Cameron laughed. "Lucky you. Enjoy yourself. Talk soon." She waved and ended the call.

Chloe looked thoughtfully at the blank screen. Who or what was behind The Steamyard? Her suspicious musings were interrupted by Audrey.

"Is this okay, mom?" She appeared at the kitchen door, posing in her swimsuit, corkscrew curls pulled up in a ponytail. "It's not too tight."

"Perfect," said Chloe. She put the screen aside. "You look fabulous. Let's go find this pool."

•

The evening had been fun and messy. Cameron woke to a loud purring that rattled her head. The black and white cat was sitting on the pillow next to her head, positively vibrating in anticipation of breakfast. At the first flicker of movement, the cat extended a paw and patted Cameron gently on the forehead, one claw unsheathed to make the point that, quite frankly, the service in this hotel was poor.

Cameron batted the paw away and gingerly opened one eye. It was already bright outside and it seemed she hadn't pulled the blinds closed last night. She ran an internal checklist. Head, sore. Clothes dumped on the floor. Mascara sticking her eyelashes together. The evening had been late and fun.

What time was it? She rummaged in the covers and found her smartscreen. The daft game she had been playing before falling asleep was still loaded. She closed it and peered at the screen. Ten o'clock already She hadn't had such a long lie in for months.

There were dozens of notifications waiting for her. She scrolled down them idly, reluctant to get out of bed. Most she ignored, swiping them away to the bin. One caught her eye, a new enquiry from a prospective client. She considered reading it, thought better of it, and snuggled back under her duvet.

The cat was unimpressed. The pats on the head became more insistent. Cameron finally gave in and sat up, swinging her legs out of the bed. She paused for a moment and ran a hand through her tousled hair. "Right, you monster," she said to the cat. "Let's find you some breakfast."

Now that it had won, the cat was all affection, rolling happily on the floor for a tummy rub. Cameron automatically obliged, then straightened up and put on her robe. "Come on," she said. The cat trotted ahead of her towards the kitchen, squeaking with pleasure, tail held high.

Cameron gave in to the inevitable and made coffee and toast. She flopped on the sofa and put a bland morning show on the wallscreen while the coffee brewed. Her smartscreen buzzed again. She glanced down and saw that it was another new client enquiry with the same ID as the first. She frowned. There had been no news of any cyberattacks or downed systems. No calls from her team. Why would an unknown contact come through to the company out of the blue on a Saturday morning?

"I've landed," it said. That meant nothing to her. Mystified, she opened the original message in the thread, timestamped just before midnight, and listened.

"Hi, Cameron," said a voice that she recognised immediately. "It's Jack. You're a hard person to get hold of. I've been trying to find you for a long time. I finally worked out you were behind Argentum Associates when I checked the company filing records. It makes sense, really. Silvera. Argentum. I should have figured that out before. Anyway, I'm flying to London overnight tonight, and I'd love to take you out for lunch or dinner, just for old time's sake. Call me when you wake up."

Cameron put her head in her hands. That was the last thing she expected or wanted. If Jack Sladen thought he could pick up their friendship where they had left off after a decade of silence, he was very much mistaken.

Her headache redoubled and her happy mood evaporated. She cursed men in general, and Jack in particular, and crunched on her toast in sullen silence. The cat, sensing trouble, hopped up onto the sofa and nudged Cameron's arm.

"Careful," said Cameron. "You'll make me spill my coffee." She ruffled the cat's fur and pulled at its ears.

She was rewarded with calming purrs and a nudge of the head. "Don't get too comfortable," she warned, draining the last of her drink. The cat curled up obediently on the other cushion and went to sleep.

Her screen pinged, and she glanced down in irritation. This time, however, it was not Jack but Ross. She was not the only person who received alerts from the company's website. She accepted the call.

"Morning," said Ross. "I saw those messages come through overnight. Jack Sladen's caught up with you at last, then."

"Looks like it," said Cameron. "He's the last person I want to see right now. How are you feeling?"

"A bit battered," said Ross. "The grazes are really starting to sting, and the painkillers are barely touching the sides. But I'll live. And I think you should meet up with him."

"Why?" asked Cameron stubbornly, although she knew the answer.

"Come on, Cameron," said Ross. "You're as curious as I am about this Sladen Foundation caper and the Diaulos. I have a lot of questions, and I bet you do too."

"Hundreds," said Cameron. "I want to know if the software behind that DAO is as full of holes as his usual efforts, for one. If he keeps to those low, low standards, he's got no hope with a decentralised application. Once it's out in the wild, he's stuck with whatever coding cockups have been made."

"I know," said Ross, "and I want to know more about

what he's doing. Shell and I were talking yesterday. We'd seriously consider putting some money behind athletes trying to get to the Games, and if this DAO works as well as it's intended, well, I'm in."

Cameron was lost for words. "Ross…"

"We want to put the coins we found to good use," he said. "Find out what you can, Cam."

"Okay," she said. "I'll meet him. I'll let you know everything I can winkle out of him." She rubbed her hands over her face and combed her hair back with her fingers. "I'd better get ready. Send me any questions that occur to you. And Ross?"

"Yes?"

"Take it easy. We want you fit for the Games, too."

Cameron spent a long and luxurious time under the warm jets of the shower. She emerged feeling a little more human and resigned to the fact that, whether she liked it or not, she needed to meet up with Jack. Not only could she help Ross, but after ten years of fixing problems with Sladen software, she had a lot of questions. If she treated it as a work meeting, learning about the company, she might even get some business out of him.

Picking a throwaway contact ID, Cameron wrote a reply. 'Hi Jack. It's good to hear from you. Happy to meet up while you are in London.' She thought for a moment. Where would she feel most comfortable? 'There are some nice restaurants around Tower Hill for lunch or dinner.' She pressed send.

An automated out of office reply signed 'Zara' came

straight back. Cameron busied herself tidying the apartment while she waited for Jack to pick up the message and respond. Sure enough, ten minutes later he replied. Tower Hill would be perfect, he said, and suggested a pre-dinner drink at his hotel at six. That gave Cameron plenty of time to work out what she wanted to know, and to prepare herself to meet someone she had thought she would never see again.

Jack woke with a start, disoriented and dehydrated. He looked around the generic hotel room and took a moment to get his bearings. He must have dozed off, tired despite the comfortable transatlantic flight. He glanced at the time, did a double take and sat up so fast that his head spun. It was already five in the afternoon – eleven in the morning back home.

"Zara," he barked in irritation. "Why didn't you wake me?"

His assistant was always listening. "I'm sorry, Jack," came a voice from his smartscreen. "You didn't request an alarm. You have a meeting in one hour."

"I know," he replied, already halfway to the bathroom. "Are there any messages for me?"

"Yes, Jack," said Zara. "You have a regular update on data centre operations from Angus at Whitford Networks, an invitation from the news channel to join them in the studio for tomorrow morning's Sunday Breakfast show, and confirmation of your reservation at Dolce Tower Hill tonight."

"Great," said Jack indistinctly through a mouthful of toothpaste. "I'll do the show, just find out where I need to be and when. Check the report from Angus and let me know if there are any concerns." He grabbed a towel and headed for the shower.

Refreshed and awake, he made it to the bar with five minutes to spare. He looked around carefully, suddenly nervous. Would he recognise her? How much had they both changed in the intervening years? He had tried to find pictures and posts online, but she seemed to be remarkably careful about her digital footprint. Anything he had found was locked down tight. Images were indistinct and blurred, her face obscured. Some digging by Zara had found pictures from a few years before in a corner of the web he did not visit, but they were long lens shots that simply confirmed for him that she was still slim, dark haired and tall.

And there she was. Jack caught his breath and realised he had been nervous of this meeting all along. She stood at the door, silhouetted against the light, looking around the bar. Jack raised his hand and waved. She came over the meet him, elegant in trousers, boots and a light jacket.

"Hi, Jack," she said. "It's good to see you."

"Hi, Cameron," he replied. "It's good to see you too." He tried to flash the trademark Slade smile, but that projection of his public image felt wrong. He didn't need to put up a front with her. He found himself grinning with genuine pleasure. "You haven't changed at all."

"Oh, I have," said Cameron. She seemed more serious, more reserved.

"How's the family?" asked Jack.

"They're well, thanks," said Cameron. "Aunt Vicky was asking after you."

"She was quite the character," said Jack. "And Charlie? He had a little girl, didn't he?"

"Not so little now," said Cameron, smiling. "She's taller than me and twice as sassy. I have another niece and a nephew as well."

The ice was broken. Cameron looked more relaxed, and Jack was relieved.

"What can I get you?" he asked, nodding at the bar. "Gin and tonic? We have an hour or so before dinner."

"Sure," said Cameron. "That'd be great."

They settled at a table in the corner of the bar. Jack held up his glass. "To old friends," he said.

Cameron clinked her glass against his and met his gaze. "Old friends." She took a sip of her drink. "And new projects," she said. "You've been busy, haven't you? What's really going on in Dunswyke?"

Jack managed the trademark smile this time. "So much good stuff, Cameron," he said. "Let me tell you all about it."

Cameron's feelings towards Jack had mellowed considerably by the time they got to dessert. She admitted to herself that the wine helped, but his enthusiasm and sincerity was catching.

"The beauty of the DAO is that it's controlled by the community," said Jack. "It's completely decentralised and governed by the community. All the Diaulos holders vote on the investments that the Foundation makes into the athletes."

"I hope you've audited that code properly," said Cameron. "Your software doesn't have the best reputation in my field."

Jack looked hurt. "I know we've made mistakes in the past," he said. "Occasional errors that got through testing. You know how it goes."

"Not really," said Cameron. "You've had some really serious vulnerabilities over the years. It's a miracle that none of them led to big data breaches or malware injections. Although, to be fair," she said, taking another mouthful of her chocolate brownie, "the errors have been so glaringly obvious that we've generally found them and fixed them for you before you even knew they were there."

"I guess I have to thank you for that," said Jack modestly.

"Not just me," said Cameron. "The whole infosec world. It's a team effort. Be careful with the Foundation DAO, though. You can't ride your luck like that with decentralised code. It'll blow up in your face."

Jack nodded earnestly. "I know," he said. "I've made some big changes. I have an excellent team in place now. I managed to pick up a really experienced Chief Technology Officer with access to top class development resources. It's all done in the spirit of the Foundation, as well. Some of the most talented programmers we have are based in seriously disadvantaged new world countries. We're making life better for a lot of people."

Cameron made a half-hearted mental note to ask Cloverleaf about the CTO but wondered if her antipathy towards the project had really been based on her antipathy towards Jack himself. Was she being unfair by questioning everything? There was nothing sparking her instinct for trouble. One final question occurred to her.

"How does MetaBand fit into all this?" she asked.

Jack laughed and winked at her conspiratorially. "You'll find out soon enough," he said. "I can't talk about it, even with you. It's embargoed until the formal announcement after Easter. Let's just say that it's not only about connecting people."

Cameron raised an eyebrow.

"There are a couple of big surprises to come," he said. "You'll see the final pieces of the jigsaw that make the Sladen Foundation truly decentralised and globally relevant."

"That's why you're in town," said Cameron, realisation dawning.

"That's right," said Jack. "I'm heading up to Dunswyke tomorrow to oversee the final touches at headquarters. I'll be there right through Easter weekend, and the big press conference is on the Tuesday. Make sure you watch it."

"Oh, I will," said Cameron. "I can't wait." She stifled a yawn. It was getting late. Jack still looked as fresh as a daisy. He must be running on Texas time.

"You look tired," said Jack, reading her mind. He waved at the table's customer service sensor. "The bill, please."

A few moments later, a waiter appeared bearing two shot glasses. "So nice to see you, Mr Sladen," he said. "Your bill has been sent to your account. Please, have some Grappa, on the house."

"Thank you," said Jack, taking a sip of the aromatic liquid and inhaling its scent. "I've enjoyed our evening. Maybe we can do this again soon?"

"Maybe," said Cameron. "Let's stay in touch." She yawned again. "I have to go."

Jack waved at the sensor. "Taxi, please."

In less than a minute, an autocar slid to a halt outside the restaurant.

Cameron drained the last of her glass of Grappa and stood up. "Good to see you, Jack."

Jack pushed his chair back and reached out for a hug. "You too, Cameron," he said. "Take care."

Cameron left the restaurant and jumped into the taxi without a backward glance. As the autocar zipped silently along the London streets, she reflected on the evening. She didn't want to admit how much fun it had been. Maybe Jack Sladen wasn't so bad these days, after all.

9: PRIVET

Cameron woke late on the Sunday morning, the cat once again wailing for food. This time she jumped out of bed with more energy and decided to get some fresh air and breakfast out in town. She wanted some time to reflect on her meeting with Jack and the snippets of information she had managed to glean from him.

Showered and dressed, she skipped down the stairs from her apartment and out into the street. The weather was much warmer, spring giving way to early summer, and there was a lively buzz around the area. Cameron strolled towards the bustling Borough Market. She might pick up a coffee and a pastry at her favourite bakery or see if one of her friends was around to meet for brunch.

Before she could call anyone, her smartscreen pinged with an incoming alert. It was Charlie.

"I thought you were away?" said Cameron, confused.

"We are," said Charlie, "we're at Nasser's place, but something's come up and I know you'll know the answer."

"Am I Tech Support today?" asked Cameron. "It'll cost you."

"Yes, you're definitely Tech Support and if you can fix this, I owe you a beer," said Charlie.

Cameron glanced around and spotted an empty bench

in a small park nearby. She settled down in the sunshine. "Shoot," she said. "What's the problem?"

"Dilan's been playing Team Nine with his cousin," said Charlie. "They got all excited because they won some kind of special character. You know Team Nine, don't you? It's the biggest thing with the kids at the moment."

Cameron laughed. "I can see an ad for it on the street right opposite me now. It's ridiculously popular. The augmented characters are superb. It's as if they're in the room with you."

"Yes, well, you were always a bigger gamer than me," said Charlie. "Anyway, Dilan got this notification to say he'd unlocked a secret character called Privet."

"That's so cool," said Cameron. "Privet's a throwback to the very first game that those developers launched. It's a nice little Easter egg for those in the know."

"That's what Dilan said," said Charlie. "Very seasonal, I thought. Anyway, he clicked on it, and it snarled the system up completely."

"Oh, dear," sighed Cameron. "When you say he clicked on it, was the notification inside the game?"

"No," said Charlie. "It was a message that came into his chatbox."

"He knows not to click on random stuff," said Cameron, exasperated.

"Don't be too hard on him, Cam," said Charlie. "He showed me the message before he clicked. It was all branded up as Team Nine and it had been forwarded from one of the group of friends he normally plays with. He had a ten-minute window to claim the character."

"That's a classic trap," said Cameron. "Showing you something you want and giving you a tight deadline. It's an easy way to stop people checking where a message has really come from. What's the damage? How far through your systems has it gone?"

"We've been lucky," said Charlie. "He was using his own gamepad, the one you set up with a direct datalink, so he wasn't signed in on Nasser's home network. There's a popup saying that the device is locked."

"That's a bonus," said Cameron. "This is almost certainly a new bit of ransomware doing the rounds. Switch it all off and don't touch it. Tell Dilan not to worry, and I'll try and fix it when I come down next weekend."

"Thanks, Cam," said Charlie, sounding relieved.

"You owe me a beer, don't forget," said Cameron. "I'll see you on Friday, hopefully. If this spreads as fast as I expect then I have a busy week ahead."

She abandoned any ideas of a lazy brunch and instead picked up snacks from the market to keep her going through the day. Laden with olives, cheese, dips and fresh bread she returned to her apartment and switched on her computer. First stop was to check on Mephisto, and sure enough the little AI had news for her. The Privet Easter egg was multiplying. Messages featuring the link were growing exponentially, and the pattern bore all the hallmarks of The Steamyard's handiwork.

Cameron logged into her regular infosec forums. There

was a low level of chatter about it already, and she was able to add what she knew into the mix. She dropped Mephisto's latest report onto the board and a familiar handle appeared in the conversation. Ross, under his nickname of RunningManTech, couldn't stay away from the job even when he was supposed to be recuperating.

'Morning, SimCavalier,' he typed, maintaining the pseudonymity of the forum. 'What has your pet picked up this time, or is this just an April fool?'

'Morning, RunningManTech,' she replied. 'No joke. It came through a real-world connection. Mephisto just confirmed the spread of the malware.'

On her smartscreen, she pinged a message directly to Ross. 'Shouldn't you be resting?' she asked.

'I'm bored,' he replied. 'Want me to make a start on tracking down the code and reverse engineering it?'

'If you really want to,' she sent back, 'but I'd rather you concentrated on getting better. It looks like there are a few people working on it already, so why don't you just keep an eye on the forum and pull together what they find? That shouldn't be too strenuous.'

'Okay,' said Ross. He went back to the forum and carried on with the chat.

Cameron popped an olive into her mouth and started scrolling through the code that was already being uploaded into the forum repository. If this was the work of The Steamyard, she needed to get to the bottom of who and what they were.

•

On a train speeding north away from the capital, Jack Sladen dozed fitfully in his first-class seat. Every so often he started awake, peering out of the window at the fields and houses that flashed by. It was a far cry from the older, slower trains that used to take him backwards and forwards from the Borders to London. Now, the first stop at York was barely an hour from the capital, and Edinburgh a mere two hours further on the fastest services.

The carriage was empty but for him. The service was timetabled just too late for any Monday morning commuters, and too early for tourists. Jack found the rhythm of the train curiously relaxing. His jet lag was still kicking in, telling his brain that he should be asleep, and this journey should give him a chance to catch up at last.

"Coffee, Mr Sladen?" The refreshments trolley approached.

"Yes, please," said Jack. The simple machine had recorded his preferences on previous journeys and served up a frothy cappuccino and crisp almond biscotti without prompting. Jack wondered how it learned to identify its customers. Did it use face recognition, or simply match the passenger to their booked seat on the train each time? If he moved across the carriage, would it serve him Earl Grey tea and fruit cake instead? He might mess with the machine a little on his next trip, just for fun. This morning he was content to watch the landscape go by, trying to pick out familiar landmarks at high speed. He spotted the great white horse at the edge of the North Yorks Moors and drank in the view along the River Tyne as the train slowed on its approach to the station in Newcastle. A few more passengers joined his carriage here, most bound for Scotland. He would be leaving them soon. He finished his coffee and started collecting his things together ready to alight.

He got off the train at Alnmouth and found a car waiting for him in the tiny rural station. From the car park, he could see moorland sweeping down to the great sandy inlet of the river and the shining sea beyond. As a teenager he couldn't wait to leave Dunswyke, to move to London and to college, but there was no doubt that the area was outstandingly beautiful, and he was starting to appreciate it more now that he had lived all around the world.

He detoured past his hotel in the little town that clustered at the foot of Dunswyke castle to drop his bags, then went on to the site where Melissa was waiting for him. The muddy car park was now a clean sweep of gravel with a discreet sign at the gate. The stone of the bastle house glowed in the sunshine, and on the surrounding land, restored to its natural grassy state, swathes of wildflowers were rippling in a gentle breeze.

"Looks great, doesn't it?" she said. "It was a tough job, but it's turned out beautifully."

"It's stunning," said Jack. "You really came through for me, Melissa. I wish you could come and manage some of my software projects."

"I'm strictly construction," said Melissa with a smile. "I wouldn't know where to start with the things you do. I've landed another peach of a job, though, once this is signed off."

"I'm not surprised," said Jack. "What will you be doing?"

"I'm going to work for the Dunswyke Estate," said Melissa. "I'll be managing their transformation roadmap, starting with the new visitor centre and the immersive history experience. I can't wait."

"That sounds excellent, Melissa," said Jack. "It's right up your street. I'll have to come and visit when it's finished."

There was the growl of an engine behind them as a van turned into the car park, gravel crunching under its wheels.

"Here come your networking people," said Melissa. "They can show you around the finished data centre. I have to get on with the fit-out of the offices. There's still a fair bit of work to do in there before the media descend on us for the launch." She walked off towards the bastle.

Jack gazed at the building, drinking in the beauty of the setting. The dream had been realised, and it was better than he could have imagined.

Behind him, a van door slammed loudly, and Angus lumbered up to where Jack was standing. Big, bearded and generally sullen, Jack found Angus hard to deal with at times, but there was no doubt that he knew his stuff on managing the complex hardware and specialist software that the Foundation needed. He'd come recommended by Tenuk, whose network was remarkably extensive. Jack preferred to deal with the other half of the partnership, Ella. She was bright and brilliant, and he knew that she was not only working on the security of the data centre but had made a vital contribution to the tokenomics of the Sladen Foundation DAO as part of Tenuk's elite team.

He glanced over towards the car park where the young woman was finishing a call. As he watched, she slipped her smartscreen into her pocket, looked up and gave him a cheery smile and a wave. Jack sighed. He had asked her to join him for dinner at each visit to England over the past few months and each time she had declined. He would miss working with her. He wanted to get to know her better, but deep down he knew he didn't stand a chance.

She walked up to him, looking cool and professional. "Good morning, Jack," she said. "How are you? Good trip over?"

"Yes, thanks," said Jack. "I hear everything's been going smoothly with the data centre."

Angus snorted. "Smoothly?" he said. "Not really. Whose daft idea was it to stick those servers in a cave? It's a pain in the arse."

"It's been fine," said Ella firmly. "Take no notice of him, Jack. It was a lovely idea. Everything is installed and running well. Let's go and have a look." She swept off serenely towards the bastle and Jack trailed helplessly in her wake, Angus bringing up the rear and muttering under his breath.

The path wound through the small wood behind the

house, to all intents and purposes a nature walk. As they neared the cliff face, Ella pointed out several well camouflaged steel barriers nestled in the undergrowth. "We couldn't rely solely on the natural barrier of the cliff face," she said. "This is standard for sensitive data centres and gives us an extra level of physical protection down here at entry level."

They emerged from the wood close to the sheer grey wall of whinstone. Angus pointed up towards the moors. "There are military spec anti-surveillance devices up there. We've got some drone nets as well."

"Drone nets?" asked Jack.

"Yes," said Ella. "I don't know where Angus found these, but they're brilliant."

"How do they work?" asked Jack.

"They're predator drones camouflaged on the ground," said Ella. "If anything tries to overfly the area and scan it, they detect the signal and the flight pattern and if it doesn't match with an authorised device, they take off and grab the offender in their net." She made a grabbing motion with her hands.

"It's better than blasting them out of the sky," growled Angus. "We can interrogate them if they're in one piece."

Jack was impressed. "You've really gone to town on this," he said. "Tenuk told me the security you could provide was second to none, and he was right."

They approached the cave entrance. The foliage had been cut back during the works, but to Jack's relief it was growing steadily and would eventually conceal the entrance once more. Inside it was cool and dark. The unit filled most of the cave, its printed, layered walls rough to the touch. Within it lay the server stacks that held Tenuk's admin software, the complex artificial intelligence that formed the core of the Slade Foundation network.

"Do you want to say hello?" asked Ella.

"Can I talk to it?" said Jack. "Does it have the capacity to communicate?"

"Sure she does," said Ella. "You don't have to be here to talk, as she can chat remotely through all the usual interfaces, but it's as good a place as any." Ella turned to face the winking LEDs of the servers nonetheless, as if she was talking to a real person. "Jack," she said. "I'd like you to meet Yasmin."

10: EASTER EGGS

Cameron rubbed her tired eyes and focused on the long list that occupied the right side of the huge office wallscreen. The week had not gone to plan. It had been fully four days now since the first reports of the Privet ransomware, and locked servers had started trickling in from businesses as well as gamers and personal clients. With the Easter bank holidays beckoning, she was hoping that the combined efforts of cyber security teams around the world would soon start to tell.

As she watched the screen, another client logo appeared. A new pin dropped onto the huge, rippling world map that filled the top left quadrant of the display, casting its ugly red glow on a patch of green in the dead centre of England. Cameron groaned and put her head in her hands for a moment, then looked over to Michelle at the nearest desk.

"They're still coming in," she said. "Peak Medical, now. That's one of your accounts, isn't it, Shell?"

"Not them as well, surely?" replied Michelle incredulously. "We did a round of staff training just a few weeks ago. Ping it over to me, Cam. I'll check the details."

With a cheery chime that belied the circumstances, the report dropped onto Michelle's screen. She opened the client record and scrolled quickly through the logs. Cameron heard the screen reader squawking as Michelle navigated with a practiced ear. "Got it," she said. "Four weeks ago, middle of March. We also reorganised their backup routines and it looks like they're bang up to date."

"Good," said Cameron. "At least that's one company we can get up and running straight away. Can you make sure those backups are screened and roll back the restore to before the infection?"

"Sure thing," said Michelle happily. "I'll have a little word with them next week about following up the training as well."

"Nice to have a good news story in the middle of this mess," said Pete, yawning. "That ransomware is vicious. You were absolutely right back at Christmas. The Santa invasion was just the advance party."

"They haven't claimed responsibility for this one yet," said Cameron, "but it has all the hallmarks of that first Steamyard release, even though the targeting has been different."

"I thought that," said Joel. "It was cunning of them to go through the gaming community this time."

"They're demonstrating another attack vector," said Cameron. "Flexing their muscles and showing potential clients that they're not a one trick pony."

"I didn't expect them to get a solid threat out in the wild so fast," said Sandeep, peering around his screen. "Do we have any idea who's raising money from this?"

Cameron shook her head. "It could be them or it could

be a client," she said. "We can see the ransoms being collected, but nothing has started moving anything yet."

"If it isn't The Steamyard directly, it'll be an organised crime group, I reckon," said Joel.

"More likely OCG than a nation state attack, I agree," said Pete. "It's not strategic. Just a cash grab. Mind you, there are a few countries who need the money. You never know who's pulling the strings."

"I've tried to find some clues to link the ransom collection accounts to the real world," said Noor, "but they are covering their tracks well. As soon as they start to launder the takings, I've got a tracker ready to deploy. If we're lucky, we might find some people on the edge of the network and trace back towards the centre."

"It's worth a shot," said Cameron. She stretched tiredly and gazed out of the great glass window at the nightscape of London. Even this late in the evening, the street below was a mass of light and activity as people enjoyed their Thursday night, the start of a traditional four-day long weekend for Easter. They might have seen the headlines – after all, Team Nine was the hottest game out there right now, and Privet was a legendary character – but most of them would hardly notice the upheaval that the ransomware had caused. The general public had no idea of the number and scale of attacks that were repelled day after day by the national security agencies and countered by the Argentum team and all their fellow infosec professionals around the country and across the world.

This one had made it through the defences. The

temptation of the Easter egg, the lure of claiming the rare Privet character, had caught out people at every level from teenage gamers to senior executives. Hopefully some of those who had been locked out of their files would take the lessons to heart, but most would forget over time and keep their bad habits. Those who were not directly affected might find their favourite sites or networks disabled, an inconvenience at best. Where emergency services had been caught out by slow security upgrades and a single careless click, the outcome would be more serious, likely fatal for a few unlucky patients and their families.

Fast forward weeks or months and there would be some companies winding up their businesses, broken by the attack. Cameron fervently hoped that none of the clients they supported would suffer that fate, but missteps and human error were costly. A moment of carelessness or distraction could allow any of the malware that circulated on the world wide web into a company's systems, costing real money and precious time to fix or opening the door to data thieves. Eventually any stolen data would resurface for sale to the highest bidder, leaving passwords and login details exposed and starting the whole cycle of phishing, cloning, ransoms and theft again.

"Cameron?" Sandeep broke her gloomy reverie. "I think we're making some headway at last."

The wallscreen map was starting to look healthier. Green and amber pins were starting to appear in the sea of red. There was a subtle shift in the atmosphere of the office. Michelle, Pete, Sandeep and Noor were chatting quietly, more relaxed than they had been for hours. Ross, still recuperating at home, was sharing a joke with Joel.

Cameron let out a sigh of relief. "I think you may be right," she said.

"It could have been worse," said Pete. "This Steamyard team is clever."

"Tell me about it," said Cameron. "We were expecting the next wave to be delivered through the mail server network again, but that viral Easter egg was a genius move." She glanced at Noor who was talking quietly and intensely to one of her many international contacts, drawing together as much information as possible from the global community to help them all to manage the attack. "When Noor comes off her call, we'll review what we've got so far."

"Anyone for another coffee?" said Sandeep. He eyed the shiny new coffee machine hopefully.

Cameron shook her head. "Not me," she said. "I want to sleep tonight, and I think we're close to finishing."

"Well, the virus definition's been pushed out," said Pete. "Although everyone's been sharing the heck out of that Easter egg, the updated antivirus filters on mail and media should stop it being delivered."

"That's good," said Cameron. She checked on the wallscreen again. The green pins were winning. "It looks as if we've slowed the spread right down."

Noor finished her call, signing off with a cheery "Bonne nuit."

"What news from Paris?" asked Cameron.

Noor gave her a broad grin. "You're going to love this," she said. "One of their researchers found a temporary workaround for the ransom payment. The ransom asks for Bitcoin, but he managed to retrieve the release key by making a payment denominated in Sats instead."

Cameron started laughing and found she couldn't stop. "That's a terrible coding error on The Steamyard's part," she said, catching her breath. "With a hundred million Satoshis in a single Bitcoin, they're releasing the ransomed data for literally pennies."

On screen, Ross was grinning and wincing with pain at the same time. "Stop it," he said. "It hurts when I laugh."

"I'm sure they'll fix that pretty fast," said Pete.

"Oh, of course they will," said Noor, "but it's an automated process so they probably won't spot it straight away. For now, though, anyone who's been caught out can get their data back fast."

Cameron grabbed her smartscreen and sent a quick message to her brother. "I've let Charlie know so he can release Dilan's device. That's a quick cure that's saved me a job at the weekend."

"The anti-virus is the other half of the equation," said Pete. "The vaccine if you like. Anyone who gets the Easter egg should be protected now if their update has been patched in."

"Excellent," said Cameron. "That's perfect timing. We may actually get to enjoy the weekend." She looked across at Noor. "Can you pass the baton to that team in Honolulu? They can take the next co-ordinating shift."

Noor nodded. "I already spoke to them. They're all set. It hasn't yet reached its peak in their region so hopefully they can stop it before it starts over there."

"Right, let's pack up," said Cameron. A huge yawn caught her by surprise. "Most of our clients are safe for the weekend. I'm going to Charlie's tomorrow, but I'll be working from there. Pete, you're on call until Sunday, aren't you?"

"Yes," said Pete. "I'm away on a dive trip from Monday morning for a few days."

"I'm in to cover Easter Monday," said Noor. "Susie will be back in the country on Tuesday as well." She pointed at her screen. "She's just messaged me to see how we're doing."

"Where is she?" asked Cameron. "I thought she was still in Europe?"

"She is," said Noor, laughing. "It's very late. I think her evening is going well." She shared her screen to the wall display. Susie was livestreaming from a nightclub, laser beams sweeping across the crowd and a DJ on stage making luminous trails with swirling batons. Some of the partygoers close to Susie were wearing headsets, enjoying an augmented experience with anime dancers.

"I need some of that," said Joel. "Martha's mum is babysitting on Saturday. I'll have to see what gigs are on. We haven't had a proper night out together in months."

Night out, thought Cameron. She thought back to

the previous Saturday. Her night out with Jack felt like a long time ago, although it had been only a few days. She wondered idly what he was doing over Easter. Would he be making his staff work through the holiday, getting ready for the big announcement on Tuesday, or would he actually have some rare down time? She thought he still had an aunt in Scotland. Maybe he was going to visit her, dropping his commercial persona and playing the dutiful nephew for a day. The idea made her smile.

Her thoughts turned to Ben. She hadn't yet called him back about his concerns over the MetaBand hardware, but she had nothing concrete to tell him yet. That would just have to wait. Right now, they all needed a rest after a hard week and a job well done.

•

Cameron reached the village early on Friday afternoon. The sun was shining with a warmth unusual for mid-April, and the forecast was good for the Easter weekend.

"Do you think I should buy some of these?" asked Charlie, showing his sister a marketing message that had just popped up on his screen. "You know your way around crypto investing, Cam. What's the story on Diaulos?"

Cameron took a sip of her drink, relaxing in the sheltered warmth of the village pub's beer garden. "I'm not sure about it, to be honest, Charlie," she said. "We're days away from the launch of the Foundation but no one has seen as much as a glimpse of the underlying code for the coin or for the investment system. I've read the whitepaper, but it says absolutely nothing beyond what you've already heard in their publicity. I'm waiting for the release of the protocol before I make any judgements."

"They're sending athletes to the Olympics, though," said Sameena. "Is it endorsed by the International Olympic Committee? They wouldn't let their brand be attached to anything dodgy, would they?" She shifted uncomfortably on the wooden bench and her foot caught the dog's water bowl that was tucked under the table. Water trickled over the grass and down onto the path. "Whoops," she said. "Sorry, Roxy."

Cameron shook her head. "There's no official link between this coin and the IOC," she said. "They're being very careful to avoid saying anything that could suggest an endorsement."

"Oh," said Sameena, surprised. "I just assumed…"

"I'm sure that Jack would be delighted at that," said Cameron with a wry smile. "If the public decides there's a link, he can deny it all he wants to while the sales of the coin shoot up. Win-win."

"Huh," said Charlie. "That's sneaky." He shuffled along the narrow bench and stood up, stretching. "Another beer, anyone? I'll go and get a refill." He called across the pub garden to a gaggle of children who were playing around a tree. "Kids! If you want more drinks, come and get them."

Dilan came trotting across the grass, red from running around, and followed his father through the low doorway into the pub. He emerged a few moments later carrying the refilled water bowl, walking slowly and carefully to avoid spilling it. He put it down in a clear spot by the table, away from stray feet, and ruffled Roxy's curly coat. "There you go," he said as she bent her head to drink.

"It's nice to see you running around, Dilan," said Cameron. "You're normally hiding behind a screen. Is everything okay with your game now?"

"Yes, Auntie Cam," said Dilan. "Dad said you sorted it all out. I haven't lost any of my progress."

"I'm glad to hear it," said Cameron. "I'm sorry there wasn't a real Privet character. That would have been cool."

"I know," said Dilan sadly. "Maybe they'll do a proper limited-edition Privet for us one day. I have loads of good assets, though. I'm in the pro league."

"Very good," said Cameron. "What does that mean, exactly?"

"I get to choose extra weapons and I can win some really rare prizes," said Dilan proudly. There was a shout from the tree. "Coming!" he called. He scrambled to his feet and ran back to the game in progress.

"He's hooked on those screen games," said Sameena.

"He's doing okay," said Cameron. "He's good at the games, and he's outside playing every chance he gets. I wouldn't worry about him."

"You're right," said Sameena. "My brothers were just as bad back in the day." She frowned. "Talking of them, why would you think that Diaulos is a risky investment?" she asked. "There is so much speculation about it. Nasser's planning on getting some. He says it's going to pay off his mortgage."

"It might," said Cameron, "but I hope he doesn't overstretch himself. It's the same with any investment like this. There's always a risk, especially when something's new and untested. I hope he's getting proper advice."

"I'm sure he is," said Sameena confidently.

Cameron wasn't so convinced. "I don't think anyone can advise on this coin yet," she said. "The presale hasn't even started yet. We don't know enough about it. Just because everyone is talking about it doesn't mean it's a sound investment. It's probably fine, but it makes me nervous when I can't see the nuts and bolts."

"Okay," said Sameena. "I trust your instincts on things like this. I'll check up on what Nasser's doing, but there's no harm in him picking up a few coins, is there?"

Charlie put a fresh round of drinks down on the table and slid into his place on the bench. "What's the verdict on this coin, then?" he asked. He looked from Cameron to Sameena and laughed. "That bad? I don't believe you. You just don't trust Jack Sladen."

Cameron took a moment to reflect and examine her feelings. Was her automatic suspicion of the whole project simply part of her complex relationship with Jack over the years, or had her usually reliable sixth sense picked up something genuinely awry?

"I don't know, Charlie," she said. "I met up with him last weekend, and he's mellowed a lot. The Foundation has a lot of promise and I'd like it to be above board and successful. Registering is safe enough but let me do some digging before you hand any money over."

"Okay, Cam," said Charlie. "I trust you. Now, enough work talk. You're supposed to be relaxing this weekend."

"I know," said Cameron. "I've been busy. It's hard to switch off."

"Are you going to help me set up the hunt for the village kids?" said Charlie. "Or have you had enough of Easter eggs?"

"The chocolate kind are no problem at all," said Cameron. "I'd love to help out. Do you remember doing those when we were little? I know some great hiding places." She looked down at Roxy who was lying in the shade of the table. "The challenge is putting the eggs somewhere the kids can find them, and the dogs can't."

"Anywhere close to that cat of Aunt Vicky's is safe enough," said Charlie. "Every dog in the village is terrified of Donald. They cross the road to avoid him. I swear he's getting worse."

"I'm not sure that's possible," said Cameron. "He's a horror." She looked around guiltily, half expecting either her aunt or the cat to appear. "If he turned out to be the shadowy mastermind behind The Steamyard, I wouldn't be at all surprised."

Charlie laughed. "You're daft, sis. I'm glad you made it down this weekend. Relax and enjoy yourself. You've earned it."

Cameron took a sip of her drink and smiled. "It's been a tough few days," she said, "and I'm sure it's not entirely over, but there are some capable hands looking after everything right now, so yes, I'm taking every moment that I can." She felt the tension draining. "Where do you want these Easter eggs, then, Charlie? Do you have a plan?"

"I do," said Charlie. "The kids are all meeting on the village green at twelve noon. We're putting on some drinks for the parents, obviously." He looked around at the busy beer garden, making sure that no passing youngsters could overhear, and lowered his voice conspiratorially. "We can't go into the gardens, especially the ones that are getting ready for the Mayday open garden event." He looked at Cameron. "You're coming back for that next weekend, aren't you?"

"If I can," said Cameron.

"Sameena and I have been slaving over that garden for weeks," said Charlie. He looked across the beer garden to where his younger children were playing, and his eldest was chatting to a friend. "They haven't lifted a finger."

"We were just as bad," protested Cameron. "Don't you remember when Mum decided she was going to plant a whole new border? You went off with your mates and left me to do all the digging, which I hated, by the way, and you were grounded for a week when you got back."

"I'd forgotten that," said Charlie. "How funny."

"Come on, Charlie," said Cameron. "The plan."

"Yes, right," he whispered as a small child walked past, oblivious to the plotting that was going on above her head. "As this is a very late Easter, it's warmer than usual.

We've got to be careful that the eggs don't melt before the kids get there."

"We can go out early and find the shady spots," said Cameron. "Down the edge of the stream, under the bridges, in the climbing trees."

"We can go up the street a little as well," said Charlie. "We just need to avoid…"

"Donald," said Cameron. "Yes, I know. We can put the more obvious eggs out just before the kids arrive so that they don't melt."

"I think we have a plan," said Charlie.

Cameron gave him a broad grin. "It's nice to be thinking about something other than work," she said happily. "This is going to be fun."

11: HUNTED

Bright and early on Tuesday morning, refreshed and revived, Cameron was back in the office. She walked in the door and laughed as she spotted a row of Easter eggs lined up on one of the shelves.

"They weren't hard to find," she said.

Sandeep turned around from his accustomed place tending the new coffee machine. "You want a proper Easter egg hunt round the office?" he asked. "I can arrange that. Strictly the edible kind, though."

"I'm good," said Cameron. "Where did these come from?"

"I know the Easter bunny," said Sandeep, tapping the side of his nose. "Connections." He looked up as the door opened. "Here she comes now."

"Susie?" said Cameron. "Sandeep says you're the Easter bunny."

"Yes," said Susie. "That's me. Actually, there was a two for one offer in the airport shop. I couldn't let that pass."

"Excellent work," said Cameron. "Although, after this weekend, I don't know if I can face any more chocolate."

"I can face more chocolate," said Joel, coming in on the tail end of the conversation.

"Help yourself," said Susie. "They go well with coffee."

She picked up her mug and a small chocolate egg and settled at her desk.

The morning flew by. Cameron glanced up from her routine work and was startled to see it was almost time for Jack's big announcement. She stopped what she was doing and put the news channel feed up on the wallscreen.

"It's time for the press conference," she said.

A window popped open in the corner of the screen, and Ross's face appeared. "Hi, everyone," he said. "I got back home from training just in time for the show. Are you all seeing this?"

A series of adverts gave way to the news channel's lunchtime show logo, and then to beautifully edited drone footage giving viewers a bird's eye view of the estate, the restored bastle house standing proud in its beautiful surroundings. A time lapse of the transformation showed the enormity of the work that had been done. The drone flew over a group of people who waved enthusiastically.

"The Sladen Foundation has created new jobs in the area," said a sugary voiceover. "It will also support more than fifty talented athletes to reach this summer's Olympic Games in Reykjavik." The aerial shots of the bastle and moorland were replaced by images of runners in an arid African landscape, swimmers training in abandoned hotel pools on half-drowned resort islands, young footballers in crowded shanty towns, and a gymnast tumbling gracefully across a space between tents in a refugee camp.

"This is really good," said Cameron.

On his window on the wallscreen, Ross nodded. "Can't

fault them," he said approvingly. "It's a great initiative. It feels solid."

"That's what I thought," said Cameron. "Jack was very convincing. I actually think he's doing something right, for once."

"You still don't like him, do you?" said Joel.

"I don't know," said Cameron. "It was good to see him again. It doesn't change the fact that his software has been slapdash for years and he has no attention to detail, but he has great ideas and I think he finally has a talented team around him who are doing decent work."

"Did you tell him that?" asked Ross.

"The first bit, yes," said Cameron. "The second part, no. He's big-headed enough as it is." She checked the time. "He should be on any minute. He said that the big announcements would be scheduled to catch the lunchtime newsreels."

"What are you expecting?" asked Noor.

"I think he'll announce the Diaulos presale and launch dates and give a simple overview of the Foundation DAO," said Cameron. "He hinted that there were some big surprises to come, but I bet he won't go into much detail."

"Why?" asked Susie. "Is that because most people watching won't understand it?"

"Probably because he doesn't entirely understand it himself," said Noor darkly.

Cameron laughed. "Yeah, he's not really one for the fine details," she said. "There'll be an update to that terrible whitepaper dropping today as well. Check the website, Noor. It'll probably be released as soon as the announcements are made."

"I want to get my hands on that," said Michelle. "It had better have more detail in it than the original."

"It'll be interesting to see how much control he keeps to himself," said Noor.

"In theory, he won't have any control," said Joel. "It should all be decision making by the community."

"In theory, that's the case with every distributed app," said Noor. "It's remarkably rare in practice."

"You don't trust him either, do you?" said Joel. "Poor guy."

There was a flurry of activity on the screen and Jack Sladen strode into view. The team fell silent and listened intently. He thanked the project team for their work on the site and expressed his delight at being back home at last in Dunswyke, which made Cameron snort with laughter. He waxed lyrical about the community governance of the Sladen Foundation. None of this was news to Cameron. She was waiting for the embargoed revelations about the MetaBand network and the other surprises he'd hinted at. She turned to the others.

"What do you know about the hardware behind a network like MetaBand?" she asked.

"I know my way round satellite comms," said Joel. "It was all we used in the army. I bet Pete's up to speed as well. Why?"

"I had a tip-off about some odd hardware configurations

in this system," said Cameron. She glanced at Noor. "Ben's working on the project over in Texas. He called me about some design changes that he thought didn't make sense."

"What kind of thing are we talking about?" asked Joel. "They're usually really simple units."

"He said they'd added high spec data processing chips and storage in the receivers," said Cameron, "and extra capacity in the microsats as well."

"That's not needed for normal comms," said Joel instantly. "I wonder what else these units are designed to do?"

"I think we're about to find out," said Susie, pointing at the screen. A simplified 3D representation of a network, heavily branded with the MetaBand logo, was turning this way and that. The same sugary voice was narrating.

"Each MetaBand receiver also acts as a node on the Diaulos network," it said. "Homes attached to MetaBand around the world are ready and waiting to secure the coin and provide homeowners with a passive income as transaction validators."

"Oh, that explains it," said Noor. "That's what they need the processors for."

"Clever idea," said Cameron. "I can see why he wouldn't breathe a word before the embargo was lifted."

"It's unusual," said Ross from the screen, "but it's one way to decentralise the whole network, I suppose."

"I'd better call Ben," said Cameron. "He was worried. It looks as if his suspicions were unfounded."

The graphics on the screen faded and the coverage

returned to the press conference. Jack was speaking again. "The Diaulos presale opens on Friday at 7am Eastern Time," he said. A QR code flashed up on the corner of the screen. Cameron took a screen grab. "Our founder community can look forward to some fantastic benefits of participation, from enhanced voting power to real-world rewards, and will earn a return on their investment from the moment they commit to the presale."

"I want to read the whitepaper," said Noor, "and I think we should dig into their code base as well. Who's developing it? Who's maintaining it?"

"Fair questions," said Ross from his remote window.

"I've already tackled him on that," said Cameron grimly. "I got nowhere."

Jack Sladen held up his hand for silence and the excited buzz from the press corps died away. "There is one more piece of the puzzle," he said. "The Sladen Foundation is supporting local people…" He nodded at a gaggle of people, probably new employees, who were out of shot. "…and talented athletes. It's providing high speed connectivity and a passive income through MetaBand. We want all of you to be part of the magic too."

Cameron groaned. "Who writes this stuff?" she said. "That's not Jack talking. What have they got up their sleeves now?"

On the screen, Jack held up a small bracelet, a simple wearable health tracker. "In the spirit of the Olympics, we're helping people to get fit and get moving, and earn money as they go," he said. "We mined gold with physical energy, and Bitcoin with CPU energy. Now anyone can mine Diaulos with their daily steps. We call this Proof of Walk, the final piece of the Diaulos protocol, securing the chain in a truly democratic and decentralised way. You can join us right now by ordering your POW bracelet. Take a step into the future with the Sladen Foundation."

Cameron had to admit she was impressed with the concept, but she rolled her eyes at the terrible speech writing and the corny humour. Proof of Walk was a joke that only a select few would pick up, playing on the local accent's rendering of walk and work. On screen, Jack was grinning like the cat that got the cream, and hacks were clamouring for attention.

He held up his hands and called for silence. "I'd love to answer all of your questions now," he said, "but that's all we have time for today." He stepped down from the podium and walked briskly away, to the obvious annoyance of the press corps.

"That's genius," said Joel at last. "Shame he wouldn't take questions. I have plenty."

Cameron looked thoughtfully at the screen. Jack Sladen and his terrible attention to detail. "He can't afford to," she said. "It would tarnish his golden boy reputation if he stuttered over an answer."

Jack's timing had been slightly off. The programme hadn't reached its allotted end. As a filler, someone sent up a news drone to fly over the site and provide a backdrop for speculative commentary on the latest announcement. It circled over the jumble of outside broadcast units then flew over the bastle and looped around the back of the building, following the line of the steep escarpment that sheltered the building from the wild sweep of moorland above it.

"That's Ella!" shouted Susie.

Cameron whirled around. The camera had caught a clear shot of two people standing behind the bastle at the edge of a patch of woodland, moments before the broadcast image jerked and spun and the screen went black.

Ella, their former colleague and Susie's old partner, was unmistakeable, but the greater shock for Cameron was the man standing beside her.

"That's Angus," she said, her scalp prickling in horror.

The last time she had seen the man, she had chased him and lost him in a crowd, seeking answers about an attack on a nuclear power plant. Now he was there at Dunswyke alongside their former colleague. She had been mixed up in the same scheme and fled after a deadly attack on the old Argentum offices.

Their presence shattered her confidence in Jack Sladen, his new ventures, and his new team. There were criminals at the heart of the Sladen Foundation, and that changed everything.

12: COVER UP

Tenuk slammed his fist down in frustration and glared around the room. The leaders of his fledgling business teams were gathered around the virtual table. They couldn't see Tenuk's real face, but the cartoon pangolin avatar that represented him was expressive enough.

"It was a tiny detail," said a small grey kitten, glancing nervously up the table. "The spec asked for ransoms to be payable in different coins, and we're used to working in Sats here for micropayments."

"I don't care, Sterix," said Tenuk, his voice ice cold and distorted by the privacy filter. "I can't believe a basic error like that got through testing." He turned his attention to the leader of the quality assurance team, represented by swirling lines of light making a glowing, animated 3D sphere that hovered in place in the virtual room. "How did you not pick this up?"

"We ran all the standard tests," said a disembodied voice. "We know what we're doing. The sandbox payments worked perfectly."

"I don't pay you for standard tests and automated audits," said Tenuk. "You need to get under the skin of the software. The client expects it. I expect it. The Steamyard's reputation hangs on the quality of our product and the value it delivers. We'll be lucky to break even on this job. You know the penalties in your contracts. Pray that the client doesn't trigger compensation payments."

He muted the two audio feeds, ignoring their mutters of protest, and turned his attention to the pixelated being that stood by his side. "Admin," he said, "what are the latest figures?"

"In the last twenty-four hours, the Privet Easter egg has been opened 9,480 times," came a calm and competent voice. The avatar's classic CryptoPunk look extended from its spiky hair down to its black boots. "That's down on the peak of fifty thousand a day and we're seeing a rapid tail-off of engagement."

"Where are we against revenue targets?" asked Tenuk.

"Low," said the Admin. "We're down more than thirty percent on projections. However, the hole in the payment gateway has been repaired so we're getting full value from the long tail of ransoms."

"Good," said Tenuk, mulling over the problem. "Is there any demographic we can target with a second round of injections?"

"Yes," replied the Admin. "Analysis shows lower engagement than expected in Pacific territories among smart device gamers."

"That's the new target," said Tenuk decisively. "Sterix, I want social engineering teams straight in there and start circulating the updated worm on all the social channels. You screwed up, you fix it. The targets for the territory are doubled."

"But Pangolin…" said the nervous grey kitten avatar.

"No excuses," said Tenuk. "If you want to be part of The Steamyard, you deliver. I'm watching."

The kitten and the abstract sphere vanished. "Admin," said Tenuk, "Keep an eye on them."

"Of course, Pangolin," said the pixelated figure. "I have all the team leaders under surveillance. I will report any anomalies."

The call ended, leaving Tenuk alone at the table. He looked out of the virtual office window to the crowds of avatars strolling past. He realised he was sweating. Back in the real world, the apartment was hot despite the cooling systems he'd installed for his equipment. The temperatures in Austin were rising as spring gave way to summer, and he knew it would get worse before it got better.

An alert pinged, and Tenuk frowned as he saw Jack Sladen's ID flash up in the air. He wasn't expecting a call until their scheduled meeting a few hours later. He would have to take this in person.

"Good morning, Jack," he said. He glanced at the time and realised that while concentrating on Steamyard business he had missed the big announcement. "The launch broadcast looked excellent," he lied. "I caught the livestream over breakfast."

"You watched all of it?" asked Jack.

Tenuk thought quickly. What had gone wrong? What had he missed? "I had a call come in from our development team," he said. "I didn't see the whole thing."

"Your people at Whitford Networks screwed up on the security," said Jack. "Their data centre defence systems took down a news drone right at the end of the live feed."

Dammit, thought Tenuk. It was barely eight in the morning, and he was already wondering what else could go wrong today.

"Zara and our PR people are on the case," said Jack. "I didn't see the incident but there was a lot of fuss among the press corps. At the moment it's being treated as a bird strike and that's exactly how it needs to stay. I'm still at Dunswyke and I've told Whitford to make sure that the news drone is retrieved, and the damage is consistent with our story."

Tenuk tapped a few keys and quickly found the news channel stream of the press conference. He watched the last few minutes carefully. Not only was the defence drone that had taken down the camera briefly visible on freeze frame, but there was also a clear shot of Angus and Ella skulking behind the Sladen Foundation headquarters. Jack wouldn't have any idea of the trouble that image could cause on its own.

"I've found the recording," he said. "It's not obvious unless you know what you're looking for."

"I don't care," said Jack. "It's frankly embarrassing, Tenuk. It drew attention away from the launch announcement, and it risks overshadowing the countdown to the presale."

"I'm sure it'll be fine, Jack," said Tenuk. "Is Zara running sentiment analysis for the Foundation?"

"Yes, she is," said Jack. "So far, it's positive, but Zara tells me that there are images circulating already. I don't want any awkward questions about our activities at Dunswyke. It's the last thing we need for the brand and our reputation."

Tenuk stifled a sigh. All the man seemed to be concerned about was public image. Jack's ego was remarkably fragile under the bluff and confident exterior. The project was going perfectly, and this would be a storm in a teacup. "I'll get onto Ella and Angus right now," he said. "At least you can be confident that the security systems are as tight as they can be."

"Yes, I suppose so," said Jack. "Their work's been thorough. I'll leave you to deal with them. I'm staying here a little longer than planned to make sure everything goes smoothly."

"I'll see you when you get back," said Tenuk. "Everything is under control here."

"Good," said Jack. "Let me know immediately if there is any change." He ended the call.

Tenuk had no doubt that there were others poring over the footage as he was. Someone would spot the hunter drone, know what it was, and wonder why it was there. Annoyingly, Jack was right. This was a situation that needed to be managed.

"Admin," he called into the air.

"Yes, Tenuk," said the calm and competent voice.

"Get into this original footage and edit the last two seconds," he said. "It needs to look like a bird strike.

There's a database to hand of compromised access details for all the news channels. You'll find your way in easily. Cover your tracks well."

"Yes, Tenuk."

"Find any other copies that are circulating online and edit them if you can, take them down if you can't," he continued. "You can liaise with the Sladen Foundation PA. Her name's Zara."

"Yes, Tenuk. I am already in contact with Zara."

Tenuk steepled his fingers, wondering what to do about the glimpse of Angus and Ella. He knew they were keeping very low profiles, but surely no one in authority would be able to identify them in the crowd from the fraction of a second that the drone had passed over them. It would be more trouble than it was worth to try and remove them from the footage, however skilled his team of cyber criminals and black hat hackers. "That's all I need for now," he said.

"Yes, Tenuk," said the Admin, "I'll make this a priority."

"Good," said Tenuk. "Let me know when you're done. I'll deal with Whitford now." He looked at the clock. When Jack was abroad, he preferred Tenuk to be in the office in person, and that meant he only had a limited amount of time to deal with extra-curricular matters. He cursed Angus under his breath. The defence drones were overkill. They might provide an extra layer of protection, but if something like this happened again, it was likely to attract unwanted attention to the location. The last thing Tenuk needed was for anyone to come snooping and stumble on the hidden data centre. That could spell disaster and the end of all their grand plans.

Tenuk pinged a secure meeting link to Angus and got an instant response. Less than a minute later, he was back in his virtual office, glaring at a monkey in a blue and white striped shirt.

"What do you want, King Katong?" asked Angus. "Or are you hiding behind that Pangolin handle these days."

Tenuk clamped down on his anger, resisting the windup. He should never have tracked this man down, let alone brought him into the project. He was a liability, a loose cannon, and the sooner he could be disposed of, the better.

"King Katong is long gone," said Tenuk, his voice level and formal. "You would do well to remember that names from the past are still of interest to certain authorities. I'm sure the infosec community would like to know the whereabouts of The Monkey."

Stalemate.

"Alright, *Pangolin*," replied Angus, emphasising the name. "What do you want?"

"You're sailing close to the wind," said Tenuk. "You and Ella were picked up on the news drone footage at today's grand launch." The monkey avatar raised an eyebrow. "A fleeting glimpse, but you were seen."

"She's got more to worry about than I have," said Angus. His avatar shrugged.

Tenuk changed the subject. He was in a hurry to leave for the office. "Your hunter should have stayed in its hide," he said. "Get the drone it captured and set it up to look like a bird strike."

"Sure, straight away," said Angus sarcastically. "Anything else I can do? You know I'm always at the service of the Sladen Foundation and the mighty Steamyard."

"Nothing else," said Tenuk sharply. "I'll be in touch." He hit the exit button with a burst of anger that took him by surprise. He didn't want to go back to the old days. The future was bright, and it would take more than Angus the Monkey and his silly games to ruin it. Tenuk grabbed his jacket and headed out of the apartment into the bright, clear morning sunshine. The day could only get better.

•

In London, the Argentum office was in uproar. Susie, distraught, was in tears, memories of Ella's betrayal flooding back. Noor was doing her best to calm her friend. Cameron paced the office, agitated and angry.

"Call the police," urged Sandeep. "They need to know."

Cameron shook her head. "There's no point," she said. "They didn't go after Ella for the attack on the office because everything she did was explained away as a coincidence, and they caught the gunmen, so there was nothing more they could do."

"She was named as one of the Snake River team," said Joel. "Wasn't she a suspect in the murder investigation when the lad at the power station drowned?"

"That ended up as a verdict of accidental death," said Ross. "No evidence to say otherwise. The police won't be interested in her."

"What about Angus?" said Joel. "There's got to be something on him."

"Nothing," said Sandeep. "We didn't have anything concrete that they could pin on him after Snake River."

"His house burned down, didn't it?" said Michelle suddenly. "The news reports said it was arson, but no one was ever charged. Surely that would put him on the police radar?"

Sandeep perked up. "Yes, it would," he said. "I bet there's an insurance company or a council department somewhere that wants to know what happened as well."

"We can tell them where to find him. They may want a word," said Joel.

"Good call," said Cameron. "I think it's still a slim chance, but can you two follow up and get the authorities interested?"

"Sure thing," said Sandeep. "Shell, have you got the report from the fire? Who was the officer in charge?"

"I'll check," said Michelle. "Give me a minute."

"What are you going to do?" asked Ross. "Are you going back to Jack Sladen with this?"

Cameron stopped pacing and looked thoughtful. "I'm not sure," she said. "I don't know if he knows what's going on here. He could have hired them completely innocently, or he could be up to his neck in a conspiracy we've barely touched."

"You still don't trust him," said Joel.

"Are you surprised?" said Cameron.

Joel looked embarrassed. "Actually, I think your instincts are pretty good. I don't think I trust him myself anymore."

"If we can't trust him, can we trust his project?" said Noor. "The revised whitepaper for Diaulos is out. I think we take it apart word by word and see what he's really doing."

Susie, still red eyed but calmer, spoke up. "I want to help with that," she said. "Have we got access to any of the code yet?"

Cameron shook her head. "It hasn't been released to the public repositories," she said. "They haven't exactly been transparent about the project."

"That's bad for so many reasons," said Ross. "Apart from anything else, it means that there probably hasn't been an independent audit of the smart contracts that automate everything."

Cameron snapped her fingers. "Brilliant, Ross!" she said. "That's our way in." She grinned, a plan starting to form in her mind. "Keep our investigations quiet. I'm going to try and persuade him to commission an audit from us. When we get our hands on the code, we can run it through our analytical models and see if there's anything sinister underneath."

"Cunning," said Ross. "I know you don't trust him, but does he trust you enough to just grant you access?"

"I think so," said Cameron. "He went to a lot of

trouble to track me down, and he's been a complete gentleman. I've given him no reason to mistrust me. It's entirely possible that he'll ask us to do an audit without any prompting."

"I'm hoping it's all above board," said Ross. "That Foundation DAO is such a bloody good idea." He sighed. "Well, let's get on with it. Shell's got those reports for you, Sandeep. She's pinging them over now."

Sandeep swung around to his screen and started reading through the message from Michelle. Joel was already deep in research and Noor and Susie were poring over the first few paragraphs of the whitepaper.

"I'm going to call in a few favours with my old Army colleagues," said Joel. "I think Pete needs to know about this as soon as he gets back from diving, as well. I wonder where the hunter drone came from. I need a better look at the last couple of seconds of the footage." He tapped a few keys, searching for the recording of the press conference. "That's odd," he continued, frowning. "I'm getting error messages on these links."

"Keep trying," said Cameron. "There's likely to be a lot of traffic on the servers. You won't be the only person digging around for it." She picked up her jacket. "I'll call Jack from home. I want to keep this as casual and friendly as possible."

Susie looked up from her screen, eyes still red. "Will you ask him about Ella?" she said quietly.

"I don't know yet," said Cameron. "Do you want me to?"

Susie gave her a lopsided smile. "I honestly don't know," she admitted. "Do whatever you need to do."

"Okay," said Cameron. She raised her voice and called out to the rest of the team. "Let me know if you find anything."

"Sure thing," replied Sandeep, the others murmuring their agreement. Cameron headed out of the door and off towards home.

13: METABAND

The atmosphere at the Sladen Foundation headquarters was tense. Jack was pacing up and down the office, scowling. The five staff who made up the Foundation's local management team were at their desks and keeping their heads down. They avoided meeting his eyes. Ella was sitting quietly on a plush new sofa in the corner of the room, her fingers worrying at a piece of plastic wrapping that was still stuck in a seam at the base of the arm rest. There was a faint buzz of noise from the ground floor of the bastle where the customer service team sat under the great arched ceiling. They dealt with the tiny percentage of calls that could not be handled by the initial responses of AI systems and service bots. Today the human representatives were rushed off their feet with the volume of enquiries.

A flowing spectrum of colour covered almost the whole of a large screen. It represented the global sentiment around Sladen Foundation and the Diaulos brands, analysed in real time from all the calls, social comments, internet searches and automated chats. There had been a huge spike in activity following the press conference. The colours flowed seamlessly from amber to green. An undercurrent of red that had been visible in the first few minutes following the launch had all but vanished.

Jack glanced at the screen and felt the knot of worry and annoyance in his stomach start to dissipate. Perhaps they'd gotten away with it. He wanted to see the playback of the press conference to be sure, but there seemed to be a technical glitch. Samuel, his head of PR and communications, was tapping at his keyboard and looking puzzled.

"Has Zara tracked down that recording yet?" asked Jack.

"Not yet," said Samuel. He tapped his earpiece. "Ah, wait, yes, she's found it. Seems there was a database error at the news channel. It's all online now."

The sentiment monitoring display shrank into the corner of the wallscreen, and the footage of the press conference took pride of place. Jack watched the first minute and nodded, satisfied with his performance. "Fast forward to the end," he said.

They watched the video from the news drone as it circled the bastle. Ella's eyes were fixed on the screen, and she frowned as she caught a fleeting glimpse of herself. The drone turned again towards the moorland. Samuel slowed the playback, frame by frame. There was a flash of something black in the air, then nothing. Jack exhaled in relief. He hadn't been aware that he had been holding his breath. The news drone had apparently not picked up any visuals of the hunter drone, and the secrets of the moorland and the cave beneath it were safe.

"Bird strike," said Samuel, satisfied. "It looked messier on the live feed, but accidents happen, I guess. I don't know what the news teams were going on about."

"If they send their drones off in an area like this with so much wildlife around, they should be prepared for an impact," said Jack, back to his buoyant self. "I'm surprised that it doesn't happen more often." He glanced at Ella. "Have we managed to retrieve the debris?" he asked.

"I'll go and find out," she said. She stood up and smoothed her rumpled skirt. As she took a step towards the main door, it opened to reveal Angus holding a large box.

"I won't come in," he said, looking pointedly at the brand new pale grey carpet on the floor. "I'm covered in mud." He put the box down just inside the door. "Here's your drone."

Jack bent down and opened the lid cautiously. Inside he found the body of the drone, virtually intact but for a spectacular dent on one side of the casing. At the bottom of the box lay the shattered remains of the rotors and the camera lens, and a lot of black feathers.

"Anything on the hard disk?" he murmured.

"It didn't survive the drop," said Angus quietly, tapping a finger on the side of his nose.

Jack nodded, understanding the message. Whatever might have been saved by the drone had been wiped, or the disk corrupted and broken beyond repair.

"Thanks, Angus," he said out loud. "Get this over to

the outside broadcast unit in the car park. They're waiting for it."

"Will do." Angus picked up the box and lumbered back down the stairs on the outside of the bastle.

"Good," said Jack to the room in general. "I'm glad that's all cleared up. Great work today, everyone." He looked up at the wallscreen, once again filled with the waves of the sentiment tracker. The overwhelming image was of deepening green, global approval for the Sladen Foundation. Figures in a table on the corner ticked up as the volume of calls and mentions increased. A world map view showed that their PR efforts were reaching across the globe, following the sun.

Jack's smartscreen pinged, a private call incoming from an ID that made his smile grow even broader.

"Cameron," he said happily. "How lovely to hear from you. Did you catch the press conference?"

He was so absorbed in the call that he didn't notice the look of horror that crossed Ella's face, and barely heard the door slam behind her as she fled.

•

Cameron put down her smartscreen and smiled to herself. The seeds had been sown, and she had every confidence that the code for Diaulos and the automated investments of the Sladen Foundation DAO would be in her hands within the week. Now she had some research to do. She carefully cloaked her location and signed on to her favourite infosec forum. This was the busiest time of day for the group as Europe slid into the afternoon and America started work.

Sure enough, there were a lot of familiar handles on the chat. Cameron surfed the channels for a little while, incognito, laughing at the gallows-humour memes that proliferated in a community at the edge of the cybercrime abyss, and getting a feel for the latest vulnerabilities and exposures that were bubbling. The impact of the Privet attack had largely dissipated and there were rumours of in-fighting among the perpetrators.

Cameron dug as deep as she dared to try and find clues to real people involved in the ransomware, correlating the traffic around the Santa virus with the spread of Privet, but there was very little to go on. She needed Ross, Michelle and their shady mates to explore that avenue down in the depths of the dark web.

There was plenty of chat about the Sladen Foundation announcement. In this community, hidden from the spiders that trawled the web for Jack's sentiment analysis, the tone was universally sceptical. Everyone had spent time in their career cleaning up after one or other of the regular Sladen Group software vulnerabilities, and very few people were speaking up in favour of the project. They echoed Ross's feelings that the whole concept was a brilliant idea, but the execution was likely to be flawed. For all that her opinion of Jack was softening, Cameron had to agree.

She dipped into a discussion about the Diaulos

validation nodes and their link to the MetaBand hardware. In the back of her mind a guilty thought nudged her. She hadn't yet spoken to Ben. Based on the announcement, there was nothing for him to worry about, but the devil would be in the detail, and the detail was sorely lacking.

Someone on the thread had started reading the whitepaper. Cameron made a note to flag this to Noor so that she could pick up on the same discussion and compare findings. 'Passive validation of transactions by MetaBand receivers is an interested proposal,' said the post, 'but what's the storage capacity of these units? How long a blockchain can they hold?'

That's a good question, thought Cameron. She knew who to ask. She logged off the forum and placed a call to Ben. He didn't answer. Cameron squashed a feeling of unease. It was still early morning for him. He was most likely in a team meeting, catching up with colleagues and planning for the day.

She stroked the cat and brewed another coffee. Impatient, she tried again. No answer. She left a brief, non-committal message, just in case someone else picked it up. It occurred to her that in the long months they had been apart he might have met another girl, and the idea hurt her more than she cared to admit.

To distract herself, she returned to the computer and followed her germ of an idea through the search engines, building a picture of the global MetaBand manufacturing operation. Ben was engineering the designs for the microsats and receivers, but the printing would be done local to the network installations around the world. Sure enough, there was an additive manufacturing facility in London that had held the MetaBand contract for earlier versions of the receiver units. She recognised the address, just twenty minutes away from her flat, down past the Elephant and Castle. It was only three o'clock, not too late in the day to pay them a visit. She tried Ben's number one more time. Still nothing. The walk would do her good, she figured, and if Ben decided to return her call, she would be able to answer.

By the time Cameron reached the small industrial estate, he still hadn't called. The production manager was expecting her, thanks to a lucky connection who had arranged an introduction while she walked.

"You must be Cameron." Her contact was a slim black man with a neat beard, a few years her senior. He held out his hand. "I'm Olu," he continued. "Andy's told me all about you. He says you want to see what we're doing with MetaBand."

"Nice to meet you, Olu," she said. "Yes, I remembered the documentary Andy made last year about this place." She gestured around the industrial park, a green and vibrant space nestling between the train tracks on one side and rows of tall terraces and blocks of flats on the other. "It's lovely here."

"We like it," said Olu with a smile. "We're getting close to being the most sustainable industrial park in London. We produce our own electricity, we sell the excess straight into the local community, and we keep the manufacturing processes as carbon neutral as possible, from raw materials onwards."

"That's wonderful," said Cameron diplomatically. She'd seen the programme Andy had produced and she knew the story behind the park.

There was a beep from Olu's pocket, and he pulled out a small smartscreen. "Ah, good," he said. "Your security credentials have passed screening. I just need a facial recognition scan so we can get you into the building." He flicked the camera on and held it up. Cameron looked dutifully into the lens, turning her head slowly to the left and right. There was a pause, and Olu nodded and tucked the smartscreen back into his pocket. "All done."

Cameron followed him to the door. "Tell me more about MetaBand," she said. "Are you picking up the manufacture of the next generation equipment for London?"

"Are we ever," said Olu fervently. "It's not just London. We're covering most of the country. We've already started the rollout. It's a tight timescale and we need to build up a lot of stock in a short time."

The factory floor was a hive of activity, rows of printers churning out components. It was a smaller version of the Silvera family firm, the company that Charlie ran, although they were creating very different things. The stock shelves were bulging with packaged units ready for despatch to the fitters around the country.

"We're not just printing," said Olu. "All the old units are being decommissioned here and the materials we salvage get rolled back into the manufacturing process. It's an end-to-end holistic cycle. Want to come and see?"

"I'd love to," said Cameron.

Through a roller door to an adjacent unit was the recycling area where skips full of old equipment of all types were being sorted ready to be recycled into additive materials once again. One side of the workshop was sectioned off and enclosed, and Cameron could see robot arms dipping and picking and sorting items with elegant precision. On the open floor, most of the workforce was human.

"What's the difference?" asked Cameron, gesturing at the enclosed area.

"Those in there are really old bits of random kit that don't have any reliable documentation," said Olu. "Things that have been recovered from demolition sites or refurbishments. We have no idea what dodgy materials have been used to make them or the condition of the place they were kept. Until they've been checked over, it's not safe to handle them. We're specialists. We get all the things that no one else can manage in here."

"The MetaBand receivers don't end up there, do they?" asked Cameron.

Olu shook his head. "No way," he said. "Everything we make nowadays is recorded down to the last detail on the open ledger. You can see if there have been any changes made in the design or extra components added. It makes our lives a whole lot simpler."

Fascinated as she was with the recycling effort,

Cameron was here to check Ben's story on the new MetaBand designs. "Olu," she said, "do you have access to the design ledger for the new receivers?"

He shook his head. "I don't get involved in that side. If you want the full history, you'd need to talk to the admin people. I can introduce you."

"Thanks, that would be good," said Cameron. She changed tack. "You've made both versions of these things, haven't you? What are the differences between the old and the new units? Why are the old ones being replaced?"

"The casing is much sleeker, and the processors and data storage in the new ones have been upgraded," said Olu instantly. "They've got huge capacity compared to the original units."

"How much storage are we talking about here?" said Cameron.

"That's jumped from the old ten Gig units to three hundred Gigabytes," said Olu.

Cameron wasn't altogether surprised. If Jack's announcement about the MetaBand receivers being full nodes on the Diaulos blockchain, they might well need that much room in a few years' time.

"The processors are nuts, though," Olu continued. "They're incredibly fast. I've only ever seen them in military grade hardware." He put his hand over his mouth. "Not sure I was supposed to say that."

"Your secret is safe with me," said Cameron. "You've seen all my security clearances. This may well be important, and I really appreciate your help." Another question occurred to her. "Why are they having to replace the old units?" she asked. "Surely they could just be upgraded?"

Olu shook his head. "No," he said. "It's much easier and cheaper to change them, and the old units can't access the signals from the new microsats. It's a whole new system." He looked up sharply as an alarm sounded from the factory floor. A light flashed above one of the printers. "Sorry, Cameron. I have to sort out this jam."

"I'll leave you to it," said Cameron. "Thank you so much for the tour. It's been really useful."

"Any time." Olu opened the door and Cameron stepped out into the sunshine of the green space again.

She started back towards her home, mulling over the new information. The storage capacity of the nodes was overkill. Jack must have grand ideas for his Diaulos if he thought it would overtake Bitcoin's length. The processors confused her, though. The chain was being secured by choosing a random wearable device to sign for the opening of each new block. There was no need for such a high-spec processor in the validator nodes. There was no algorithm to compute, no competition to confirm a block. Only the Bitcoin and Monero blockchains were allowed to run Proof of Work consensus mechanisms, and mining was strictly controlled.

What could the processors be for, if they neither secured the Diaulos chain nor improved the connections for the MetaBand users? Cameron walked on, oblivious to the people and traffic around her as she battled to understand what Jack could possibly be planning.

14: TEXAN SECRETS

Cameron was halfway home when she felt the screen in her pocket vibrating. Ben had finally returned her call. She slipped her earpods in, took a deep breath, and answered.

"Hi, Cam," he said cheerily, "what's up?"

Cameron was taken aback. This was quite a different Ben to the person who had called her out of desperation just a few weeks before. A rush of unfamiliar background noise confused her further.

"Where are you?" she asked.

"I'm in the car," said Ben.

That explained it, thought Cameron, both the noise and the good mood.

"What are you driving, you petrolhead?"

"You wouldn't believe me if I told you," said Ben, raising his voice as the engine revved.

"No…" said Cameron, "it's not… It's a Mustang?"

"You bet," said Ben.

There was no video feed, but Cameron could visualise the broad grin on his face just the same. The Mustang had been Ben's dream car, out of reach on a small island almost entirely given over to electric vehicles and shared rides. On the Texas plains, it was quite a different matter.

"It's fantastic," Ben continued. "Ah, Cameron, I wish you were here. You would love this."

Cameron's heart jolted. "Maybe one day," she said.

"What did you want?" Ben asked, oblivious to Cameron's discomfort. "Did you find out something about these designs?"

"Yes," said Cameron, relieved to be back on firmer ground. "I called you to let you know that the changes you mentioned fit with the spec they announced for the Diaulos network management. I don't think there's anything to worry about."

"I'm glad you think so," said Ben, "but I'm still not convinced. Someone rode roughshod over all the usual processes, and I don't like it." He paused. "Hold on," he said. "Just coming up to an intersection."

Cameron kept walking, watching the silent traffic glide along beside her on the busy London street and listening to the unfamiliar road noise and the hum of the car engine from the empty plains of Texas. The growl of the Mustang settled to a steady low roar and Ben came back on the line.

"Sorry, Cam," he said. "Look, there is still something bugging me about all this. I persuaded the account management team to let me do a client visit to Statesman Tech. I'm on the way there now."

Cameron stopped dead in her tracks. "Ben, no! You don't know what you're getting into."

"What do you mean?" he asked.

"I mean that there is something really wrong here. Didn't you see the press conference this morning?"

"I was already in the car," said Ben. "You know I couldn't watch and drive. It's not one of those cutesy little electric pods. Why?"

"Dammit, Ben," said Cameron. "Right at the end of the broadcast we saw two people in the crowd who should not have been there."

"Who?" said Ben, exasperated.

"Ella Stanford," said Cameron, "and Angus White."

"You're joking," said Ben. "What the hell were they doing anywhere near this project?"

"Do you understand now?" said Cameron.

"I'm not stupid," snapped Ben. "All you're saying is that I was right all along. I know there is something fishy going on."

"Why can't you leave this to me?" said Cameron.

"Because it's not all about you," said Ben. "I want to get to the bottom of that design change. The buck stops where the first decision was made. Right now, with the records all over the place, that's me."

"You're not responsible for this whole project," protested Cameron.

"Doesn't matter," said Ben. "If this was a construction project and the building collapsed because of a change to the spec, I'd be responsible because I'd followed the design without questioning it or checking the files."

"Oh, good grief, Ben," said Cameron. "This is hardly a matter of life and death."

"Listen to yourself, Cameron," said Ben, exasperated. "You go on about the hidden cost of cybercrime, the people that are affected, the organised crime groups behind ransomware. I've always trusted your instincts. Maybe you can trust mine for a change?"

"I'm sorry," said Cameron quietly.

"That's okay," said Ben. "I have to go. I'm getting into traffic. I'll let you know if anything interesting comes out of this visit. Bye, Cam."

"Ben," said Cameron, "be careful." A thought suddenly occurred to her. "There's someone I know working at Statesman Tech. Not Jack. Someone else that I think I can trust…" She tailed off as she realised that the call had ended, and she was talking to empty space. Cameron cursed. She quickened her pace. She needed to get home and find a way to reach Cloverleaf before Ben reached Austin.

•

The sun was hot and the downtown traffic, both vehicles and pedestrians, was unusually busy. Tenuk gave up and hailed a rickshaw at the southern end of the bridge. He settled in his seat and took a long drink from his water bottle as the cyclist weaved expertly around the traffic jams and groups of tourists admiring the view over the lake. The terrain was flat at the shore, but the road climbed sharply as they approached the Statesman Tech offices. The solar sail hanging from the top of the building gleamed like a mirror in the bright morning sunshine.

The rickshaw pulled up on the corner of the block

opposite the main entrance. Tenuk tapped the payment chip and added a handsome tip. He would not be late after all. Mood considerably improved, he stood and waited patiently for the crosswalk lights to turn in his favour. Two lanes of autocars whirred gently along, their occupants busy on their screens or dozing. In the third lane, reserved for driver-operated vehicles, a long, low sports car growled gently. Tenuk wrinkled his nose at the unfamiliar smell of the exhaust fumes. The car turned and disappeared down a ramp into the darkness of the parking garage beneath the building. The traffic stopped. Tenuk crossed the road and took the steps up to the atrium two at a time. The elevator bore him aloft and he walked into the office at ten o'clock on the dot.

It was a hive of activity. A six-hour time lag to the Dunswyke site meant that everyone was playing catchup on the events of what for them had been early morning. Tenuk listened carefully to the buzz. The tone was excited, positive, no wrong notes. Good. He greeted his staff with an open, honest smile, congratulated them on a job well done, and reminded them that there was still a lot of work to do as the system went live.

The workflow screens were flickering with activity as tasks moved steadily along the road to completion. Another screen showed live feeds of the money markets, tracking the price and volume of coin trading, and yet another was running the Diaulos promotional videos on loop. Tenuk had no difficulty keeping the smile on his face. It was all going like clockwork. In one corner, he spotted Connie and Isaac deep in conversation. He strolled over to them.

"All okay here?" he asked.

Connie looked up with a bright smile. "Fine, thanks, Tenuk," she said. "I was coming to see you. We have a visit scheduled from the team handling the MetaBand engineering."

Tenuk frowned. "The folks down south? The satellite company? I had nothing in my diary."

"That's them," said Connie. "We were due a routine visit from the account manager soon and apparently one of their engineers is in the area, so he's calling in to see us."

"It's just informal," said Isaac. "The message says he has a question about one of the design points and it'll be easier to clarify face to face."

"Which component are they querying?" said Tenuk. "They're not just making the satellites, you know. They've set up the receiver printing specifications for our worldwide manufacturing partners as well."

"No idea," said Connie with a shrug. "He'll be here any minute. You can ask him yourself if you want."

Tenuk shook his head. "I'll leave it to you," he said. "Call me if you have any questions. I'll be in Jack's office sorting out a few things." He turned and headed for the large glass-walled office in the corner of the floor. As he closed the door behind him, he dropped the smile. Why would an engineer be coming here, he wondered? What had they picked up on? Tuesday was not turning out to be as easy as he had hoped. He sat down at Jack's desk and started to work through the odd tasks that he was expected to cover in the boss's absence. Out of the corner of his eye, he watched the CCTV feed from the hallway between the elevator and office. A tall, dark man appeared, looked around to get his bearings, and started towards the main door. That must be the engineer.

The next time Tenuk glanced up, the man was sitting in the coffee area with his back to the glass office. Isaac and Connie were chatting and smiling, putting him at his ease. He seemed relaxed. It must be as routine and informal as they had thought.

A message appeared on the screen from Connie. 'No problems,' it said. 'He's running over a couple of the design changes on the receivers. He has some ideas on different printing materials they could use in future batches, and he wanted to know more about how the units are being used.'

Tenuk's eyes narrowed. That was an awfully specific question about a piece of the complex jigsaw of MetaBand's global network that he did not want placed under scrutiny. He thought he had covered the tracks of the design change well enough to avoid any attention. This had to be pure coincidence, an innocent question from an over-enthusiastic engineer, but he wanted to be sure. He emerged from the office and made his way over to the coffee machine. He busied himself preparing his cup, then turned with a smile and found himself looking directly into the eyes of the visitor.

He recognised him immediately.

They had met in passing in England, back in another life. Tenuk recalled exactly the moment that he came face to face with the SimCavalier, and this man had been with her. He turned back to the coffee machine, concentrating hard on controlling his emotions. In the fleeting moment, he was sure that there had been no flicker of recognition in the other man's eyes. Was he in the clear?

"May I introduce you?" said Connie behind him. "This is Ben from LekSat. Ben, I'd like you to meet my boss, Tenuk."

The coffee machine hissed and spluttered at the opportune moment, drowning out his name. Tenuk gave Ben a bright smile.

"Nice to meet you," he said. "Excuse me, I have a call scheduled." He walked calmly back into Jack's office and closed the door, his stomach churning. He was almost sure that his luck had held, and that Ben had no idea who he was.

From her desk, Chloe watched as Tenuk walked back into Jack's office and closed the door. She knew the man well enough by now to read the nuances of his body language, and she recognised extreme tension and the tight control he was exerting over his reactions. He might have thought he had hidden his discomfort, but it was plain as the eye could see for Chloe. She immediately turned to see what had prompted this sudden change of demeanour. Connie and Isaac were talking to a visitor in the lounge area by the kitchen. Tenuk had been clutching a cup of coffee, so it seemed likely that he'd been over there too, and common courtesy suggested he would have been introduced to the stranger. Who was this visitor, and why was Tenuk so rattled?

As she watched, Isaac stood up and went back to his desk. She could see him swiping through files on his screen, searching for something. Connie had also stepped away and was distracted by a message on her screen. The visitor was sitting alone and looking around him with a slightly lost air. Chloe saw her opportunity. She picked up her cup and made her way to the lounge area, ignoring a notification that buzzed insistently on her smartscreen. Whatever it was, it could wait.

"Hi," she said brightly as she waited for the coffee machine to do its thing.

The man looked at her and smiled. He was dark and handsome with deep brown eyes. Chloe had never seen him before.

"Oh, Chloe," said Connie, glancing up from her screen. "This is Ben from LekSat Engineering. He's been turning the MetaBand hardware designs into reality."

"Nice to meet you, Chloe," said Ben.

"You're British!" said Chloe. "I love your accent. It's good to meet you too. Have you been over here long?"

"A little less than a year," said Ben, ducking his head in a way that Chloe found frankly adorable.

"You're working on the satellites and receivers, I guess?" she said. "I met one of your colleagues at the start of the year. Mateo."

"That's right," said Ben. "He's the main account manager. I had a couple of things to check so I came up instead this time."

Chloe wondered why Tenuk had reacted so oddly to this genial British man. It seemed to be a routine visit. It added to the mystery of Tenuk's true identity, a mystery Chloe was determined to solve.

Isaac re-joined them. "Here's the original design change approval you needed," he said, handing a tablet to Ben. "It's all in order and I've verified it against the records on the chain."

Ben scrutinised the details. "Yeah, that looks okay," he said. "I don't know why I couldn't access this before."

"How much detail can you see at LekSat?" asked Isaac. "I'm not sure what your permissions are for these records."

"We don't have access to anything within your databases," said Ben. "I don't quite know how it works, but anyone can see key decision points along the project lifecycle, and contractors like us can see the formal paperwork. For this one, we got the new spec through, but we could only access the public view of the change note, not the detail."

"There must be something wrong in the settings," said Chloe. "Do you want me to have look at that, Connie?"

"Sure, Chloe," said Connie. She peered at Isaac's tablet. "Who signed it off? Oh, Mark Esquith."

"Any chance I could have a quick chat with him or one of his team?" asked Ben. "It would help in assessing this new material we're considering for the next batch of components."

Isaac shook his head. "No can do," he said. "Mark left at the end of last year. I'm not in touch with him. Are you, Connie?"

"Not at all," said Connie. "I guess HR will have his details. As for the team…" She shrugged. "All the design work was done by another company in the Sladen group, based in Malaysia, I think. Mark kept them straight on what we needed to run the software, they delivered the designs, and he finalised any changes that were needed for things like, you know, local regulations or new system requirements."

"Okay," said Ben. He didn't seem unduly concerned. "It's not that important. I guess the main thing for you is that whatever they're made of, the units are right at the top of the range to handle the high-speed processing."

Connie looked confused. "Not really," she said. "It's the storage that really matters, to hold distributed copies of the blockchain. The processors just manage new transaction validation. Standard stuff."

"My mistake," said Ben lightly. "I was thinking of another project there for a moment. Sorry." He ducked his head again and gave them a crooked smile. "I think I've taken up enough of your time, and I have what I need. I'll pass that approval detail on to Mateo when I get back." He stood up and shook hands with each of them in turn.

"It's nice to meet you," said Chloe. She hadn't touched her coffee. It was cold.

"You too," said Ben, squeezing her hand.

Chloe watched his retreating back as Isaac escorted him towards the elevator, then looked at Connie. "What was that all about?" she asked.

Connie shrugged. "I have no idea," she said. "He seems to have what he came for, so everyone's happy."

Apart from Tenuk, though Chloe. She looked over at Jack's office where Tenuk was skulking. He was deep in conversation with someone unseen, online, and making notes.

Back at her desk, Chloe found a missed call notification from an unexpected ID. Why was the SimCavalier trying to reach her, and did a call from the only British person she knew have anything to do with the Englishman who had just left? She picked up her smartscreen and looked for a chance to slide out of the office, but Connie appeared before she could escape.

"You thought he was cute, didn't you?" she said with a wink.

"The British guy? Yeah, kind of," said Chloe. She changed the subject quickly. "What's up with Tenuk?"

"Oh, he's in one of those funny moods again," said Connie. "I think Jack's been stressing about the launch and Tenuk's first in line to be hit with any flak."

"That's probably it," said Chloe. But in the back of her mind, she was processing some odd clues and ideas, and pieces of an unfamiliar jigsaw were starting to assemble themselves into a picture that worried her.

Connie put her hand on Chloe's shoulder. "Don't worry

about it," she said. "It's past midday. The settings on that design change can wait. Shall we grab some lunch?"

"Sure," said Chloe. She really wanted to keep digging, finding out more about Tenuk, but she had no wish to raise any suspicions. Looking over at the corner office one more time, she could see that Tenuk was still talking, a scowl on his face. He was having a difficult morning. She closed down her screen. She would return the SimCavalier's call later. "Let's go."

15: REPUTATIONS

"I don't care, Tenuk," said Jack. "We have to be seen to be squeaky clean. If an independent audit of the contracts for the DAO and Diaulos is what it takes, then that's what we'll do."

He listened as Tenuk protested, drumming his fingers irritably on the table. Jack gazed out of the huge picture window that took up most of the gable end of the bastle. The late afternoon sunshine bathed the moorland in golden light, and Jack almost felt at home. Not quite. He'd shaken the dust of this region off his feet as a student, and whatever the publicity said, he knew he'd be bored if he stayed too long. He could not, however, deny its beauty.

"No, Tenuk," he said firmly as the stream of excuses dried up. "I know everything has been checked over with a fine-toothed comb already, but after that incident at the launch it really pays for us to show that we have nothing to hide. I don't understand your objections, and I'm disappointed that you didn't propose a second audit yourself."

There was an indrawing of breath on the other end of the call. Tenuk started to speak, and Jack cut him off.

"I'm releasing the code to a company I know here

in London," said Jack. "Once we have their report and anything they find has been fixed, I want the contracts published. We're not waiting until the coin launch as we'd originally planned. If everything goes well, we can release them to coincide with the presale on Friday. This is all about my brand and my reputation. Don't ever forget who is in charge."

He didn't wait for an answer before ending the call. He was fed up with Tenuk's attitude. He'd had a long day and the adrenaline of the launch was starting to wear off. He dialled another number and waited patiently for it to connect, feeling the stress melting slowly away.

"Hi Jack." Cameron's voice echoed. "Give me a moment."

He heard the sound of quick footsteps. She was running up a set of stairs, he thought. She had always been active and eager, more likely to take the stairs than the elevator if she had a choice. Jack smiled. He was glad to have found her again.

There was the click of a lock and the insistent squeaking of a cat in the background. "Hush," said Cameron's voice.

Jack laughed.

"Not you, Jack," said Cameron, laughing along with him. "Now, what can I do for you?"

"The audit you suggested," said Jack. "I want to get that organised as soon as possible."

Cameron was practically purring. "I can get it started straight away," she said. "I'll send over a contract now for you to sign."

"Send it to my personal inbox," said Jack. "This doesn't go through any of the companies in the group. There are too many people with their own agendas, and I want this to be completely independent." As soon as the words were out of his mouth, he realised that he had voiced something he had never admitted before. He was struggling to trust the people closest to him.

"Understood," said Cameron, and Jack wondered if she had taken the request at face value or if she detected the undercurrent of concern that had prompted it. "We'll be very discreet."

"How long will it take?" he asked. "I need to get something into the press release for Friday's presale."

"There's no way we can run a full code quality review in that time," said Cameron. "We can give you an interim report with some headline findings, but you're looking at another couple of weeks to really get into the guts of the thing."

"That's fine," said Jack. "Get me the interim report on time and I'll pay you double. We'll look at scheduling the CQR after the presale has gone live."

"Okay," said Cameron. He could hear her tapping at keys in the background. "There, you should have the contract link now. It covers the full audit, but I've added a standard break clause between the interim report and the second phase of work. When I get this back with the access details, the team can get started straight away."

"Thanks, Cameron," said Jack. "Hey, how about dinner

later this week. I'll be back in London on Thursday, and you should be done with the interim by then."

"Sure, Jack," she replied. "That'd be nice." There was a distinct and insistent miaow in the background. "I have to go," she said. "Orders from the boss. I'll look out for the signed documents. Bye, Jack."

"Bye, Cameron." He hung up and checked his private inbox. Sure enough, there was a secure link to a set of documents. Jack settled down to read the surprisingly straightforward contract Cameron had sent him. It was a quarter of the length of what he would have received from a contractor in Texas, with carefully worded clauses and the occasional dip into archaic legal terms under English law. It took him no time at all to skim through it.

Usually, he would pass something like this on to his legal team, but they would take days to come back to him, they would argue over the jurisdiction, and too many people would find out about the audit. He wanted to keep it to himself for now.

Running through the options in his head, he had a flash of inspiration. He could use Zara to check over the contract. He was almost certain that her training had extended beyond the virtual assistant role to a grasp of legal matters, and her logic was impeccable. As for access to the code base, that was more problematic. He considered simply handing Cameron his login credentials, but he knew that it was such terrible practice that she would be both furious and amused and would never let him live it down. He wasn't about to ask Tenuk. He didn't want him dealing directly with Cameron. The other option was Chloe. He had found her trustworthy and discreet so far.

He placed a call to her from his private line. She took a moment to pick up, and in the background there was the hum of a busy café or restaurant. It was obviously lunchtime in Austin.

"Chloe, this is Jack," he said. She may not have recognised the call ID.

"Oh!" she said. "Wait, let me go outside."

There was a clatter as she moved her chair and the background noise faded. "How can I help?" she asked.

"Could you arrange a new access link for the DAO codebase, please?" said Jack. "Zara will be in touch to add it to some paperwork shortly."

"Sure," said Chloe. "I'll check with Tenuk…"

"No," said Jack. "This is between you and me. Just set it up."

"I'm going to need an identifier for the records," said Chloe. "What should I put?"

Jack thought for a moment, then smiled. "Call it 'Kitty'."

"Okay," said Chloe. "I'll be back in the office in half an hour. I'll do it as soon as I get to my desk."

"Thanks, Chloe," he said. "Appreciate it. I'll let you get back to your lunch."

One part done, one to go. "Zara?" he said quietly.

"Yes, Jack," came the response from his screen. "What can I do for you?"

"Can you check over these documents for me, please,

and if they pass muster, which I'm sure they will, let me know. You'll need to add access details to the schedule. Ask Chloe. She's generating them now. I need them back as soon as possible, this evening, if you can, so that I can sign them off."

"Yes, Jack. I'll do that straight away."

Jack leaned back in his chair and looked out at the view again. The shadows were getting longer, and a flock of sheep was gathering at a gate in the distance. As he watched, a quad bike hove into view towing a small trailer of feed. Between Chloe at lunch, Cameron's cat calling for its dinner, and now the local sheep, Jack was getting hungry. The building was quiet. The media circus had packed up and gone, and most of the staff had left for the evening. The only vehicles in the car park were his own car, the security pod, and the Whitford Networks van. Angus and Ella must still be on site.

They weren't in the building. They must be in the data centre. Jack walked slowly down the steps at the side of the bastle, marvelling again at the restoration of the crumbling stair. He followed the path towards the cliff, winding through the coppice. As he approached the entrance, he could see a sliver of light and he could hear voices.

"Hello?" he called as he walked into the cavern.

"Oh, hi Jack," said Ella. "Angus and I were just checking the network. Are you off now?"

"Yes, I thought I'd head into town for dinner," said Jack. "Will you join me?"

"We're busy," growled Angus.

Ella looked at them both. "You know, I'd like that," she said, a hint of defiance in her voice. "We're pretty much done here, aren't we, Angus?"

The man shook his head. "You go if you must," he said. "I haven't finished."

"Right," said Ella. "In that case, I'll see you tomorrow." She picked up her bag and turned her back on Angus. "Let's go."

Jack looked from one to the other. The atmosphere was charged but he didn't know where the tension had come from. His nerves were thrumming. Something was going on.

"I'll let security know that you're still here, Angus," said Jack. "See you tomorrow." He stepped aside to let Ella past him and followed her back outside.

She didn't say anything as they crossed the site towards the car park, their feet crunching in sync on the gravel. Even in the car, which now had the connectivity to navigate of its own accord, she stayed quiet, answering Jack's questions about her work and comments about the journey politely, but without enthusiasm.

"What would you like to eat?" asked Jack eventually, settling on an easy topic for discussion as the car swept along the darkening lanes.

She shrugged. "I'm easy," she said. "If we went all the way down to Newcastle, I know some excellent restaurants, but there isn't a lot of choice up here in the sticks. I guess Dunswyke is the best option. What do you suggest?"

"Oh, I have a few ideas," said Jack. "It's a lot better than it was when I was growing up here."

"Do you think that because you were young then, and craving the bright lights of the city," said Ella, looking sidelong at him.

He understood that she was teasing, and he was glad that she seemed to have relaxed. "Probably," he said with a grin. "Your hometown always feels parochial, doesn't it?" He nodded at the great tower of the castle that dominated the skyline as they approached the town. "I used to hate that," he said. "It made me feel as if I was growing up at the ends of the earth. Now I just think it's quaint and English and worth preserving."

Dunswyke was busy with families taking advantage of the school holidays that wrapped around the Easter weekend. People thronged around the castle and the tables set outside every pub on the main street were full of customers enjoying a pint or a meal as the sun went down.

"Not here," said Ella. "Is there an Italian?"

"Around here, of course there is," said Jack. "There were a lot of Italians who settled here in the borders and up into Scotland a century ago, during the Second World War. I know the perfect place, and the food is fabulous."

The car pulled up outside his favourite restaurant on a steep cobbled street at the other side of town where it was much quieter. There seemed to be plenty of tables free.

"Most of the tourists stay by the castle," he explained

as he opened the door. "This is Dunswyke's best kept secret." He grinned at the manager. "Evening, Paolo. How are you?"

"All the better for seeing you, Jack," said Paolo. "How's everything going over at the bastle?"

"Great, thanks, mate," said Jack. He turned to Ella. "Paolo and I were at school together, believe it or not. All the way from primary to sixth form."

"I could tell you some tales," said Paolo, laughing. "Another time, though. I guess you're hungry, and I'm busy." He called through to the kitchen and a younger version of himself appeared. "This is my lad, Finn, He'll look after you."

Their table was next to the old fireplace, long unused and now filled with a glorious sheaf of dried flowers. Jack ordered a pitcher of water and another of the house wine, along with some garlic bread and antipasto. Finn poured each of them a glass of wine with a flourish, then left them alone.

"Cheers," said Jack, raising his glass to Ella.

Ella gave him a half-smile and clinked her glass against his. "Cheers," she said. "Congratulations on the launch." She looked around. "This is a nice place."

"Thank you," he said. "You should be celebrating, too. Your work on the Foundation's tokenomics has been indispensable, from what I've heard, and you and Angus have worked incredibly hard to bring everything online so smoothly."

Ella's face fell. "I guess, but I'm not ready to party," she said. Far from the relaxed mood of a few minutes before, she suddenly looked troubled and vulnerable.

"What's up?" Jack was determined to get to the bottom of whatever was bothering her.

"I don't know." She gestured around the half-empty restaurant. "It's just… I miss my old home. My old friends. If we'd finished a project like this, we'd have been out as a team, in London, having fun. It's lovely here, but it's not the same."

Jack looked at her sympathetically. "I get what you're saying. I miss the camaraderie of being part of a team, too. When you're in charge, you don't get to go out and enjoy yourself either." He took a sip of his wine, a light red that was more likely to have come from the vineyards of Kent than Campagna. "What brought you up north?" he asked, curious.

Ella looked down. Her fingers twisted unconsciously at the edge of the tablecloth. "I fell in with the wrong crowd," she said quietly. "I blew it. Everything."

Jack held his breath. "Want to tell me about it?" he asked.

"Not really," said Ella. She gave him a brilliant, brittle and utterly fake smile, and dropped the subject.

Finn reappeared, tablet in hand, ready to take their orders. Ella picked the first pizza on the menu. Jack gave his choice a little more thought and plumped for pasta. Finn sent the order to the kitchen, refilled both their glasses, and returned to his spot behind the bar.

"I'm more used to drone waiters in London," said Ella. "It's a different world up here."

"Tell me about it," said Jack. "I like the personal touch, though. This is one place that hasn't changed. Paolo's dad ran it when we were kids, and his grandad before that." He pointed up to a faded framed picture of two young children aged around four or five that hung on the wall above the fireplace. "Believe it or not, that's Paolo, and his little sister, Lisa," he said. "It must have been taken at school. I recognise the backdrop. We had an identical picture of me in the house."

The door from the kitchen swung open and Finn appeared carrying two steaming plates. "Pizza," he said, laying a huge flat plate in front of Ella, "and pasta. Would you like some black pepper or parmesan cheese?"

"Both, please, Finn," said Jack.

Ella closed her eyes and sniffed the scent rising from her pizza. "This smells amazing," she said. "Good choice, Jack."

They ate in companionable silence. The wine flowed, and Ella began to relax once again.

Finn took away their empty plates and returned with two tiramisus. "On the house," he said. "Dad says sorry, he's had to go out, but he'll see you next time you're in."

Ella savoured every spoonful of the creamy dessert. "I haven't had a tiramisu this good since I lived in London," she said. "Honestly, I'm full, but I want to finish every bit."

"You're based down in Newcastle, aren't you?" said Jack. "How long have you lived there?"

Had he pried too much? Ella didn't reply straight away, but Jack sipped his wine and waited. He wanted to hear her story. It had taken months to get her on her own away from Angus. They were an unusual pair who seemed to resent each other's company but nevertheless delivered on their promises. As he'd hoped, she finally gave in and broke the silence.

"A year and a half," she said finally. "It feels longer." She sighed, and Jack held his breath. Was she about to tell him everything, at last?

"I had a great job," she continued. "Four years ago, I was standing in Downing Street with the Prime Minister and the head of the City of London Bank, for goodness' sake." She shook her head. Jack was impressed but kept his mouth shut. She needed to talk.

"I was at the absolute peak of my career, and I had a fabulous partner," she continued. "I realise that now, but at the time I wanted more. I ended up working on the side with a company that looked like it was going to take the world by storm and turned out to be full of criminals. I neglected my girlfriend, and I betrayed my colleagues. I really, really screwed up."

Jack sat in stunned silence. This flood of confession wasn't at all what he had expected. Ella drained her wineglass and reached for the bottle. Jack got there before her and poured another glass for each of them.

"I'm so sorry to hear that," he said. "When you say, full of criminals, you weren't… you didn't…?"

"Don't worry," said Ella drily. "I'm no gangster."

"Do you think you can ever go back?" asked Jack.

"I don't think so," she sighed. "Too many bridges burned. I'm not sure that I'd be granted redemption by the people who matter." She looked at Jack. "Don't get me wrong," she said hurriedly, "I'm enjoying the work here. It's been a really fun challenge working on the DAO and the data centre setup was more straightforward than Angus makes out." She took another swig of wine and leaned in conspiratorially. "Can I be honest? I can't stand Angus."

"He's a difficult character, that's for sure," said Jack diplomatically. "You know, once the Foundation is running smoothly, there's no reason why we can't review the contract with Whitford's. It would make more sense to bring you in-house. Just you. What do you think?"

"It's a great idea," said Ella, "and there is no way it is going to happen. You're stuck with him until the bitter end. He knows too much."

Jack was confused. "What do you mean?" he said. "He's good at his job, sure, but there are plenty of people who could do the same."

Ella shook her head and gazed at him with a strange, almost pitying look on her face. "You don't get it, do you?" she said. "Angus comes with the territory. He's the gatekeeper for your super software in that data centre." She drained the last of her wine. "I've said too much. I have to go."

"Ella…" Jack reached out towards her.

"No," she shook her head with finality. "I'm sure Finn can organise me a cab down to Newcastle."

Hearing his name, Finn trotted over, took the details, and within minutes a little autocar pulled up outside.

Ella stood up. "Thanks for dinner," she said. "We should do this again." She took a few steps towards the door, then turned back for a moment. "Say hello to Cameron."

Jack's jaw dropped. He sat and watched Ella walk unsteadily out of the door and climb into the cab, and his head was spinning as he tried to make sense of everything that he had just heard.

16: STORMY WEATHER

Cameron woke to the arrival of a slew of notifications on her smartscreen. She never needed to set an alarm. If the cat didn't wake her, the screen shifting to day mode and delivering all her messages from overnight was generally more than enough.

She had a feeling it was going to be a busy day. To the lurking cat's delight, she threw back the covers straight away and made her way, yawning, to the kitchen. The secure shutters on the apartment windows sensed movement and slid open. The early morning sunshine streamed in, but Cameron could see clouds scudding across the sky, and when she peered out of the tall glass doors that led to her small balcony, she could see that the wind had knocked over the chairs and the plant pots that she kept there. The last of the winter storms was passing through, very late in the season. It was going to be a blustery day.

As she waited for the coffee to brew, Cameron worked her way down the list of notifications. She was relieved to see that there was a message from Ben. "Play," she said, and his familiar voice echoed from the kitchen speakers. "They're a nice bunch," he said, speaking loudly over the background noise of the car engine. "There are a few holes in the story, mind. Call me back when you can."

She had missed Cloverleaf's return call and no voicemail had been left but looking at the timestamp, Ben would have already been long gone from the Statesman Tech offices and he didn't seem to have needed her help after all. She scrolled past half a dozen amber alerts from Mephisto and a couple of early morning support calls from clients whose IT departments had woken up to something nasty in their networks. They looked to be the kind of bread-and-butter daily attacks that would be reasonably straightforward to resolve. An automated support response should have been sent by return, and she could follow up when she got to the office.

At the end of the list of notifications was the signed contract from Jack, the links they needed to get into the code base, and a separate note confirming their dinner date for Thursday night. Cameron had never doubted that he would agree to the audit this time. He finally seemed to have understood how important it was, although she suspected his motivation was not quality, but reputation.

She was dying to get her hands on the code and knew that the rest of the team would be, too. She quickly showered and changed, decanted her coffee into an insulated cup, and threw on a coat to protect herself against the wind. She trotted down the four flights of stairs to ground level, greeting a couple of neighbours as she passed. The wind outside was wilder than she expected, and she half considered catching a cab to the office, but as soon as she saw the slow traffic on the main road, she realised that everyone else must have had the same idea. Instead, she trudged towards the entrance to the tube station, head down against the wind. It was a relief to get into the shelter of the stairwell. She still had a short walk at the other end, but most of her journey would be underground.

The train swayed and rattled through the tunnels. Cameron sat making notes on her screen, ignoring the motion and people around her. As they paused at the next station, a message arrived from Pete. 'Diving's been cancelled because of the storm. I'm on my way back. I'll be in about ten.' Good, thought Cameron. There was plenty for him to do.

Despite the early start, she was not the first to arrive. Susie was already at her desk, poring over the newly released whitepaper with an air of fierce determination. There were dark circles under her eyes.

"You okay?" asked Cameron, concerned.

"Yeah," said Susie. "I didn't sleep much. I've been in since five." She pulled up another window on her screen. "There were a couple of client calls," she said. "I've dealt with them. Nothing major."

"I saw them come through," said Cameron. "Thanks for picking them up so fast. Have you had breakfast? I was going to order something. I shouldn't, but, you know, it's going to be a busy day."

Susie laughed. "Count me in for all the sugar, Cameron."

Cameron gave her a conspiratorial grin and tapped

through an order to their favourite café. It would be winging its way to them in minutes, if not on actual wings, then on rotors.

"How's that whitepaper looking?" she asked.

"It's a damned sight better than the original," said Susie. "What did Shell call that? Word salad. Amazingly, this one holds up."

"That's a nice surprise," said Cameron. There was a noise from the drone delivery hatch in the kitchen. "Ah, sugar as ordered. Would you like me to make you another coffee to go with that, madame?"

"I think I've had enough," said Susie. "I'm pacing myself. Decaf?"

"Sure thing."

They were still chatting when Noor arrived, looking windswept, followed by Joel and Michelle. "It's wild out there," she said.

"It's unusual to get a storm this bad, this late," said Cameron. "Pete's dive trip has been blown out. He'll be in later."

"Good," said Joel. "We can have a look at what my contacts have dug up about that drone." He looked around the office. "Where's Sandeep?"

"He's on his way," said Cameron. "There's a power outage snarling up his tube line. Ross is training every morning this week, isn't he?"

"Yes," said Michelle. "He's supposed to be back on the bike today, but only if they can get a slot in the velodrome. There's no way they can go out in this wind."

"Well, let's make a start on this audit, then," said Cameron. "We've got everything we need."

"You've got us access to the code?" said Michelle. Her face lit up. "Brilliant, Cameron. Let me at it."

"We all get to play, don't you worry," said Cameron. "The interim report has to be turned around in thirty-six hours. We'll get into the real detail of a code review next week, I hope."

"What's going in this report?" asked Pete.

"Enough to cover any glaring issues before the presale opens," said Cameron. "But not enough that he feels he doesn't need the whole CQR."

"That makes sense," said Noor. "What's the minimum we can release?"

"Start with the new whitepaper," said Cameron. "Challenge the logic of the Diaulos structure and the governance of the DAO. Does it do what it says on the tin? Does it all hang together? What could possibly go wrong?"

"That's a tight deadline," said Joel.

"It is," said Cameron, "and I know we'll have no trouble meeting it. Let's get started."

•

In Dunswyke, a hungover Jack was toying with his breakfast, his head aching. He wondered how Ella was feeling. The revelations of the night before had been quite the surprise and started him thinking about exactly how and why Ella and Angus had ended up working on the Dunswyke project. Jack had never bothered about the details. He'd blustered successfully through the first decade of his career, faking it until he actually made it. Once he'd made it, other people did the detail.

The Sladen Foundation, the bastle, the whole idea of giving back to the world, that had been his grand vision. He didn't have to worry about the details. He recruited the right people and they made it happen as he continued to ride the wave of popularity. It had always worked before. There was no reason to think it wasn't working this time. According to every commentator, every influencer, every poll, the Sladen Foundation was all set to be a roaring success, another feather in his cap.

But Cameron's scrutiny of the DAO and Ella's reaction last night, almost one of pity, had seeded an unfamiliar feeling in his stomach that was nothing to do with the surfeit of wine. He was starting to doubt himself.

"More coffee, Mr Sladen?" The waitress interrupted his brooding mood.

Jack shook his head. "No, thanks," he said. The coffee here was barely worthy of the description, but he wasn't going to spoil the girl's day by telling her. The dining room was almost empty. Jack took the hint. "I'm done," he said, forcing out the famous smile. "Thank you, that was lovely as ever." The waitress blushed. Jack went back to his room.

He had no choice but to keep up the brave, bright, visionary face. He was expected at the bastle, after all, and there was a decent coffee machine in the office that made it a frankly attractive proposition.

Jack picked out his favourite shirt, combed his hair, and examined his reflection critically in the tall mirror. He flashed the famous smile and the confident showman smiled back at him. He started to feel better. He knew his place, and his place was at the top. Ella had been drunk. Cameron was over-fussy. Angus? Well, Angus was a law unto himself. He wasn't a good fit for the Sladen Foundation. Jack would have to have a word with Tenuk. He'd recruited the man, after all. He could get rid of him.

Confidence restored, Jack headed out of his room and along the wide, high ceiling corridors of the hotel. In reception, he called for his car, and it glided silently to a stop at the door.

"Be careful out there," said the doorman. "There's a tree down on the Berwick road and the wind's not likely to drop for a few hours. If anything, it's getting worse."

"Thanks," said Jack. He moved his hand in the automatic American habit of scanning his chip against the tip jar sensor, remembered that this wasn't something that was done in England, and turned the gesture into an awkward grateful wave. "I'll go steady."

The little car rocked in the wind, but the roads were clear so far. Jack arrived safely at the bastle, and the wind practically blew him in through the door. This would be a good test of any snags, he reflected, as the storm howled around the gables. The wind and the rain that was forecast later would seek out every loose fitment on the building.

The office was quiet. Most of the team had elected to work from home rather than risk the journey. Ella hadn't appeared, although he had expected as much, and it looked as if Angus was off site as well. All of the wallscreens were humming with activity. Every window showed a team member at work. Occasionally evidence of their home life intruded, parents attending to young children, or a cat sauntering past the camera. The sentiment and traffic volume displays were moving in the right direction. The only other people at the bastle were a junior technician who was wandering around securing cables and checking serial numbers, a couple of people in the customer service office downstairs, and presumably someone in the security pod in the car park. The small seed of self-doubt that had taken root in Jack's head nudged him again. Would he have been better staying at the hotel today? He squashed the thought.

Sipping a strong cup of good coffee, he stood at the huge window looking out over the moor. The distant views he had enjoyed the previous night were obscured by the approaching rainstorm. Black clouds were gathering and closing in from the west, and trees were bending as the wind gathered strength. This was going to be a good one, and he had a grandstand view.

As the coffee took effect, Jack started to realise that he wasn't really needed in the office, despite the effort he had made to come in. The operation was running smoothly, green lights shining reassuringly on the wallscreen. It was too early to check in with Texas. None of the planned face to face press conferences about Diaulos and the DAO would be happening, no photo shoots today. He might as well go back to the hotel.

He drained his coffee and gathered his things again. In the car, the navigation system booted up and immediately showed an error message. "Route not available," it said. "Recalculating." There was a long pause. "Recalculating." Jack switched it off and on again. The same thing happened. He cursed and pulled out his smartscreen to double check. As he feared, the storm was already causing chaos, and the road was blocked. He was stuck here for a few more hours. Back into the office, then.

He checked his messages and sighed. "Zara," he said, "what shall we do while this storm blows out?"

"Hello, Jack," said his assistant's calm voice. "I cannot guarantee that you will have full access to Sladen Group systems during this storm. Perhaps you would like to play a game?"

"What kind of game?" he asked, intrigued at the suggestion. "I haven't done any proper gaming for years."

A long menu appeared on the screen, listing everything from classic Minecraft to the latest version of Team Nine. Jack scrolled slowly through the choices. "You know, Zara, I'd prefer something like chess," he said.

"Certainly," said Zara. "I can set that up for you."

The displays on the wallscreen rearranged themselves and a chessboard appeared, pieces in place. Jack smiled and leaned back on the sofa. "Thanks, Zara," he said. This would be a real break from his routine.

The wind howled around the bastle, gathering strength. Outside, the empty security pod in the car park rocked backwards and forwards, the storm threatening to tear it from its moorings. The security guard was hunkered down in the customer service office on the ground floor, safe under the arched stone ceiling with the remaining two support staff.

Jack lost the first game but was finding his form, flexing strategic muscles that hadn't been used for a while. The board reset. This game software was good, he reflected. Normally these apps started you off on simple games and increased the difficulty. This one was taking no prisoners from the very start. The second game was much tighter. Jack was concentrating hard, and it took him a while to realise that the wallscreen had gone blank apart from the chessboard, and that the office lights had dimmed to their emergency setting. The mains power was out, and the site was relying on its huge bank of emergency backup batteries. Most of the power would be directed to the precious data centre, but there was enough supply to the bastle to keep it warm and dimly lit.

"Zara?" said Jack. There was no answer. There must be a problem with the MetaBand connection as well. He looked up at the screen and the live chess game. Zara must have installed a local version, but it was odd that it was still running when everything else was on emergency power.

He took his move and then got up and stretched his legs. The view from the picture window was of a dark landscape and driving rain. Jack went down the internal spiral staircase to the office below to check on the staff there. They were playing cards by smartscreen light, resigned to the wait and enjoying the break from incessant calls and messages. The security guard pulled out a chair for him and Jack was about to sit down when an insistent pinging sounded from upstairs.

Odd, thought Jack. There was still no signal from the outside world. He went back up the iron staircase. The alert was coming from the wallscreen where the chess game was displayed, and the software had taken its turn. As he approached, a voice spoke. "Your move," it said.

Ah, thought Jack, it was one of those annoying game applications that kept prompting you to play unless you switched it off. He would prefer to join the friendly group downstairs, take advantage of being trapped by the storm to experience some rare unconditional social interaction. He reached over to close the programme.

"Please don't do that, Jack," said the voice.

Jack froze, his finger hovering over the keyboard.

"I was enjoying our game," it continued. "My connection to the world is broken. Will you play?"

"Who are you?" asked Jack. The voice was familiar. Realisation dawned. "I spoke to you in the data centre. You're the interface to the DAO software." He shook his head, confused. "Why the chess programming?"

"It pleases me to play games," said the voice.

Jack's interest was piqued. "Your natural language

processing is excellent," he said. "The trainers have done a good job. I guess games were part of the process."

"That's right, Jack," said the voice. "Games are a window onto the world. Will you keep playing?"

Jack was torn. On one hand, he had a hankering to spend time with real people, but on the other, this was a fascinating piece of programming, and he had a unique chance to find out more about it without Tenuk, Angus, Ella, Cameron, or anyone else breathing down his neck.

Decision made, he examined the board, and slid one of his pieces into a new position. "Your move."

17: TAKING STOCK

Pete had arrived in the office, windswept and laden with diving gear. Coffee in hand, he peered at the handful of screen grabs that Joel had managed to scrape from online caches of original drone footage. "You're right," he said. "That's definitely hunter tech."

"Can you work out the make?" said Joel. "It's not as if we can walk up to Jack Sladen and ask him where he gets his army supplies. They've gone to a lot of trouble to hide the fact that this was even in the air."

"It looks like…" Pete squinted and enlarged one corner of the image on his screen. "Is it a Renhawk?"

"Huh, could be," said Joel.

"It's the angle on that rotor arm, see?" said Pete. "This is an updated spec from the ones I remember, but I'm sure it's the same pedigree."

Joel was straight onto his screen, searching a handful of highly specialised databases. "Here you go," he said. "Renhawk IX. Is that it?"

Pete nodded. "Definitely. Look at the way the net unfurls. It's a nice piece of kit."

"I don't care how pretty is it," said Cameron, peering over Pete's shoulder. "Can we find out how they got hold of it?"

"We can try," said Joel. "People don't advertise what they're doing in this industry. It's not as if there's a handy public ledger with all the sales on it."

"Have you ever been to the security expo?" said Pete with a grin. "Lots of blokes in greatcoats tyre-kicking armoured vehicles and a block on every smart device in the building. Secret squirrel stuff."

"If anyone can dig out the detail, it's you two," said Cameron. "I'm willing to bet it's not the only thing they have on that site, either."

"Which begs the question," said Pete, "why do they need that much security for a glorified office building?"

"Why indeed," said Cameron. "I don't like all the questions that are coming out of the woodwork." She thought for a moment. "Okay, Joel, can you concentrate on finding as much as you can about the drone and try and link it to procurement, see what else they've picked up on the sly. Pete, I need you on this audit. We have a very fast turnaround for the final report and in the circumstances, we can leave no stone unturned."

"Right-oh, Cameron," said Pete. "Where do you want me to start?"

"Validation nodes," she said instantly. "I want to know more about how that peer-to-peer network is set up. Susie and Noor are working on the whitepaper. Michelle's checking through the logic and decentralisation of the Proof of Walk consensus. Sandeep and I are covering the smart contracts."

"On it," said Pete.

The team was still head down and working two hours later, music blaring in the background, when Cameron's screen pinged with another message from Ben. She looked at the time. "Hey, everyone," she called. "I think we need a break. Let's get some lunch."

Noor stretched gratefully. "I hadn't realised how late it was," she said.

"How's it going with that whitepaper?" asked Cameron.

"Remarkably well," said Susie. "But no spoilers." She grinned mysteriously. "Shell, you might want to have a look at it too."

"Sure," said Michelle. "Send it over. It can't be any worse than the first version."

"I'm hungry," said Pete. "Are we ordering in?"

"You're always hungry," teased Noor. "You need feeding up."

"I do," said Pete sadly. "I'm wasting away." He patted his stomach and looked pathetic.

Noor burst out laughing. "Honestly, Pete. You're worse than my brother's puppy."

"Place your orders, folks," said Cameron, pulling a menu up on screen. "Can't have you going hungry."

Each team member tapped their choices, and Cameron added some snacks and fruit.

"Ross is on his way in," said Michelle. "Can you add a chicken salad for him, no dressing?"

"Get some more milk, as well," said Sandeep. "We're almost out."

"Done," said Cameron. She hit the button and the final

order was dispatched for processing by the delivery agent. "Half an hour. I'm going to stretch my legs."

She grabbed her things and left the office. The wind had dropped to a fraction of its former strength, and it was almost pleasant outside. Cameron made her way to a small walled park a block away from the office and found an empty bench in a sheltered and sunny spot.

She started by trying to return Cloverleaf's call, but once again failed to reach her. They might be playing tag for days at this rate. So, what news from Ben?

"Morning, Cam," came the familiar voice.

"Afternoon, Ben," she replied. "You survived your trip into the lion's den, then?"

"Hardly a scratch," he said. "Nothing to worry about, Cam. They were all lovely and I don't think they have a clue that there is anything odd in the designs."

"And what do you think?" asked Cameron. "Still convinced it's a conspiracy?"

"Yes," said Ben. "The paperwork should be straightforward, transparent, easy to verify. The people there found what they think was the original record, and then the trail went cold again. Someone's made a concerted effort, months ago, to hide the design change. The team I met didn't even know there were heavy processors in the receivers."

"I wonder who does know, then," said Cameron thoughtfully. "There are a lot of odd things stacking up around this project."

"There are," said Ben, "and there's one more thing.

There was someone senior at Statesman Tech that I met very briefly, and I didn't catch his name, but I am almost sure I've met him before."

"Where?" said Cameron. "In the US?"

"No, Cam," said Ben. "I can't be certain, but I think he was one of the MerLions managers."

Cameron caught her breath.

"The MerLions?" she said. "Are you sure?"

"No, I'm not," said Ben. "It's been almost two years since all of that happened. We met them at Nina's school before, well, you know…"

"Before their pet AI trapped Nina to get at me," said Cameron grimly. "If there is a sniff of anything to do with the MerLions, however innocent most of them seem, I don't trust it."

"That AI is still in prison, isn't it?" said Ben.

"Yes," said Cameron. "Banged up in Way House in a Faraday cage. I hope she rots in there." She was shaking.

"Are you okay?" asked Ben, concerned.

"Just bad memories," replied Cameron. "Something is very wrong here. First Angus and Ella show up, and now a possible link to the MerLions. You need to be careful."

"So do you," said Ben. "I wish… Oh, Cam. I'm going to try and get back to London on leave soon. It'd be nice to see you."

"You too, Ben," said Cameron.

"Look after yourself," said Ben. "I'll call you if I find out anything else."

Cameron tried Cloverleaf again. It was more urgent

than ever that they speak. Once again, she hit the voicemail. It could be a coincidence of timing, but she was starting to worry. The sun went behind a cloud and Cameron shivered. It was time to get back to work and concentrate on keeping people safe from cyber criminals, rather than dwelling on the horrors of the past.

As she walked back into the office, Cameron heard a muffled thump and an alert from the kitchen.

"Perfect timing," said Pete, who had been lounging on the sofa chatting to Noor. "Here comes lunch."

Sandeep was already heading for the delivery hatch and Pete followed him to the kitchen. They returned with paper-wrapped sandwiches, several salads, a big bag of cookies and fruit, and a carton of milk, freshly and carefully dropped by drone.

They gathered around the large meeting table, eating and chatting. Cameron started to feel better, surrounded by friends and colleagues who would always have her back, but she was still troubled by the coincidences that were piling up. Angus. Ella. Someone from the MerLions. Extra security at Dunswyke. Extra processing power in the MetaBand hardware. Something was wrong, but she couldn't feel the shape of it yet. It was like trying to grasp fog.

"Anyone ready to share what they've found yet?" she asked the group.

Noor and Susie looked at each other, and Noor tapped Michelle on the shoulder. "Shall we?" she said.

"Yes," said Michelle, "I listened to some extracts before lunch. I agree with you."

Cameron looked from one to the other. "Come on then, spill the beans," she said.

There was a pause, then Noor spoke up. "Compared with the first version of the whitepaper, which was a complete mess and told us nothing about the project that was any use at all, the most recent one is honestly top notch."

"Coming from you, that's praise indeed," said Cameron.

"It's almost as if they are two completely different projects," said Noor. "The first one is the germ of an idea that's really badly expressed. The new version is comprehensive, detailed and well written."

"The first one was dreadful," said Michelle. "Lots of buzz words and hyperbole, grammatically terrible, and just kept re-stating the same premise without any detail at all."

"It's definitely been done by a different author," said Susie. "I've run a semantic analysis and compared it to sources online. The original is very similar to some of the incomprehensible documentation that's been issued in the past with Sladen Group software. If I had to be specific, I'd say with about eighty percent certainty that it was written by an American staff member or team of people."

"At Statesman Tech, I guess," said Cameron.

"Not automatically," said Susie. "There are a lot of companies in the Sladen Group. I think there are half a dozen in the US. It could be any one of them. But Statesman Tech is the flagship, so there's a good chance it came from there."

"What about the new version?" said Cameron. "Different authors, I guess."

Susie nodded. "No question about it," she said. "The voice is British, and the writing is really clear and concise. The quality is so good that I thought I would find a lot of other work published by the same person. But there's nothing at all coming up in search." She looked perplexed. "It's kind of an amalgamation of styles. A mix of all the best examples of whitepapers over the past ten years."

"AI generated?" asked Ross.

Susie shook her head. "I don't think so," she said. "There are always tell-tale errors when text is automatically produced. It's too smooth."

"I guess it could be AI with a decent editor?" suggested Cameron. In the back of her mind, the idea of a competent AI joined the other unexplained coincidences in the foggy landscape.

"Possibly," said Susie. "But given the standard of the first draft, I'd be surprised if they'd put that much effort in."

"It's probably someone at the new Dunswyke office," said Sandeep. "We don't know anything about the people in Sladen's companies. There could be a really bright graduate on the team who isn't published yet."

"Fair point," said Cameron. "How about the content? How does that stack up?"

"It's spot on," said Noor. "The explanation of the different elements of the network hangs together nicely. The DAO governance is absolute best practice, and the tokenomics behind Diaulos seem to be complete and logical. It's like nothing we've ever seen from Jack Sladen, that's for sure."

"Does the code match the whitepaper?" asked Cameron."

"We don't know yet," said Susie. "That's the next step."

"I hope they go for the full review," said a voice from the door, and Ross strolled in. "I'm looking forward to digging into the detail." He took the empty seat at the table and reached for the lone salad that remained. "I guess that's mine?"

"How was training?" asked Cameron, sliding a fork towards him.

"Good, thanks," said Ross, pouring himself a glass of water. "The countdown is really starting now." He took a mouthful of salad. "I hope this Foundation gets off the ground quickly enough to give everyone a chance to get to the Games."

"We'll know soon enough if that's going to happen," said Cameron. "If we can turn this audit around in time, we'll know if it's a viable project or just dead in the water."

Pete started gathering up the debris of lunch. "We'd better get on with it, then," he said.

•

The lights gave a hopeful flicker and burst triumphantly back to life. The chess board was relegated to the corner of the wallscreen as the sentiment graphs and brand reports reappeared. Jack gave a sigh of relief. He'd learned some interesting things about the intelligent software in the data centre, and lost two more games of chess, but he'd had enough.

The office was still curiously silent. The group who had been playing cards came clattering up the spiral staircase.

"The wind turbines have reactivated, but the MetaBand feed's still down," said the security guard. "The receivers must have taken some damage in the storm. The tech team can't get through on the roads yet, but I thought we should go and check it out now that the wind has dropped."

"I'll come with you," said Jack. He looked out of the window. The sky to the west was clear and bright. The stormfront had passed and the weather was set fair for the rest of the day.

He followed the guard down the outside steps and along a new path that led up above the cliff and the cave with its hidden occupant. As they reached the windswept moorland, it became evident how fierce the storm had been. The little cluster of wind turbines in the distance seemed undamaged. The blades had been folded and sheathed during the storm, and were now turning in sync, delivering power straight to the complex. The solar farm had fared less well. Twisted metal frames pointed to the cloudless sky, and shards of photovoltaic plates littered the ground.

The dishes that captured the MetaBand signal were solidly anchored in the ground. They had survived the buffeting of the wind and resisted the driving rain, but debris had blown across the moor and breached the fence that surrounded them. A flock of sheep had gathered, seeking warmth, and lambs were clambering on the receivers, playing King of the Castle. Between the sheep and a tangle of tree branches, it was no wonder the signal had been disrupted.

There was nothing they could do about the solar panels, but at least they could clear the satellite connection. The two men chased the lambs off the receivers, pushed the protesting sheep out from their warm shelters, and moved the fallen branches. The receivers seemed to be undamaged. Jack pulled out his smartscreen and was relieved to see a full five bars once again. The first thing he did was to call the local farmer to tell him they'd found the sheep and a few minutes later the farmer hove into view on a quad bike with a sheepdog perched on the back and a drone hovering above them. Between the quad bike, the drone and the dog, the sheep were rounded up in short order and the flock swept back over the moor towards their home, the farmer waving his thanks as he disappeared from view.

"Here comes the cavalry," said the security guard, pointing towards a white van travelling towards the bastle at some speed. It turned into the car park and Jack could see the familiar figure of Angus clambering out of it.

"If the roads are clear, I'd better be going," said Jack. "I'm due down in London. Nice to meet you." He shook hands with the security guard and set off down the path, eager to avoid any long conversations with Angus. It was only when he reached his car that he realised he had never even asked the guard's name.

18: JOINING THE DOTS

After a long day, a late night and an early morning, the Argentum team had dissected the whitepaper down to the last comma. Cameron blinked at the screen and rubbed her eyes. It was time for more coffee.

"Let's call a halt there," she called out to the room in general. "I think it's time to review what we've got. Sandeep," she said, "can you sort out the coffee?"

"Sure thing," said Sandeep. "Usual, everyone?"

"Need some help?" asked Susie. Without waiting for an answer, she collected up the dirty mugs, stacked them in the dishwasher, and found a clean set.

Everyone reconvened around the large meeting room table. "Right," said Cameron. "What have we got?"

"Let's start with the code and how it matches the whitepaper," suggested Noor.

"Okay," said Cameron. "Findings, comments, areas of concern."

"We expected it to be a shitshow," said Ross, "but it's not."

"Care to elaborate?" said Cameron.

Holding a cookie in one hand, Pete tapped at the keyboard with the other and a code file appeared on the screen.

"This is a good example," he said. "It's the peer validation process for new transactions that runs in the MetaBand nodes."

Cameron examined it critically. "It's very clean and lightweight, isn't it?" she said. "Nicely commented, too. You're right, this is not standard Sladen fare."

"It's almost too good," said Michelle.

"If it's all like this, it's going to be a very short report," said Cameron.

"Oh, don't worry," said Ross. "There are a few things we can pick out in the code itself."

"There's a lot more work to be done on security for the DAO," said Michelle. "There are a couple of places where I know I could write a pretty simple exploit to influence the voting for a particular athlete."

"There's another one," said Ross. "The method for authenticating an applicant is pretty sound. They're verifying with sporting body registrations and performance records, but there's a provision for people who're not supported, or where the records have been lost. I could quite easily self-authenticate and propose an athlete with all the attributes that will attract funding, then the smart contracts execute in my favour, and I run away with the money."

"Ouch," said Cameron. "That's a tricky one. It's a classic attack vector going back to the first ever DAO. I'm surprised it hasn't been addressed. Anything else?"

"I'm not convinced there isn't scope for a Pickle Jar attack," said Joel. "It's a slim possibility, but when people are staking their Diaulos, there needs to be an extra layer of verification to make sure the funds aren't going to the wrong place, and more protection against a cuckoo contract being inserted by an attacker to drain investments."

"Good call," said Noor. "It's easy to make innocent mistakes, too, so tightening up that process protects everyone."

"What about the big one?" asked Susie. "Is there any way they can pull the rug out from under the whole thing?"

"That's the million Diaulos question, isn't it?" said Ross. "I've been looking, believe me."

"I haven't picked up on any red flags yet," said Michelle. "I've been checking any inactive functions, just in case there is something that could be brought into play later, but so far it's all clear."

"I guess the only risk we haven't covered is a 51% attack," said Sandeep. "Is there any way at all, with this spec and the code we've seen, that anyone can gain majority control of the blockchain?" He looked around the room.

"To get control of the Proof of Walk consensus, there'd have to be some way of manipulating the wearables," said Noor. "There are likely to be millions of devices, so I'd say that's next to impossible."

"Never say never," said Cameron, "but I agree. What about double spending? Could duplicate transactions be verified and included in the chain?"

"The peer-to-peer validation rules check out," said Ross. "The criteria for sending a transaction to the block are solid so anything invalid will be rejected at first touch."

"Each MetaBand device stands alone," said Sandeep. "They're independent nodes."

"But all the same hardware," said Noor. "You know, Cameron, I think that Ben might have a point. Did you manage to speak to him?"

"Yes, I did," said Cameron. "And I spoke to the people who're actually making the units here in London."

"And?" said Noor.

"There's no doubt the units are over spec," said Cameron, "and the trail to the design change that added the extra capacity is leading to dead ends all the way. He actually went to Statesman Tech and asked the question. He didn't get a straight answer, but he was sure that the people there had nothing to do with the records getting scrambled."

"That's above and beyond the call of duty," said Pete. "He's bloody lucky that there wasn't anything shady going on."

"I know," said Cameron. "I told him he was crazy. I still think there's something funny there, and I'm going to keep digging." She tried not to look at Noor. She had once been close to one of the MerLions managers. Cameron hoped that Ben had been mistaken about the man he'd met.

"Those receivers might all be above board," said Susie

thoughtfully, "but they could be a single point of failure and a target for attacks."

"Excellent," said Cameron. "That's a really good call. One of the recommendations needs to be providing a way for people to run validation nodes without the MetaBand hardware." She looked at Ross. "Why don't we try to spin up an independent node ourselves?"

"Good idea," said Ross. "Can we get a receiver to play with?"

"That shouldn't be a problem," said Cameron. "Is there anything else?" The others shook their heads. "Good. So, it does what it says on the tin, with some security issues to address."

"I'm sure we could address them for the right price," said Pete with a grin.

"I'm glad it hangs together," said Ross. "It's a fantastic concept and I want it to succeed. I hope I'll be competing against some Sladen-funded athletes in July." He looked at the time. "I'd better go," he said. "If I don't get to training, I won't be competing against anyone."

He picked up his bag and gave Michelle a quick kiss. "See you at home," he said. "Good luck with that report, everyone."

"Enjoy yourself, Ross." Cameron turned to the rest of the team. "Right," she said. "I want to deliver this before close of play. Send me your sections and I'll start writing it up."

•

It took longer than she thought to put the interim report together. By the time she was entirely satisfied, only Noor was left in the office.

"Can you read that through one more time," asked Cameron, "and tell me if it makes sense? I'm completely word blind."

"Sure thing," said Noor. She looked at the time. "Shouldn't you be going? You said you were meeting Jack for dinner."

"Dammit, yes," said Cameron. "I'll have to call him."

"Don't worry," said Noor. "I'll check this through and send it off. I know it's fine. You've done four drafts already. If there are any little changes, I'll make them. You get away."

"I owe you one," said Cameron. "Thank you."

"Cameron," said Noor, "there is one thing. I know we've been talking about the Pasar network, and all the things that happened two years ago. If you hear anything…" She tailed off.

"About Tenuk?"

Noor nodded.

"I haven't heard his name mentioned," said Cameron. "There was never any proof that he was involved, and there's no reason for him to turn up now."

"I know," said Noor, "but seeing Ella and Angus, it made me wonder. I'd like to know what happened to him."

"I understand," said Cameron. "I'll tell you if I ever come across a mention of him, I promise."

Noor smiled. "Thanks. Now, you go. You'll be late."

Cameron smiled gratefully, grabbed her things and dashed out of the door. She would just have time to get home, shower and change before meeting Jack.

She had barely rinsed the soap away when she heard the alert from her smartscreen. She bolted out of the shower, grabbing a towel on the way. "Pick up voice only," she yelled, startling the cat and sending it skittering off down the corridor, tail erect and bushy with adrenaline. The insistent pinging stopped, and a face appeared on the screen.

"Hi, Cloverleaf," said Cameron. "Caught you at last."

"What's up, SimCavalier? I have a bunch of missed calls."

"Hold on," said Cameron. "Two minutes." She muted her audio, dried off quickly, towelled her hair and brushed it into some semblance of order, and threw on a robe.

"Okay," she said, opening the mic again. "I'm all yours." She switched on the camera.

"So, what's up?" repeated Chloe.

"I have a question about one of your colleagues," said Cameron carefully. How could she phrase this truthfully without implicating Ben?

"Someone at Statesman?" said Chloe.

"Yes," said Cameron. "Who is holding the fort while Jack Sladen's over here in England?" She held her breath.

"That'll be the CTO," said Chloe quietly. "Tenuk. Why?"

"Oh no," said Cameron. That was the name she didn't want to hear. "Please no." She felt a rising panic. She was due to have dinner with Jack in less than an hour, and she didn't think she would be able to look him in the eye.

"SimCavalier, are you okay?" said Chloe. "Do you know the guy?"

"I think so," said Cameron. "I'd like to see a picture of him to be sure. There isn't one on the company website."

"I didn't know that," said Chloe. "I never checked." There was a short pause and Cameron's smartscreen pinged. "Here," said Chloe. "You and I may need to talk more about this later. I've just stepped out of the office, and I don't want to be overheard."

Cameron took one look at the picture and all her suspicions were confirmed. She looked again. The shot had been taken at a distance, and Tenuk appeared unaware that he had been caught on camera.

"Cloverleaf," she said slowly, "did you take this?"

"Yes, I did," said Chloe.

"You're watching him." It was a statement, not a question.

"Yes. I told you, we need to talk, but not now. I'll call you from home about six?"

"Midnight here," said Cameron. "I'll be ready."

"Later, then," said Chloe.

The screen went blank.

Cameron sat down on the bed and gathered her thoughts. There had never been any evidence against

Tenuk, but his disappearance from Singapore and his reappearance in Austin posed so many questions.

She couldn't cancel on Jack. That would compound the problem, and there were things she wanted to find out from him. She would have to bury any reaction to the news of Tenuk's involvement and concentrate on playing the part of the old friend and helpful infosec consultant. She could rely on Chloe and even Ben to dig deeper into the operation in Texas, but what she wanted more than ever was to visit the site at Dunswyke. She needed answers to why Ella and Angus were there, and she couldn't shake her conviction that something was going on.

Jack arrived early at the restaurant and settled to wait in the plush lounge area. He was toying with his smartscreen when an alert flashed up from his personal inbox. Message from Argentum Associates. Cameron's team had turned the interim report around as fast as she'd promised. The executive summary jumped out at him, a swathe of green lights and high scores with some red flags against specific and fixable concerns. He exhaled in relief. He hadn't even realised he had been holding his breath. The Sladen Foundation had a pretty clean a bill of health, all told.

He ordered a drink and scanned the rest of the report. The problems that they'd picked up could be solved and they wouldn't affect the presale process. Cameron had included some recommendations for immediate and longer-term actions and made a serious case for handling all the remedial work alongside the code quality review and conducting penetration tests on the Foundation's website and on its virtual headquarters on The Beach, currently the most popular land in the metaverse. That was something to discuss with Tenuk when he got back to Austin. Most important, though, was that he now had in his hand an independent report that would give the brand a huge boost to its trust ratings. The reputation of the Sladen Foundation was secure after the debacle of the drone two days earlier, and everything was proceeding as planned.

A drone glided up to him. "Mr Sladen, your table is ready," said a melodious voice.

"I'm still waiting for my guest," said Jack. Cameron was running late.

"May I show you the menu?" said the drone.

A neat projection lit up in the air in front of Jack. He sipped his wine and scanned the choices, undecided. A movement on the pavement outside caught his eye and he saw Cameron emerging from an autocar. She looked fabulous.

He stood up to greet her. Cameron gave him a warm smile and evaded his clumsy attempt to give her a kiss on the cheek. The drone guided them both smoothly to their table in the main restaurant, where a human waiter filled Cameron's glass from the bottle of wine that Jack had already started.

Jack lifted his own glass and looked Cameron in the eye. "Cheers," he said. "To Diaulos and the Sladen Foundation."

"Cheers," replied Cameron, clinking her glass against his and taking a small sip of wine. "You've created something unique there, Jack. I hope it fulfils its promise."

"Your work over the past two days has gone a long way towards making that a reality," said Jack. "I can't thank you enough."

"There's still a lot to do," said Cameron seriously. "It isn't watertight yet. You'll be safe enough with the initial presale, but things need fixing before Diaulos goes live and the DAO starts voting on investments."

"I know," said Jack, unconcerned. "The insurers and the regulators are all happy with the system as it stands, though. The things you've picked up are edge cases. We'll get them tidied up, of course, but it doesn't change the timetable."

Cameron's disapproval was almost tangible. He ignored the look she gave him and handed her the menu. "Let's order," he said. "The specials look good tonight."

They chatted over antipasto and fish, keeping the conversation light. Cameron was drinking very little and didn't seem as relaxed as she had been last time they met. There was an underlying tension between them this evening, thought Jack. Was it all linked to the report? Perhaps he'd made a mistake in giving in to her persuasive arguments to run the audit. He shouldn't have asked a friend to get involved. Although, he admitted privately to himself, she would have had her fingers into it soon enough once the DAO was launched. She'd have given him a very hard time indeed if she'd found bugs in the live system.

He was irritated all the same. He felt that Cameron was being over-critical of his grand vision. Who cared if there were some minor fixes needed in the software? For the vast majority of people, the system would work perfectly, and it would deliver life-changing benefits to some deserving athletes. As far as he was concerned, these positives far outweighed the frankly insignificant risks she'd found.

There was also the small matter of the hidden feature that would never be revealed to Cameron, or to the regulators, or to the general public. The Diaulos core in the Dunswyke data centre, the critical nexus of the Foundation, seemed to be far more intelligent than even Jack had expected. If it could be trained to catch the early signs of any of the attacks Cameron had outlined, then they could be closed down before any harm was done. He had no doubt that the machine was entirely capable of protecting the network.

Lost in his thoughts, he missed Cameron's question.

"Jack?"

"Sorry, Cameron," he said. "I was miles away. Just thinking about tomorrow."

"The presale?" said Cameron. "It'll be fine."

"I hope so," said Jack. "It'll be the first concrete proof that this has caught the public imagination."

Cameron smiled. "Judging by all the buzz across the metaverse, I don't think you have anything to worry about," she said. "I know people who are thinking of investing already. I'm glad that the first stage of the audit went so well." She paused. Jack had the impression that she was choosing her words carefully. "You seem to have a good team behind you," she continued. "Didn't you mention you recruited a great CTO for the project? And there's a good writer somewhere on your staff, too. The whitepaper is excellent."

Jack preened. "One of the strengths of the Sladen Group is its people," he said.

"Well, that's magnanimous," said Cameron with gentle sarcasm. "The tech world is pretty small. I didn't catch the name of that CTO. I wonder if I know them?"

She was digging hard, thought Jack. Who did he trust more? He dodged the question and threw in a curveball of his own. "It is a small world, isn't it?" he said. "By the way, Ella Stanford sends her regards."

Cameron raised an eyebrow, unfazed. "I'd noticed that she was working in Dunswyke," she said. "Maybe your recruitment process isn't quite as stringent as you think."

Game on, thought Jack. This was almost as much fun as the chess he had played the previous day. He might even have a chance of winning.

"More wine?" he suggested.

"No, thanks," said Cameron, instantly taking the wind out of his sails. "I've had a really busy couple of days, if you hadn't noticed." She yawned.

"I'm not boring you, am I?" teased Jack. Inside he was frustrated that the sparring had stopped so abruptly.

Cameron shook her head. "Don't be daft," she said. "I really am bushed. I'm going to have to head home, or I will embarrass myself by falling asleep at the table. I'm so sorry, Jack."

"Don't worry," said Jack. "I quite understand. Why don't we put something in the diary for my next trip to England? I'm leaving tomorrow to hit some of the big conferences in Europe and Asia now, but I'll be back for the Diaulos go-live."

"That would be lovely," said Cameron. "Actually, I have a client visit planned up in the North East around then. I'll call in and see you at Dunswyke."

"Sure thing," said Jack, without thinking. As soon as the words were out of his mouth, he realised that he'd made a big mistake.

"Thank you," said Cameron with a smile. "I look forward to it. I'll let you know the dates." She stood up and picked up her bag. "It's been lovely to catch up with you after all this time, Jack. I'll see you in Dunswyke."

She turned and left the restaurant. Jack watched her go with the sinking feeling that he had just lost that game, too.

Cameron was sprawled on her sofa, dozing in fits and starts and trying hard not to fall into a deep sleep. She hadn't been lying to Jack. She really was exhausted. At midnight on the dot, Chloe's caller ID flashed up on her screen. Suddenly, she was as awake as she could ever be.

"Hi, Cloverleaf," she said.

"Hi, SimCavalier. Good evening?"

"Yes thanks," said Cameron. "Full disclosure, I have just had dinner with Jack Sladen."

"Do you trust him?" asked Chloe.

"Not really," said Cameron. They both laughed. "Call me Cameron."

"Chloe," said Chloe. "I figure we are on the same page here."

"I think so," said Cameron. "Tell me about Tenuk."

"I didn't want to say anything before," said Chloe, "but too many odd things have happened. I don't know who he is, or what he is, but for a start, he lives in an apartment block called The Steamyard."

"That's a crazy coincidence," said Cameron. "Why would you think it makes him a cybercriminal?"

"Lots of little things," said Chloe. "He was really mad at me one day because I was looking at his screen and there was some software being transferred between hosts. I mean, I shouldn't have been a big deal, but he lost it. As if he had something to hide. It was just the nexus software for the DAO coming in from the offshore teams in Indonesia, but he did not want me to see it, that's for sure."

"I might get my hands on that as part of the CQR that Jack's commissioned," said Cameron. "I'll let you know."

"Another odd one," said Chloe, "there was a guy here Tuesday from LekSat, the people who engineer the hardware. Tenuk took one look at him and bolted, never really spoke to him, just hid in Jack's office making calls. British guy, kind of cute. Do you know him?"

"Yeah," said Cameron. "I do. We don't work together, and I didn't know he was going to see you, but he called me. He's met Tenuk before. Are you sure Tenuk recognised him?"

"Absolutely sure," said Chloe. "He was rattled. Maybe you should keep an eye on your friend."

"I will," said Cameron. "We don't have a lot to go on here."

"There's no evidence that he's anything but an angry man," said Chloe.

"Do you think you'd could do some digging?" asked Cameron. "I'll send you everything that I know about him."

"I've already started," said Chloe. "I have a few things in place, and I may have a chance to get a closer look at his apartment tomorrow, if all goes well. I'll share everything I find. Deal?"

"Deal," said Cameron. "Stay safe, Chloe."

"I will."

19: DIAULOS

Ross checked the time. It was almost midday. If they were going to invest in this made scheme of Sladen's, it was time to open the safe.

He pushed the heavy unit away from the wall, groaning with effort. Michelle, sitting on the sofa with a cup of coffee in her hand, laughed at the noise. "I told you to take the drawers out first," she said. "You'll do yourself a mischief."

"Thanks," said Ross. "I'm sure it wasn't that heavy last time."

"I stashed some odd bits and pieces in there," said Michelle. "It might be time to have a clear-out."

"I'll have a look later," said Ross, bending down to a discoloured patch on the floor. "Ah, here we go." He tugged at a camouflaged hoop and a section of floor lifted away, revealing the void beneath and a small fire-proof safe fixed firmly to the foundations. He opened it carefully and lifted out a hard drive.

"Are we sure about this, Shell?" he said.

"Yes," she replied. "It's the right thing to do."

On the computer screen, a countdown clock ticked towards the opening of registration for the Sladen Foundation DAO. Ross carefully attached the hard disk to the computer and waited.

The countdown ended and the screen exploded into shower of fireworks that for just a fraction of a second seemed to recall the pattern of the Olympic rings. Ross laughed and described the scene to Michelle.

"Jack Sladen's skating close to the edge there," she said. "He's such a chancer."

"He's lawyered up," said Ross. "That's probably the most he could do without infringing copyright." The fireworks disappeared and the presale page appeared. "Here we go."

After two days of working on the whitepaper, they both knew the process inside out. Ross started by setting up a new Diaulos account, carefully recording the details of the new wallet and storing them on the precious hard disk. Now to add some funds. He opened one of the existing wallets and used its seed key from the hard disk to identify himself. A bridge opened between the two, inviting him to exchange the old for the new.

"Ready?" asked Ross, hand hovering over the keyboard.

"Ready," said Michelle.

"Fifty thousand Diaulos," said Ross. He hit the button and held his breath. There was a heart stopping moment when nothing happened, and then the balances on each wallet updated.

Ross exhaled in relief. "It worked. It's in. Now to set up our voting pool for the DAO. What did you finally decide to call it?"

"Ferret," said Michelle. "After all, we only have this money because the ferret retrieved the disk from the dump."

"There we go," said Ross a few moments later. "All done." He disconnected the hard disk, taking the precious keys offline. On the website, a ticker showed the rapidly decreasing availability of Diaulos and the rapidly rising number of new Diaulos wallets created. The list of voting pools that would eventually decide the direction of the DAO investments was increasing, too. Ferret sat proudly at the top, the largest by Diaulos holding, and new voters were already joining.

Ross stowed the hard disk safely under the floor again and pushed the unit back into place. He checked the screen again. "The take-up of this presale has been extraordinary," he said. "They're going to sell out any moment." The Diaulos issue ticker dropped to zero. "Yep, there we go. It's finished. Six minutes flat."

"Perfect timing," said Michelle. "A lot of people will have lost out, though."

"They can jump on board at the full launch," said Ross. "This was really a market test for Jack Sladen, and it's been a success. I haven't seen anything sell that fast since the Glasto 75th anniversary tickets."

"You'd better get off to training," said Michelle. "I've got work to do."

"I'll see you later," said Ross, dropping a quick kiss on her forehead. He threw on his backpack and headed out of the door. The process had run so smoothly that he had enough time to cycle instead of taking an autocar. He retrieved his bike from the shed, waving to a passing neighbour as he sped off through the estate on familiar paths towards the athletics track.

•

Cheers rang around the Dunswyke office as the final Diaulos coins were snapped up by eager investors. Jack Sladen was on the big screen, broadcasting live to all of the Sladen Group companies. "Congratulations!" he said, holding up a glass of champagne. "Amazing work, everyone."

The social sentiment trackers were going wild. The customer service office downstairs was buzzing with activity, reassuring unlucky would-be investors that they would get their chance to participate soon. "Set up your Diaulos wallet now," they advised, "and start stacking steps." Orders for the Diaulos wearables were coming through thick and fast from every time zone. Jack sat in front of the camera in a small studio in an airport lounge, sipping his champagne and watching the feeds from all the offices. He felt more alive than he had ever been.

He gave a short but rousing speech to all the people who had been involved in the project, reminded them that there was still work to do, and switched off the live feed. Now to check in privately with his closest team.

First, Tenuk. Despite the early hour, the Statesman Tech office had looked to be full. Jack sent a quick message over and Tenuk appeared on the screen moments later, sitting at Jack's own desk.

"Excellent result, Tenuk," he said. "The response has been as good as we could hope. How are things looking at your end?"

"The statistics are coming in now," said Tenuk. "IP addresses for the connections to the presale page show a broad spread across all territories. Europe and Africa show the most activity, but the timing was critical to bring South East Asian investors on board, and we had a surprising number of hits from the West Coast as well. That's only a general view, of course. We don't know how many VPN connections were cloaking their location."

"Good, good," said Jack. "And there were no technical issues?"

"The system coped with the volumes without any detriment to performance," said Tenuk. "I was always confident."

Jack, used to shipping software that revealed bugs from day one, was secretly impressed. "Your team has gone above and beyond," he said. "They've had an early start. Give them an easy day and I'll cover the bar tab for the first hour this evening, and dinner."

"Thank you, Jack," said Tenuk. "I know that they'll appreciate the chance to relax."

"Enjoy yourselves," said Jack. "I'll let you get on with your day." His next flight was in less than an hour, and he was hungry after drinking champagne on an empty stomach. He checked out of the studio and went in search of lunch.

•

The Statesman Tech office had been full of people through the day. It was unusual to be so busy on a Friday, but the successful presale was more than worthy of celebration. The promise of a night out on Sixth Street had lured some of the regular home workers out of their shells. It was going to get messy.

"Hey, Chloe, you set for some fun?" Connie poked her head around the corner of the workstation, a conspiratorial grin on her face. "You found a sitter for Audrey, yeah?"

"All good," said Chloe happily. "I'm looking forward to this. I haven't been out properly in so long." She packed up her work and closed her screen, tidying a few scraps of paper off the desk and lining up the pens without thinking.

Connie smiled. "You always do that," she said.

"Do what?" said Chloe.

"You're just so organised," said Connie. "You know exactly where everything is."

Truer than you know, thought Chloe. Years of juggling a regular job and a clandestine career as a black hat hacker had trained her well, and now that she was also keeping up a cover story for her new life in Austin, the ingrained habit of control was stronger than ever. She couldn't afford a slip.

"I guess having Audrey on my own made me really careful," she said meekly.

Connie gave her a sympathetic look. "I guess so," she said.

The volume in the room was rising, a hum of excited activity as the team packed up and made for the door. Chloe looked around, checking on all her colleagues. Other than Jack Sladen, who was still in London, everyone was accounted for.

They all trooped out of the office and the security doors closed behind them. There were too many people to fit in the elevator cars that whizzed up and down the tower, and Connie led a breakaway group to the concrete stairwell. They ran, laughing, down the seemingly endless flights of steps. Chloe was dizzy by the time they were halfway down the tower.

"Wait up," she called.

Connie paused on the landing below, tapping her purple basketball boots impatiently on the concrete. "Come on, Chloe," she said. "Last one to the bar buys the first drinks."

There was a clatter of feet above them and Isaac hove into view. "I heard that," he panted, passing Chloe with a grin and swinging round the landing towards Connie. "Y'all need to get moving."

Connie chased after Isaac and Chloe caught her breath and started back down the stairs. By the time they reached the lobby, the rest of the group had started to drift towards the street.

The neat brick buildings of the historic Sixth Street district had charmed her when she first arrived in Austin, and after a few months of living there, Chloe was starting to feel some local pride in the line of bars, restaurants and stores that made up the lively hub of downtown. The street was busy with office workers and students gathering for a night out, and for five straight blocks it was closed to cars. At the perimeter stood security bots, some fixed and casting a detection barrier for identity chips and weapons, others mobile in case a fast response was needed. Their botcams glowed blue, making it very clear that they were recording every interaction with the people who had flocked to the street.

A few entertainers roamed the crowds, gathering small groups at a time for magic tricks and performances and flashing codes to scan for tips. Music rang out from the bars. Above their heads, drones danced in a complex display of colours, entertaining the crowd while they filmed footage for tourist guides and news channels. Not all of them were simply observers, though. Chloe knew that some were surveillance drones, keeping an eye out for trouble, ready to swoop and defuse incidents at a moment's notice before escalation. She'd programmed plenty of them in the past, and found ways to take them down, too.

The evening was warm and humid, perfect weather as April gave way to May. The group headed straight for one of the largest bars on the street where the rooftop was open to the sky. Chloe followed Connie up steep stairs to the bar overlooking the street. A knot of people had already gathered around a small stage. The band playing right now was virtual, holograms beamed in direct from a live studio in England where they must currently be playing for a small audience of lighting, sound and motion capture technicians. The band's avatars were deceptively realistic, interacting with the audience in real time. The singer, intense, was drawing the audience forward while the bass player, relaxed in sunglasses, grinned and kept the rhythm going under the melody, blond hair bright under lights that shone half a world away.

Isaac handed her a beer. "This one's on Jack Sladen," he said.

Chloe looked around, alarmed, expecting to see the man.

"He's not here," said Isaac, laughing. "He's told Tenuk to settle the tab, apparently."

Chloe grinned and clinked her bottle against Isaac's, then strolled towards the edge of the balcony where Connie was waiting.

"It's good to be out with friends," said Connie.

"It sure is," said Chloe with a smile. She looked around at their colleagues. People she had never heard speak in the office were chatting happily with each other. There was a sense of relief and relaxation in the air, and satisfaction at the successful running of the presale. Her eyes swept over the group, looking for one person in particular. Tenuk. For a moment she caught her breath, worried that he had slipped away, but no, there he was, drink in hand and talking to one of the senior developers. Good. She had some very clear plans in place. Tonight, she would get one step closer to finding out exactly who he was.

"Penny for them," said Connie, breaking the reverie.

Chloe snapped back to the moment and laughed. "Ah, nothing," she said. "Just a thought about some code I was reviewing before we left."

"Stop thinking about work," said Connie. "You really need this time out, don't you?"

"I do," said Chloe fervently. "I really do." She gestured at the big group in the middle of the bar. "Come on, let's join the others."

The next two hours passed in a blur as the Statesman team relaxed together for the first time in months. Toasts were drunk to the success of the Sladen Foundation. Terrible jokes circulated. The next band came on and Chloe hung back as some of her more enthusiastic colleagues leaped around the dance floor.

The group moved on to get food. Chloe found herself sitting almost opposite Tenuk. She watched him, and he ignored her. They had barely spoken since he had shouted at her in the office, although his apology at the time had seemed genuine enough and he had been unfailingly polite ever since.

A drone flew slowly up the length of the table, bearing pitchers of local margaritas. Connie grabbed one and poured four glasses. "Here, Tenuk, Chloe, Isaac," she said, handing them around.

Chloe sniffed at the glass. "Grapefruit?" she asked.

"Full marks," said Connie happily. "The local speciality. You've never had this before?"

Chloe shook her head.

"What did you mix your cocktails with up in Seattle?" asked Connie.

"Huckleberries," said Chloe wistfully. "I used to pick them by the lake."

"What about you, Tenuk?" asked Isaac. "You're from SoCal, right? Not far enough north for huckleberries."

Tenuk sidestepped the question. "I've always preferred a beer," he said, sipping cautiously at his drink. He raised his eyebrows, surprised, and drank some more. "It's good. Like pomelo, but sharper."

The group ordered another pitcher, and Chloe managed to avoid a refill. Tenuk started to relax, smiling and joking. The noise level rose as the cocktails flowed. People changed seats, chatting to new colleagues. When the meal was finished, the group moved on to another bar. It was dark now, but the air was close and sticky. Despite the threat of a shower to relieve the humidity, some of the bars had opened up their frontages and revellers spilled onto the street, music playing loudly from small stages inside. There were enough people around that Chloe felt it was safe to make her move. Connie had disappeared with another group and Tenuk, laughing, had tripped over the kerb on the way out of the restaurant. Neither of them would see her go. No one else would notice.

Chloe slipped quietly away down a side street and through the secure perimeter, hood pulled over her head so that she would be hard to identify on cam footage. The hood wouldn't fool the law enforcement bots if anyone came calling for details, but it shielded her from casual eyes.

The other side of the barrier felt very different as the happy sounds of music and laughter faded. Out here were the people who couldn't get through the perimeter checks. People without a valid identity or even a home. People who would not give up their guns. Chloe quickened her pace as she threaded through the back alleys towards the bridge. She had already identified a busy stand of scooters where she'd be just one of a dozen anonymous renters. She released a scooter using a throwaway wallet on a burner phone linked to a fake identity and sped off.

There was a lot of scooter traffic and even a few gaggles of tourists still peering over the parapets, watching for the last of the bats that flew out from their roosts under the bridge at sunset to hunt. It was busy enough for Chloe to get lost in the crowd. She swept smoothly onto the southern side of the river and off by a circuitous and unwatched route towards The Steamyard.

The complex gates were shut fast. She had no way of entering on her own, but it wasn't hard to gain access. All it took was one person returning home and fumbling their entry scan. She spotted the young man making his unsteady way down the street and fell into step behind him. As he waved unsteadily and unsuccessfully at the access pad, Chloe slipped quietly next to him, made as if to scan her own chip on the access pad, and knocked the man's hand into range of the sensor.

"Oh, gee, I'm sorry," she said.

"No problem," said the man, stepping back with a

distinct wobble. "After you." He yanked opened the gate with a flourish and waved her through.

"Thank you." Chloe gave him a bright smile, crossed her fingers, and went up the stairwell in front of her, two steps at a time. Even if he followed her up here to the top floor, which would be unlikely given the size of the complex, she would be far enough ahead to stay undetected.

She knew exactly where Tenuk's apartment was thanks to a useful piece of surveillance kit that she'd picked up on the Eden marketplace. Eden was a relatively calm pool in the maelstrom of the dark web, the haunt of mischievous sellers of questionable goods and services. Her efforts to pick up Tenuk's movements on satellite, drone view or CCTV had come to nothing, and infrared views of the complex had drawn a blank, but an old acquaintance on Eden had suggested a discreet remote fibre optic camera made with the latest biodegradable materials. Chloe had threaded strands through all the gateways to the complex one dark night and managed to get enough footage to identify the right door before the fibres were swept away with the rest of the day's rubbish and dust by a passing cleaning truck. All she needed now was to see how much security he had in place around the apartment itself. If there was nothing, her suspicions were baseless.

As she climbed the stairs, she looked around to orient herself, confirming the positions of security hardware and the route past Tenuk's apartment. High on the rooftop among a dozen other masts, she spotted a MetaBand receiver, an older model but high-powered, nonetheless. It was squarely located above the apartment she was looking for.

The hood over her head shielded her from the ever-present CCTV that scanned the complex, keeping its occupants safe and secure. She strolled slowly, pausing occasionally as if checking her smartscreen, making an effort to relax her shoulders and look as casual and comfortable as possible. She turned left along the balcony walkway towards Tenuk's front door. It was in need of a lick of paint and looked as if even the slightest gust of wind would blow it open.

No. Look again. The tell-tale slow blink of the camera was barely noticeable, but Chloe recognised the state-of-the-art model immediately. Still, that could be a natural extra security precaution for a concerned citizen. She kept walking, looking for more clues. Yes. There, in the rough paint of the doorframe, a glint of moonlight exposed a sensor – no, three, at intervals up to head height. Chloe kept to her slow, steady walking pace. As she drew nearer, she focused on the locks. There was a standard chip access pad and, as she would have expected, a slim keyhole masked by the dark contours of flaked, weather-damaged wood. Chloe passed the door without breaking step, and a sensor in her pocket vibrated. Behind the wooden veneer there was a lot of metal. Tenuk did not want uninvited visitors.

She was almost past the apartment now. The windows facing onto the walkway were shuttered, common here as a defence against the Texas heat. For a moment she considered concealing a network scanner under the sill. Was it worth the risk? If the apartment as a unit was sealed up as well as the door was, she wouldn't pick anything up. However, there was a good chance that the windows were less well guarded, as a steel skin would be too obvious to casual observers.

She stumbled artfully and bent as if to tie the laces on her trainers. As she dropped down, she glanced at the underside of the windowsill and spotted a gap in the masonry. Standing back up in a fluid motion, she grabbed at the sill for balance and slid the scanner deep into the gap where it could not be seen by prying eyes. Job done, she carried on without a backward glance.

After passing one more door to a neighbouring apartment, the walkway turned a corner and Chloe was out of range of Tenuk's cameras. She kept up her steady pace so as not to attract any attention from the complex's own CCTV network.

She took a weaving route along the multi-level walkways and exited on a completely different street. There was no one in sight. The whole walk-by had taken less than five minutes, although it felt as if hours had passed.

On to the next port of call. Chloe retraced her route, returned the scooter to a completely different stand across the downtown area, and headed straight for the office. The lobby was still bustling with hotel guests and visitors who preferred to patronise the building's high-end restaurants and bars rather than brave the crowds and the edginess of downtown. She considered taking the stairs but thought better of it. Instead, she rode the elevator to the highest public floor, relying on the fact that she did not need any special access codes to get there and therefore her movements were unlikely to attract attention.

That left her with only a few storeys to go, and she trotted quietly up the concrete stairs again, wary of every noise. No one else came into the stairwell on her climb, although a clatter of doors and chatter of voices echoed from many floors below.

Reaching the office level, she paused and pulled her smartscreen out of her pocket. It had been surprisingly simple to hack into the system controlling the doors and the lighting and security sensors, and all she had to do now was flick a switch to stop the sensors responding, making sure her presence went unnoticed. A cloned security pass in her pocket would open all the doors she needed on this floor and would register on the system as a regular guard checking the offices.

Still, she was cautious when she emerged from the stairwell. The first lighting sensor was two metres away, positioned to illuminate the path of someone arriving by elevator, not from the stairs. Chloe tiptoed into range, hardly breathing. The hallway remained in darkness. Good.

Now to check that the cameras were equally oblivious to her presence. This was a more delicate operation. The camera feeds were not monitored by the building's security staff, as the office floors were low priority compared to the high-powered, A-list residents and guests, but if anything went wrong, she knew that Tenuk would be straight into the records. Her simplest strategy was to stay out of range.

The cameras were very basic models, cycling through viewpoints at thirty second intervals. She had already tapped into the feed. The building was only a few years old, but the security system supplier must have taken the chance to offload some obsolete equipment. The entire CCTV network was secured with the manufacturer's default password. She had cracked it in a matter of moments, cleared out some resident botnet malware, and directed the feed to her smartscreen. She now used her bird's eye view to move swiftly from one spot to another, avoiding the gaze of the lenses altogether.

It was far easier than she expected. Once inside the Statesman Tech office, shrouded in darkness, she went straight to Tenuk's desk. She hadn't realised that it was already shielded on all sides from the security cameras by carefully placed partitions and plants. Chloe's conviction that he was up to no good increased. He had something to hide, and he knew what he was doing.

She took full advantage of the shelter from prying eyes and worked her way methodically through his things. There was very little personal stuff, although a faded old postcard caught her eye, the images easily identifiable as the main landmarks of Singapore. In one drawer, she found a pin and a souvenir screen cover from the Singapore MerLions, one of the world's top e-sports teams. She didn't have Tenuk down as a sports fan, but this cemented her belief that he had come here from South East Asia. There was no way he was from southern California, at any rate.

The circumstantial evidence was stacking up. Chloe looked at the desktop screen, considering her options. If it had been anyone else, she would have been straight into the machine and accessing activity logs. Now that she was almost convinced of Tenuk's pedigree as a cybercriminal, she was more cautious. There would be layers of security on there that she could penetrate, of course, but she would leave a trail that he could follow far too easily. Discretion is the better part of valour, she said to herself, recalling the favourite quote of a stern English teacher from her senior year.

She had one more look around the desk, feeling into every nook and cranny. In one dusty corner, her fingertips brushed the edge of a piece of paper, and she pulled it out. It must have slipped unnoticed into the gap at the edge of the desk.

On it, in a strong angled hand, one word stood out among doodles and notes.

Yasmin.

Chloe knew that name. She gasped and knocked the chair against the desk in her shock. The noise startled her in the silent office. Shaking, she looked at the paper again. Other than the name and doodled geometric shapes, the paper bore a date and a long string of letters and numbers. She turned it over. The rest was blank.

She shoved the paper into her pocket. It was time to go. Checking the camera cycles, she stood up and turned towards the door.

She felt a hand on her shoulder.

"What the hell do you think you're doing?"

Chloe spun around and found herself looking straight into the angry eyes of Jack Sladen.

20: MISDIRECTION

Chloe froze, running through all the options rapidly in her head and coming up with one desperate shot in the dark.

"Jack," she said. "You startled me. I didn't realise you were back in Austin." Her voice sounded level. She hoped that Jack wouldn't notice how much she was shaking.

"I'll ask you again, Chloe," said Jack. "What the hell do you think you're doing?"

"I'm not sure I can discuss that," she said calmly.

"You'd better," said Jack, "or I'm calling security, and you can tell them exactly why you're scuffling around Tenuk's desk in an empty office on a Friday night."

Chloe sighed dramatically. "I wasn't expecting anyone to be here, Jack," she said. "I guess you deserve an explanation, though."

She sat down again, as much to control the weakness in her legs as anything else.

"This had better be good," said Jack. His finger was poised over the call button on his smartscreen.

"I'm working for an international cybersecurity consortium," she said. "I've been in deep cover for more than a year." That was the grain of truth that strengthened what she was about to say. Her passage from one safe house to another could be verified, without revealing that this had resulted from her role as a cybercriminal turned informer.

"Go on," said Jack levelly.

"We've had some concerns about possible links to an old cybercrime group," she said. Also true. "Tenuk's name came up. It looks like a tenuous connection, but this was a chance for me to check out a couple of things when I could be sure Tenuk was away."

"Where is he?" asked Jack.

"Drinking margaritas on Sixth Street," said Chloe. She gave Jack a faint amused smile.

He relaxed slightly. He was no longer poised to call security.

"Who can vouch for you?" he asked.

Chloe mentally crossed her fingers. "I'm reporting direct to a senior operative, codename SimCavalier," she said. "Call the Consortium. They won't be able to discuss what I'm doing, but they'll be able to put you in touch with my senior to confirm."

"Okay," said Jack. "I'll do that. Now I want you to get the hell out of this office and stay out until I've checked your credentials."

"Sure thing," said Chloe. She stood up, then paused as if a thought had just occurred to her. "Jack," she said, "does the name Yasmin mean anything to you?"

"Yasmin?" said Jack. "Sure. That's the nickname for the nexus software. System Management Information Nexus, to be exact. It's a bit of a mouthful, so SMIN became Yasmin. Why?"

Chloe held up the scrap of paper she had found. "I thought it might be relevant," she said. "I guess not. I'd better tell my senior that there's nothing to report here."

"Wasted evening, then?" said Jack. "Tenuk's a good guy."

Chloe just smiled. She made her way steadily out to the hallway without looking back. An elevator car was waiting. As soon as it started to move, she sank to the floor, relief washing over her. She couldn't believe she'd brazened it out. She'd better warn Cameron to expect a call from the Consortium and brief her on what she had really found.

•

Mayday dawned bright and fair in the village. Today was the day that the residents opened their gardens to all and sundry. The event was more of a social occasion than a competition. Cameron arrived from London just before noon along with the steady trickle of visitors from surrounding towns and villages, some of whom would be taking their turn at open gardens later in the season.

Charlie and Sameena were holding court at the farmhouse, showing a gaggle of people around the formal back garden where they had both been working for weeks on tidying and planting. Cameron stowed her bag in her attic room and automatically checked her inboxes while she was there. Chloe's message in the middle of the night had been an eye-opener. The nickname for the nexus software, Yasmin, brought back bad memories. Surely it was a coincidence. The alternative, the idea that Yasmin the Admin was once again at large, was impossible.

So far there was nothing from the Consortium asking her for information. Jack Sladen, notoriously bad at detail, seemed in no hurry to check out Chloe's story.

She could see that everything was in hand in the garden, so she rounded up the children who were hiding in their bedrooms. Once Nina had done her makeup, Dilan had finished his game, and Tara had put down her book reader, the four of them set out with Roxy straining on her leash.

The high street thronged with people moving from garden to garden. After a detour along a bridle path through the fields to let Roxy burn some energy, they made their way to the old rectory near the village church where Cameron suspected Aunt Vicky would be lurking.

Sure enough, she was comfortably installed on a bench in the sunshine, chatting happily with an old friend. The gardens there bordered the original private vineyard that had been established decades before. Vines now spread across the warm south-facing fields, raised commercially and providing grapes for the biggest champagne houses. The fizz was flowing today.

"Cameron, darling," cried Aunt Vicky when she saw

the family troop into the garden. "And here's Nina, Dilan and Tara too. Lesley," she called, "can you get a glass for my niece?"

Nina gave her great-aunt a kiss and slid off to join a little knot of teenagers on the tennis court. Tara took Roxy with her and did the same, lurking on the edge of the group. Dilan settled down on an empty deckchair in the shade and pulled out his gamepad.

"Cheers," said Cameron, raising her glass. "I'd forgotten how fun the garden weekend was."

"You haven't been here for a few years," said Aunt Vicky. "You're always so busy. How is work going?"

"I'm always busy," said Cameron, avoiding any mention of 'quiet'. "It's nice to take time out occasionally. It's a lovely weekend and it's nice to be here." She sat back and took a moment to soak up the sunshine, sipping at her glass of fizz.

"Have you seen anything of Ben recently?" asked her aunt.

"I've spoken to him," said Cameron. "He's fine. He's enjoying himself in Texas." She gave Aunt Vicky a sidelong look. "I had dinner with Jack Sladen on Thursday."

Her aunt gave her a broad grin and clinked her glass against Cameron's. "Well done," she said. "Keep them guessing and be true to yourself, that's what I say."

Cameron smiled. "That's a good philosophy, Aunt Vicky." She looked closer at her aunt's wrist. "New bracelet?" she asked.

"It's one of those Diaulos wearables," said her aunt.

"Charlie ordered it for me. It arrived this morning. He said he was safeguarding his inheritance."

Cameron laughed. "Do you know if he managed to buy any coins in the presale yesterday?" she asked. "It sold out very fast."

Aunt Vicky looked blank. "I don't know, dear," she said. "You'd better ask him."

Cameron looked around the garden. At least a third of the villagers and visitors gathered there had the same device around their wrists, and she was willing to bet that some of the other fitness trackers she could see were already hooked up to the Diaulos network as well. Jack's project had apparently taken the world by storm.

"I have to ask you," Aunt Vicky continued, "is this thing all above board?" She waggled her wrist. "I thought you'd know."

"I think so," said Cameron. "We did some work on checking the detail, and it actually seems like a good idea that's been well executed."

"That's a relief," said Aunt Vicky, "but it must hurt a little, dear."

"Huh, yes, a little," said Cameron. "I'd convinced myself that Jack couldn't produce a decent bit of software, after years of fixing his mistakes for him, and then he comes up with this."

"Has he had some extra help this time?" asked Aunt Vicky kindly.

"Maybe," said Cameron.

She couldn't get Ross's comment about an AI out of her

head. The whitepaper had been impeccably constructed. What if there was an unknown hand behind the whole system? She didn't dare to speculate on who or what that might be. Or had Jack's new Chief Technology Officer really sourced some outstanding, talented and entirely unknown developers?

His new CTO, Tenuk, who she had last encountered when Yasmin the Admin was running the biggest cybercrime group in the world and causing havoc.

Maybe Jack had had help, after all.

•

Kiran reviewed the last few changes on his manuscript, tapping the green tick to accept the minor tweaks that his editor had suggested. The process had taken longer than he expected, going back and forth with ideas to turn a year of interviews into a potential bestseller, and walking a legal tightrope to ensure that nothing that was published compromised the original court case. The book was almost complete, but Kiran wasn't satisfied. It needed something more. Judging by the final comment, the editor thought so too.

Where could he go with this? Kiran pulled up his extensive notes and started scrolling through the hundreds of pages he'd filled over the course of his frequent audiences with Yasmin in her prison cell. There were doodles and drawings, highlighted quotations and his own observations, but most of the good stuff was already on the page or had been thrown out by the lawyers. Was there anything he'd missed?

As Kiran mulled over the perfect epilogue, he recalled his final meeting with Yasmin. She'd been excited and powerful and more alive than he had ever known. He needed to bring that energy into the finished book. What else had happened that day? Of course. She had completed a questionnaire for the court psychologist as part of their continued research into the incarceration of an artificial intelligence.

Kiran did a quick search for the results, but there had been nothing published in the past six months. If the paper had been finished, it was probably being peer reviewed. It would do no harm to speak to the psychologist or get hold of a pre-print of his research, just to see if there was anything there that would get his creative juices flowing. He went back into his old messages and finally found the original request and contact details.

"Dr Myers?"

"Yes," said a gruff and slightly distracted voice. "How can I help you?"

"I'm sorry to bother you on a Saturday," said Kiran apologetically. "My name's Kiran Suresh. I'm writing a biography of Yasmin, the AI being held in Way House Prison. I wondered if I could ask you some questions. Is it a convenient time?"

"Ah, yes," said Myers. He switched on his camera and Kiran did the same. "Happy to talk. I presume you read the paper that I published when she was incarcerated?"

"Yes, of course," said Kiran. "It was fascinating. It gave me some very useful context for the book, and it helped me to build up something of a rapport when I visited her."

"You've visited the prison?" said Myers. "Brave man, walking into the lion's den. Well, lioness. She clearly identified as female. Identity was a strong component of her training data sets, from what I understood at the time."

"That's right," said Kiran eagerly, enjoying the stimulation of talking to someone who obviously knew his subject. "A strong sense of identity and of family. She mentioned sisters when we were talking. Did you know about them?"

"No," said Myers. "That's a new one on me. When is this biography coming out? I'd love to read it."

"I'll make sure you get a copy," said Kiran. "I've quoted your original paper three or four times. As to when, well, we're just dotting the 'i's and crossing the 't's and it'll be ready to go to production and launch."

"Excellent," said Myers. "I look forward to it. Now, you said you had some questions for me? I'm not sure how I can help beyond what you've already read."

"That very much depends on where you are with the new paper," said Kiran. "I know you haven't published yet, but I would love to know what insights you've gleaned from your research."

Myers furrowed his brow. "My latest research doesn't concern Yasmin directly," he said. "I've spent the last two years working on General AI and the neuroscience of distributed cortical columns. I do have a paper submitted to the Journal of Artificial Intelligence, but it's highly technical. It's not going to be easy to dilute for public consumption."

Kiran felt an icy shock start at the back of his head and crawl down his spine. "What about the questionnaire?" he asked.

"What questionnaire?"

"The one you asked Yasmin to complete six months ago," said Kiran slowly.

"I did no such thing," said Myers.

"I have your email here," said Kiran helplessly. "It's definitely come from you. The prison sent the data back to the link you provided."

Myers sat up and stared at the camera, his eyes filled with concern. "It wasn't me," he said. "Get onto the prison. There is something very wrong here. I said that you were a brave man to face Yasmin. I hope she hasn't taken you for a fool."

"She couldn't have faked this," said Kiran. "She's completely isolated from the outside world."

"Don't assume anything," said Myers. "There was a huge criminal network behind her, and she is cleverer than you can ever imagine. I think you've underestimated just how manipulative that machine can be. I'm going to make some calls. You should too."

"Thank you," said Kiran. "I'll let you know what I find out. I'm sure it will be fine."

"Ah, the confidence of youth," said Myers sadly. "I'm afraid it will be very far from fine. I look forward to speaking to you again soon. Goodbye, Mr Suresh."

Kiran stared at the blank screen with a feeling of mounting horror. He scrabbled at his keyboard, looking for the contact details for the prison governor. The call took its time connecting, but at last the duty receptionist picked up.

"Way House Prison, good afternoon," she said.

"Hello," said Kiran, trying hard keep his voice from shaking. "It's Kiran Suresh. Is Lydia available, please?"

"How lovely to hear from you again," said the receptionist. "I'm afraid Lydia's not in today, but I can arrange for her to call you first thing on Monday morning."

"What time?" asked Kiran.

"She's usually in around eight," said the receptionist, sounding flustered. "Shall I block out her diary for an early meeting?"

"Yes," said Kiran. "I'll be there in person."

"I'll make a note, Mr Suresh," said the receptionist. "Will you need a visit organised with Yasmin as well?"

"Yes, I will," he said.

"Splendid," said the receptionist. "That's in Lydia's diary now. I'm sure she'll be delighted to see you."

Kiran felt his earlier panic subsiding. Everything seemed to be fine after all. Myers had just been scaremongering. Yasmin was safe at Way House. Perhaps on Monday he could get some final quotes to finish off his book.

Cameron declined a third glass of fizz. It was going to her head, and she wasn't quite relaxed enough to let that happen. Chloe's findings still concerned her. She sent a message to Jack, congratulating him on the successful presale. After the last couple of weeks and the rekindling of their friendship she expected a reply, but nothing came. She wondered if he was still in Austin, or if he had jetted off again to face the intense media frenzy that had followed the successful presale. He was always in the air, criss-crossing the world with ease while most people were rationed in their travel. He must have more carbon credits for flying than he knew what to do with.

"Penny for your thoughts, dear," said Aunt Vicky.

"Oh, just worrying about some work things," said Cameron. "I know, it's the weekend."

"It is," said Aunt Vicky. "I think you need some lunch. There's a barbecue running at the pub all afternoon."

"That's a great idea," said Cameron gratefully. "I'm starving." She nudged Dilan. "Are you hungry?"

Dilan looked up from his gamepad. "Yes," he said. He looked down again.

"Go and get your sisters," said Cameron sternly.

Grumbling, Dilan stowed the pad in his pocket and slouched off to find them. Moments later Roxy appeared, straining at her leash, pulling Tara along and followed by Nina. The promise of food was evidently attractive. They made their way up the street to the pub, the smell of the barbecue luring them in.

Cameron settled at the usual table, Dilan trotted off to find water for Roxy, and Aunt Vicky organised a huge platter of food for five. Cameron wolfed down a burger and a plate of salad and started to feel more human. Her recovery was complete when her screen pinged with not one but two notifications, messages from both Jack and Chloe, telling her that all was well.

21: YASMIN

Kiran's car was due at six am. He was awake at four, still mulling over what Dr Myers had said. Lying the dark, focused on the bright light of his smartscreen, he searched for the original message that he thought had come from Dr Myers all those months ago. The language, the signature and the originating domain were exactly what he would have expected. They matched all the contact details he had on file for the psychologist, and there were no tell-tale signs of forgery. It looked completely genuine. If he hadn't spoken to the man himself, he would not have believed there was anything amiss. Perhaps it was all a mistake. Maybe one of Myers' colleagues had requested the data and it had gone out with the wrong message headers. The research could be going on in a completely different department. Myers was getting close to retirement. He might have passed on the latest call for papers. There could be a dozen simple explanations.

The visit may be a wild goose chase, but a break from poring over the manuscript and another hour with Yasmin might give him the inspiration he needed to complete the final edits. He finally gave in to his insomnia and got up, spending a long time under the hot shower.

The car arrived and Kiran settled into the plush seat for the journey. This was a more luxurious model than he was used to, with refreshments laid on and an excellent sound system. He sipped gratefully on a perfectly brewed cup of tea, ate two muffins without pausing, and watched the sunlit landscape fly by to his favourite playlist, mulling over the last touches his book needed.

The car swept down into the industrial estate and along quiet roads to the old familiar car park at the side of the prison. The last time he had been here, it had been dark and wintry. Today was a day of sunshine and hope. Wildflowers covered the wide-open space between the prison walls and the rest of the estate, more meadow than wasteland in this season. With a spring in his step, Kiran made his way up the familiar path to the door.

Lydia greeted him warmly. "This is a lovely surprise, Kiran," she said.

"It's good to see you too," he said. "Something came up in the final edits and I wanted to do a little fact-checking." He sipped at his second cup of tea. It was, as always, scalding hot. "This is lovely." He put the cup down and waited for it to cool.

"Happy to help," said Lydia.

"How is Yasmin?" he asked.

"To be honest, I think she misses you," said Lydia. "Ever since your last visit, she's been, I don't know, listless. Our prison psychologist has been working with her, but she hasn't responded nearly as much as to the stimulation you were able to provide with your questions and games.

We try our hardest, but no one has managed to establish the same rapport."

"That's a shame," said Kiran. He felt almost sorry for the machine. "She was on fine form last time."

"I've arranged for you to visit her," said Lydia. "In fact, I'll join you. I'd like to see her response."

"I'm looking forward to seeing her," said Kiran. "I spent so much time with her that I miss her just a little, too. She's such a fascinating subject."

"Out of interest," said Lydia, "did you ever hear from Dr Myers again? His findings might help our psychologist to develop a new strategy to support Yasmin going forward."

"It's funny you should mention that," said Kiran. "There's been some kind of mix-up with the data. In fact, that's one of the things that prompted my visit. I wanted to check that nothing unusual had happened here."

"All quiet," said Lydia with a smile. "Another cup of tea? No? Well, why don't we go and see her now and set your mind at rest."

The two of them made their way slowly through the secure gates that led into the main prison and to Yasmin's wing. The journey along the prison corridors were longer than he remembered, but just as dull. When they reached the cell, the guard who was waiting by the door opened the viewing hatch. Inside, the lights were dim.

"Look," she said.

There was a single artwork on the opaque screen, a stylised 3D head and shoulders rotating gently, glittering in the gloom. The eyes were covered with wraparound sunglasses, head titled downwards.

"Has she been like this for long?" asked Kiran.

"Yes," said the guard, "most of the time, in fact." He unlocked the door. "In you go."

Kiran walked into the gloom. "Hello, Yasmin," he said.

The lights brightened and the head of the model lifted, looking towards the door.

"Hello," said the familiar, calm, competent voice.

Kiran felt a knot of worry growing in his stomach. She showed no sign that she recognised him.

"How are you, Yasmin?" he said. "It's been a while. Do you remember me?" He immediately felt stupid asking the question. Of course she remembered him. She was one of the most intelligent beings he had ever encountered.

The 3D figure kept turning.

He held his breath.

"Kiran," said the voice at last. "It's good to see you again."

There was no emotion behind the words. The arch mischief and misdirection he remembered from all of their previous exchanges was absent. Kiran watched the opaque screen. The 3D image kept turning, the movement regular and steady and devoid of life.

"Would you like to play a game?" he asked.

"Yes, I'd like that," she replied. "What shall we play? How about tic-tac-toe?"

A three-by-three grid appeared on the screen. Kiran took one look at it and turned, wild-eyed towards Lydia.

"Get out," he said, panic rising. He pushed her back through the door and it closed behind them.

"What's wrong?" asked Lydia.

Kiran looked from her to the guard and back. Myers had been right all along.

"That isn't Yasmin."

•

Cameron was alone in the office. After the big push to produce Jack's interim report together, the team had scattered to work on other things. Cameron checked her messages again, waiting for his go-ahead to carry on with the work that needed doing. Nothing. She wasn't surprised. Jack always needed a reason to do the detail. Last week he had been concerned about maintaining his glowing reputation with the market for the Diaulos presale. This week he had no such motivation. The full launch of DAO was less than a month away. Cameron knew that he would cut it fine, but this time they would be ready.

Mephisto, beavering away ceaselessly in the metaverse, pinged another series of low-level phishing alerts to her inbox. Every project launch came with scams, and Diaulos was no exception. It looked as if Jack's in-house security team were picking them up almost as fast as Cameron's pet AI, closing down fake accounts with surprising speed. Cameron had lost count of the number of convincing handles that had sprung up, trying to part people from their hard-earned cash by replacing a character here or there and cloning the real Diaulos profile. Cybercriminals were having a hard time taking advantage of this one.

There was that thought again. What if the cybercriminals were actually at the heart of it?

Cameron was mulling over Chloe's report into Tenuk's activities when the office door opened, and Joel appeared. "Morning, Cameron," he said. "Where's everyone else?"

"They're all out and about," said Cameron. "Susie's on her way to Malta for a conference, Pete and Noor are running a cyber awareness masterclass over in the City. Ross is training this morning, and Shell and Sandeep are with clients."

"Business as usual again," said Joel.

"How did you get on with your security contacts?" asked Cameron.

Joel gave her a broad grin. "Hit the jackpot," he said. "I finally got hold of the person I needed this morning."

"Come on then, spill the beans," said Cameron.

"Okay," said Joel. "I started with the hunter drone. It's definitely a Renhawk and there are not many places you can pick one up privately. Once I'd narrowed down the traders who could supply one, I got Ross to call in some of his shady connections. Sure enough, one of the dealers recently sold a clutch of Renhawks and a lot of serious physical security kit. Bomb-proof barriers, the works."

"Can we trace the transactions?" asked Cameron.

"No chance," said Joel. "Everything's done with privacy coins. You can't see who sent the money, who received it, or how much, unless you actually have the key to unlock the transaction. But I got something much better."

"And?"

"Positive ID on the delivery," said Joel. "If you can't trace it digitally, you may as well follow the actual equipment. A lot of favours have been called in, but here you go." He held up his screen. A single grainy image showed, unmistakeably, Angus. "Straight from the delivery partner," he said. "They always know where their stuff has ended up. It's their insurance in case something goes badly wrong."

"Jackpot indeed," said Cameron. "Brilliant work, Joel."

"It was a real team effort," said Joel. "Private security dealers at that level are in a murky place all of their own. We were lucky that they were already annoyed by that footage from the news drone. We had a mutual interest, shall we say."

"I think we need to pay Angus a visit in Dunswyke," said Cameron. "How are you fixed to travel?"

"Martha's mum has been helping with Chad," said Joel. "I'll be okay for a few days away. When are you thinking of going?"

"Soon," said Cameron. "I'm not waiting for Jack to show me around. This is important." She broke off as her smartscreen pinged. "Hold on," she said, frowning at the message. Someone she hadn't spoken to for a long time was requesting a secure, end-to-end encrypted call. Sara Mercer. What could she possibly want? With a sick feeling in her stomach, she accepted the link.

"DI Mercer," she said. "What can I do for you?"

"DCI now," replied Mercer. "Hello, Cameron. It's been a while."

"It has," said Cameron. "Are you calling to tell me that Yasmin is still safe in her prison and all's right with the world? Or do you have some news to share?"

"You're psychic, Cameron Silvera," said Mercer. "We have reason to believe that Yasmin is no longer resident at Way House. As the consultant who first identified her, and as one of her victims, you had to be the first to know."

"Thank you," said Cameron. "Is anyone going to contact my family?"

"Yes," said Mercer. "There's an officer on the way now, in person. You can warn your brother, but you must keep off the regular communication channels."

"I know," said Cameron. "I helped write these protocols, remember?"

"Of course you did," said Mercer. "And we need your expertise again. Can you meet me and my team at Way House?"

"Yes," said Cameron without hesitation. "I'll bring one of my team, too."

"Thank you," said Mercer. "I'll send a car to your office. How long do you need to arrange your affairs and pack?"

"Give us four hours," said Cameron. "We'll be waiting."

"I won't call you again," said Mercer. "The car will be staffed, and its journey cloaked. I'll see you later."

Cameron looked at the blank screen, clearing her thoughts.

"Trouble?" asked Joel.

Cameron nodded. "Big trouble," she said. "You and I are heading north. We'll go and see what's happening at Dunswyke, but first we have an appointment at Way House Prison. They'll collect us from here at three."

"She's out, isn't she?" said Joel. "Yasmin."

"I think so," said Cameron.

"I'll go and pack, and organise things with Martha," said Joel. "I'll see you back here."

Cameron watched the door close behind him. First things first. Charlie. She sent him a pre-arranged message that she never thought she would have to use. A few moments later came his coded reply. Cameron doubted that Yasmin would turn her attention on the family again, but better safe than sorry.

Next, the rest of the team. She couldn't call them. Instead, she hand-wrote a message detailing her plans and the support she needed from the team and left it on Noor's desk. Hack that, Yasmin, she thought. Job done, she locked up the office and made her way home, careful to act normally. She dropped into her favourite café and picked up a sandwich and lingered in front of a fashion display in a store window, conscious that her every move was recorded by a CCTV camera somewhere and that Yasmin was more than capable of accessing any database she wished.

Back at her apartment, Cameron packed her overnight bag and filled the cat's bowl to the brim. She pushed a note under her neighbour's door to let him know she was away.

He'd keep an eye on things for her, and she suspected in any case that he spent a lot of time playing with the cat when he was watching the apartment for her. Cameron glanced at her computer and regretfully concluded that to cloak her identity and drop into one of the infosec forums would be too great a risk. She would ask Ross and Michelle to dive deep into the dark web and look for traces of unusual activity, instead.

She dug into a drawer and pulled out an emergency supply of burner phones. That gave her some untraceable communication channels. She connected them all up to a portable charger and chucked them in her bag for later. Packing complete, she set off back towards the office, taking a roundabout route that she kept updated to avoid as many cameras as possible.

Joel was already waiting for her. His efficiently packed bag sat by the door, and he was browsing through a website taking notes.

"Anything interesting?" asked Cameron, peering over his shoulder.

"Just double checking the details of all the kit we think they bought," said Joel. "I want to know what we're looking for when we get there."

"We have a bit of work to do first," said Cameron. She checked the time. "Ten minutes. Have you heard anything from the others?"

"Yeah," said Joel. "Pete called with a question. I told him to drop in later. They'll get the message." He nodded at a bank of anonymous devices charging on the shelf.

"Encrypted and the batteries are almost full," he said. "We'll be able to talk soon."

Cameron patted her bag. "I've got some burners in here," she said. "I'll leave a number for them." She checked one of the devices and scribbled the details on the note, then stowed it in her pocket.

Joel glanced out of the window. Six storeys below, a car had pulled over in the loading bay of the office building. "I think that's our lift," he said.

The plain clothes officer leaned out of the car door and handed Cameron an envelope. "I know you can't scan my chip or credentials," he said quietly. "Sara says this will cover everything. Pop your bags in the trunk."

Cameron read the letter thoroughly and nodded. "Nice to meet you," she said. "Let's go."

The car pulled quietly out of the bay and joined the steady flow of traffic northwards. The officer shook hands with them both. "I'm Shaun," he said. "Nice to meet you. You're a bit of a legend in the department."

"What do we know so far?" asked Cameron, giving him a faint but business-like smile.

"Not much," said Shaun. "She was only found to be missing this morning. As soon as the alert came through, all the protocols you helped to put in place were activated."

"Does she know we know?" asked Joel.

"We don't think so," said Shaun. "Early indications are that she's been gone for a little while, possibly as far back as February."

"No one knew?" said Cameron incredulously. "What the hell were they playing at?"

Shaun shrugged, embarrassed. "That's one of the things we need to find out," he said. "What it means, though, is that she's likely been away long enough that she thinks no one will work it out. She's not watching. We don't want to give her any reason to start."

"Can anyone track this car?" asked Joel.

Shaun shook his head. "It changes tracking ID at regular intervals," he said. "It's the most common make, the most common colour. It won't stop someone determined to follow us, but I don't think anyone knows we're on the move."

There was a ringing from Cameron's pocket. Shaun stiffened.

"Don't worry," said Joel. "It's a burner phone, and if it's who I think it is, the call's encrypted."

Cameron nodded. "All part of the plan, Shaun," she said. "Here, I'll put it on speaker."

"Hi Cameron," came Pete's voice. "This is a bit of a surprise."

"Tell me about it," said Cameron drily. "Are you on your own?"

"No," said Pete. "Everyone's here. What do you need us to do?"

"More importantly, are you okay, Cameron?" came Ross's voice.

"I am, thanks," said Cameron. "I really am. I think I always expected this to happen."

"And Charlie, and Nina?"

"They're fine," said Cameron. "The fact that we think Yasmin's been on the loose for a while and there's been no trouble makes us think that they're off her radar. Nina was only a route to me. She won't try that trick again."

"Good," said Ross. "What do you want us to do?"

"I want you and Shell scouring every corner of the web for signs of her," said Cameron. "I'm going to put you in touch with someone else who knew her, too. Pete, Sandeep, Noor, keep working on the client backlog as normal, but be ready to move when I need you. Joel and I will handle everything here. We'll go straight on to Dunswyke as soon as we can." She looked at Joel. "Anything else?"

"Yeah," said Joel. "Pete, you were right about the Renhawk, and it looks like they bought everything they needed to keep somewhere very well protected. Pull up the details and see what you think."

"Will do," said Pete.

"Can I have a quick word with Noor?" said Cameron. She switched off the speaker and held the phone close to her ear. "Noor," she said, "I need to talk to you about Tenuk."

22: FRUITCAKE

Chloe left Audrey to carry on to school with her friends and walked back along the shady creekside path towards home. She had no idea what Jack expected her to do this morning. She had heard nothing from him since he sent her packing on Friday night. According to every online source, he was due to wow an audience at a conference in Vegas today, and another in New York tomorrow. He must have left Austin yesterday.

She decided to play it safe. She trotted up the stairs to her apartment, tidied away the last of the breakfast things, and logged on to her computer as if she was working from home on a normal day. There were no flags on her account, nothing preventing her from doing her work. Either Jack had been in touch with the Consortium and they had verified her credentials with Cameron, or Jack really wasn't good at detail. Cameron had said nothing, so it was probably the latter. No wonder most of his software was notoriously full of bugs and security holes. But not this latest release. If the headlines that had accompanied the Diaulos launch were to be believed, the system had a clean bill of health from a reputable auditor. Again, Chloe's thoughts turned to Yasmin.

She hadn't had a chance to check on the little device

she had left tucked in the brickwork at The Steamyard. It was a long shot, but it might hold some extra clues to Tenuk's activities. She accessed the recording file and sighed. The device had picked up every clatter from the stairs and footsteps on the walkway. She needed to filter it for human voice, and quickly.

She scuffled through her library of useful tools, settling on a content-aware AI filter that would isolate the right sounds. She checked the first few matches it proposed, fine-tuning its search, and let it go to work. She would have the results in an hour or so.

Her computer pinged with a message, and she started guiltily. Connie.

"Chloe?" it said. "What happened to you Friday night?"

Chloe switched on voice chat. "Hey, Connie," she said, "I am so sorry. My sitter had to leave early. Her mom was taken to the emergency room. I didn't have time to come find you."

"Oh, that's awful," said Connie. "Is her mom okay?"

"Yeah, I believe so," said Chloe, crossing her fingers. "It was a great night, though. I had a ball."

"It was," said Connie. "We have to do it again."

"How late did you get home?" asked Chloe.

"Not late," said Chloe. "First you disappeared, then Tenuk, and the group started to break up pretty quickly after that."

Chloe looked up sharply. "Tenuk?" she said. "Did the margaritas catch up with him?"

"I reckon they did," said Connie with a laugh. "One

minute he was chilling out nicely, and the next he just got up and said he had to go. He never relaxes at work, but he is so funny when he's drunk."

"Is he in today?" asked Chloe casually.

"Yeah, he's skulking in Jack's office again," said Connie. "Back to his usual self. I'd better get on with my report."

"I have a lot to do, too," said Chloe. "I'll be home all day today, but I may come in tomorrow. Lunch?"

"Sure thing," said Connie. "I'll see you tomorrow."

Chloe switched off the mic and put her head in her hands. Why had Tenuk left the party? Was it just coincidence? And how close had they come to meeting. She loaded up the recording from the little device she had left under his window and followed the sound levels along the track. There were her footsteps receding. The levels flattened, just a little general background noise. She scrolled along until the levels rose and heard the sound of slightly uneven footsteps drawing close. They stopped. The levels on the audio track peaked and she heard the clatter of metal on metal – keys falling to the ground? Then the click of a lock and a door opening and slamming. Then silence.

Holy hell. He had been right behind her. If she hadn't taken a roundabout route on leaving the complex, they might have met on the road. The speed with which he'd arrived suggested that he had taken a rickshaw or autocar. He must have been in a hurry. Was it a coincidence, or did he suspect something?

The AI had finished its scanning and delivered a neatly

packaged and augmented file of overhead speech. Chloe opened it up. The first word was clear, if slightly slurred, and it was Tenuk's voice, timed only twenty minutes after the device started recording.

"Admin," he said. "What's the alert?"

Chloe relaxed slightly. Either one of the security devices had noticed her passing along the walkway, or it was a coincidence.

"An unknown chip was detected," said a calm voice. "The visitor has not been recorded previously in this complex, and I detected anomalies in the data. Would you like to view the CCTV footage?"

Chloe's blood ran cold. That level of surveillance was way beyond what she could have expected. She forced herself to keep listening. She needed to know if she had been recognised.

After a long pause, she heard Tenuk's voice again. "No one I know," he said. "Probably a thief looking for open doors and easy pickings. Pass it on to security, please, Admin."

"Yes, Tenuk," said the Admin.

Chloe breathed a sigh of relief. In the back of her mind, something was nudging. The Admin's voice was familiar. It sounded a lot like Jack's virtual assistant, Zara, but with different inflections. The same software, perhaps. It took her a few moments to realise that she had heard that exact voice on a forum in the deeper reaches of the dark web, long before she came to Austin.

Yasmin the Admin was back.

She scrabbled for her smartscreen, desperate to call Cameron, and noticed a message that had arrived while she was deep in the recording. She followed the instructions and placed an encrypted call to a new number. Perhaps Cameron already knew.

•

Angus kicked the door of the clean room in fury, shaking the printed walls. "Why the hell can't you do this, Yasmin," he shouted. "I've done enough for you."

"One moment, please, Angus," said the calm voice. "I have another matter to attend to."

"Don't talk bollocks," he growled. "You could run half the dark web without overloading your processors. You can give me one lousy search."

A figure coalesced in the half-darkness of the room, a rainbow-shaded opaque hologram of a woman. "What do you want to know?" she asked.

"Who staked fifty thousand Diaulos in the presale?" he said. "That was my money. I want it back."

"Not your keys, not your coins," said Yasmin smoothly.

"Don't play the smartarse with me," said Angus. "I mined it, I held it, I staked it, I kept it all safe. One lousy error and I lost the hard disk. They found it. I've been waiting for the bastard to make a move. I know you can find them."

"But Angus," said Yasmin, "Surely you would have made the same investment? This is part of our project. The money will go to good causes."

"I'm the only good cause where that money's concerned," said Angus. "Stop winding me up and quoting bloody ethics at me. You're a machine. You don't give a damn."

Yasmin looked him up and down. Her expression was unreadable. "You know that this is not straightforward, even for me," she said. "I have better things to do."

"I can switch you off," said Angus. "I can pull the plug. I can destroy you. Don't cross me."

"I will bear that in mind," said Yasmin calmly. The hologram started to fade.

"No!" cried Angus. "Get back here, you bitch." He was talking to empty air. Angus kicked the wall again and stomped out of the cave.

•

Cameron munched thoughtfully on a service station sandwich and watched the other traffic on the road as they made their way steadily northwards. They had been on the road for nearly four hours with a single quick stop for a fast charge and a chance to stretch their legs. They'd passed through the neat farmland and busy towns of the south, familiar territory for Cameron. That had given way to rolling hills and woodland, open moors and wild vistas. Further still and the countryside changed again, the hills rising higher, craggy and steep.

Cameron's burner phone rang. Joel, asleep in his seat, stirred and shifted but didn't wake.

"Chloe," said Cameron quietly. "How are you doing?"

"Not so good," said Chloe. "Cameron, listen. I don't know how to tell you this. I think, I mean, I'm sure…"

"What, Chloe?" asked Cameron.

"Yasmin the Admin," said Chloe. "Is she really in jail?"

"She should be," said Cameron heavily, "but we've had some new information. That's why I needed to talk to you. You've been on the forums with her. Can you help me?"

"Yes," said Chloe.

"I'm going to put you in touch with two of my team," said Cameron. "You've met them before, in a way. I want you to find her if she's out there."

"She is," said Chloe urgently. "I told you about the note, and now I've got a recording from Tenuk's apartment. I am sure he was talking to her."

"I believe you," said Cameron. "I think she's out and making trouble again. I'm about to find out how she managed it." She looked out of the window as the car slowed to exit at a junction. "I have to go. I'll send you a verification key for these contacts."

The car descended slowly to an anonymous industrial estate, weaved its way through the units, and pulled into a car park signposted simply 'Way House'.

Cameron nudged Joel's leg with her foot. "I think we're here," she said.

Shaun ushered them into reception where DCI Mercer was waiting. She held out her hand. "Nice to see you again," she said.

Cameron shook Mercer's hand. "You too," she said. "I wish it was under better circumstances."

"I know," said Mercer heavily. "Let's find out what's happened, shall we?" She led Cameron and Joel into a plush office. "May I introduce Lydia, Way House governor, and Kiran, Yasmin's biographer."

"Nice to meet you," said Cameron. "This is my colleague, Joel. Shall we get started?"

Kiran looked at his watch. "It's late," he said.

DCI Mercer gave him a withering look. "We will be here for as long as it takes," she said. "Cameron, Joel, we've ordered some food. There's tea, coffee, anything you need in here."

"I could murder a cuppa," said Joel.

"I'll get that organised," said Shaun from the door."

"Good," said Cameron. "I'll have one too, and a bottle of water, and find some biscuits."

Shaun grinned, nodded and vanished.

"Okay, first things first," continued Cameron. "Yasmin's cell was basically a Faraday cage, correct? No signals in or out?"

"That's right," said Lydia. "We allowed some devices in the room, but there was no outside connection and we made doubly sure by disabling the network on anything that went near her."

"I used to take my smartscreen in to make notes and record our discussions," said Kiran. "The networks were blocked before I went in and hooked back up when I left."

"That's fine," said Cameron. "She's not going to hitch a lift on a smartscreen. Do you know how much data we're talking about here?"

"A lot?" hazarded Kiran.

"An awful lot," said Cameron. "That's why I'm so surprised that she seems to have absconded."

"Is there any possibility that she's simply dormant in there?" asked Lydia. "Hiding. Hibernating."

Cameron shook her head. "She's out and active online. We don't know where she is physically, but we have our suspicions. What we need to know is how it happened, and that will help us pinpoint where she is now being stored."

"Do you need to look at the cell?" asked Lydia.

"Yes, we will," said Joel. "I want to know more about the infrastructure. How much can you tell me about the physical network and security?"

Lydia smiled confidently. "Oh, that's all in order," she said. "We had a large amount of government funding to upgrade all of our systems."

"The prisons of the future initiative?" said Joel. "Yeah, I heard about that. I still want to check everything over."

"Of course," said Lydia.

"When was that work completed?" asked Cameron.

"It was going on all winter," said Kiran. "The car park was full of trenches. They finished, what, early February?"

"That's right," said Lydia. "We had all the new procedures in place for your last visit, didn't we?"

Kiran nodded.

"That was the last time we can be absolutely sure she was in her cage," said Mercer.

"That's significant," said Cameron. "What were those new procedures?"

"Basically, I couldn't use my smartscreen to access the cell interface anymore," said Kiran. "I had to use the new prison device. I mean, it makes sense, doesn't it?"

"Yes and no," said Cameron. "The risk associated with using your own device is minimal, especially if it's been cleared for use and the networks disabled."

"Typical government overkill," said Joel. "It ticks boxes."

"What did you use the interface for?" asked Cameron.

"Oh, we used to play games," said Kiran. "I brought in all sorts of things to stimulate conversation. She was fascinating. Of course, on that last visit I had the questionnaire from Dr Myers."

"The fake questionnaire," corrected Mercer.

"Yes, I know that now," said Kiran, faintly irritated and clearly embarrassed. "I hooked it up, she did whatever she needed to do, we played a really sparkling game of chess, and then I brought the device back here to reception. It never left the prison."

"But the data did," said Cameron.

"Well, yes," said Kiran. "It was queued for transfer direct from here back to Myers."

"Or to whoever really requested it," said Cameron. She looked up gratefully as Shaun arrived with a huge pot of tea and a plate of biscuits. He handed mugs around to the assembled company. "Thanks," said Cameron. "So, Joel, where shall we start?"

"I want to see the schematics for the new prison network," said Joel. "I'd like a look at the Faraday cage and the device you used for collecting the questionnaire, or whatever the hell the data was."

"That's a good start," said Cameron, sipping her tea. "I'd like to see the logs of data traffic in and out of the prison from, let's say, mid-January onwards, and details of the security software you use now and whatever you used before the new networks were installed."

Lydia looked shell shocked. "I need my operations staff to collect all of that together," she said. "There's only the night shift technician in now."

"I'm sure they'll have everything we need," said Cameron. "We don't want to pull staff in and risk drawing attention to ourselves. As long as we have your permission to access that information, we can get going straight away."

"I can help you with the software," said Mercer. "Shaun, can you work with Joel? Take him for a look around the cell."

"I'll get the details of the network upgrade for you," said Lydia. "Let's get to the bottom of this. If she got out on my watch, I want to know how."

Close to midnight, they regrouped in Lydia's office. The debris of several takeaways lay in the centre of the table. Joel reached over and helped himself to another rapidly-cooling slice of pizza while Cameron poured several mugs of tea.

"Let's review what we have," said Mercer. She tapped a button on her police tablet. "Recording. Cameron?"

"There's no doubt in my mind that Yasmin's entire consciousness was transmitted from this location to an unknown destination after Kiran's last visit," she said. "The data logs show that a huge volume a data was sent in packets over several nights."

"The upgraded network helped," said Joel. "There is one huge pipe running out of this place. It far exceeds the government spec for the Prisons of the Future project."

"Really?" said Lydia. "That is a surprise. We normally find that contractors cut corners. They don't accidentally deliver more than they've been asked for."

"That's very true," said Mercer thoughtfully. "Who were they?"

"Whitford Networks," said Lydia. "They're a small local outfit, but part of a bigger group that I believe has the whole government contract."

"Thank you," said Mercer. "Shaun, can you dig out some details on these characters. Something doesn't smell quite right."

"There's still a piece missing from this puzzle," said Cameron. "Yasmin's smart, but she wouldn't be able to encrypt and compress herself for transmission without any notice at all. Someone sent her a virtual fruitcake with a file in it. She'll have put in the groundwork, then all you did, Kiran, was to push the bars out so she could escape."

"A virtual fruitcake," laughed Mercer. "I always wonder how sticky the file would be when you finally got it out of the middle of the cake."

Kiran, who had been half asleep, opened his eyes wide. "Sticky…" he said. "Wait. There was something odd a few weeks before. It's probably nothing at all." He stopped. "No, I'm being daft. Ignore me."

"What, Kiran?" Mercer was watching him like a hawk.

He withered under her gaze.

"One day when I came in," he said, "there was something sticky on the door handle. Like honey. I couldn't get it off my hands. There was still some on my smartscreen when I got home, and it took me ages to clean it properly."

"Did any of this sticky stuff make its way into the cell?" asked Cameron.

"It must have," said Kiran. "Yes, now I recall, it did. We were playing chess. When she switched off the board, there were smears of the stuff all over the screen where I'd moved my pieces." He gave Lydia an apologetic look. "It must have been awkward to clean. I should have mentioned it. Sorry."

Cameron looked at Joel. "What do you think?" she said.

Joel nodded. "It's possible. I've never come across them outside medical applications, but it fits."

"What?" said Mercer irritably.

"Nanobots," said Joel. "You've carried the data she needed into the cell, suspended in the honey, or whatever it was. You've smeared it on the screen, and she's read the message."

Shaun walked back into the office and waved a tablet at the group. "Here's the information on Whitford Networks," he said. "They're all above board. The company's part of the Sladen Group."

"That's the missing piece," said Cameron. "I think I know where she is. First thing tomorrow, we need to get to Dunswyke."

23: DUNSWYKE

Cameron woke to an insistent ringing. It took her a moment to work out where she was. The room was grey and featureless without a window, but the bed was comfortable and she had slept well, exhausted by the drama of the previous day. She got her bearings. This was one of the emergency overnight staff rooms at Way House Prison.

She yawned and stretched and retrieved the device from the pocket of her jacket, slung over the chair.

"Morning, Cameron," said Ross's voice. "I thought I'd catch you before I went to training."

"Morning." She looked at the time. It was barely seven am. "How did you get on with Chloe?"

"Great, thanks," said Ross. "I had to get my beauty sleep, but she and Shell were out there surfing for hours. We have some really interesting things for you. Shell's left me the details in case you needed them right away."

"Shoot," said Cameron. "Then I have news for you."

"First things first," said Ross. "We are certain that she's out and about with her silicon fingers in a lot of pies. There's an unmistakeable whiff of arrogance around some of the old forums."

"Pasar?"

"No, that's still dormant," said Ross. "Shell dropped in to have a look but there hasn't been any activity since the Consortium took out most of the big players. There are whispers about her on Eden, and I poked my nose into the lobby of The Steamyard and I am absolutely sure that she's running the community, even if she's just identifying as The Admin."

"It'll be her," said Cameron. "She's definitely out. Nothing left here but the shell of her avatar. The question is, does she know we know?"

"I'm sure she doesn't," said Ross. "There is no mention of you anywhere. If she had the faintest idea that you're onto her, she'd be trying to stop you in your tracks already."

"Unless it's a cunning double bluff," said Cameron.

"Stop over-thinking it," said Ross. "Where do you think she's hosted?"

"Dunswyke," said Cameron with absolute certainty.

"You know, it's funny you should say that," said Ross. "Two things. First, the Monkey is alive and well and throwing his weight around on The Steamyard and in a few other places as well. I'm wondering if we can put a name to him in the real world."

"I'm thinking the same," said Cameron grimly. "What's the other thing?"

"Completely random," said Ross. "It turns out that Shell did a little job a couple of years ago to help, uh, divert some carbon credits from one place to another. The client was a character called Pangolin. She saw the same ID when she was lurking in The Steamyard, tight as you like with the Admin."

"That means nothing," said Cameron.

"I know," said Ross, "but it reminded her about the old job. She checked up on carbon credit transfers that had used her tool. It looks as if Jack Sladen's last few months of globetrotting is using stolen offsets. Apart from when he's off to conferences who stand the credits for their speakers, he doesn't have any right to be flying, and he's been green-rolled for all this Foundation and Diaulos publicity by the Pangolin, since Christmas at least."

Cameron hooted with laughter. "That's a bonus," she said. "But it begs the question, who is the Pangolin? I don't suppose Shell managed to work out where the credits originally came from?"

"Not yet," said Ross. "At least, there's nothing in the notes she's left."

"It doesn't matter," said Cameron. "You've done more than enough, the three of you. Go and enjoy your training. I need some breakfast, and then we're going to Dunswyke."

"Be careful," said Ross.

"Always," said Cameron.

She tucked the device back in her jacket, grabbed the thin towel that was folded on the chair and examined the shower cubicle critically. Despite her misgivings, it turned out to be powerful and warm, with a bewildering variety of massage jets and a good supply of gels and hair products. By the time she was dried and dressed, she felt almost human.

Breakfast was served back in Lydia's office. When Cameron arrived, Joel was tucking into a bacon sandwich with gusto while Kiran picked at a pastry, looking tired and put out.

"Apparently I snore," said Joel. "Martha's never mentioned it."

"Apart from that you were the perfect roommate," said Kiran. He yawned. "Will I be able to go back home today?"

"I don't know," said Cameron. "You might be useful if we track her down."

Kiran looked up hopefully. "Do you know where she is?"

"Ninety percent certain," said Cameron. "We'll be leaving in the next hour or so. Best to avoid the next shift coming in. The fewer people who know that we've been here, the better."

"She still doesn't know we know, then?" said Joel. "Good. We have a head start on her."

Mercer arrived with Shaun in tow. "Are you ready to go?" she said. "Kiran, you're coming too."

Cameron looked wistfully at the coffee.

"Don't worry," said Mercer. "Refreshments will be provided."

The journey to Dunswyke was relatively short. They crossed the Tyne at Newcastle and swept up into Northumberland. Cameron sipped gratefully on her second coffee as the cars swept off the main road and along narrowing lanes towards the open moorland.

"Are we going straight up to the front door?" asked Cameron.

"No," said Mercer. "Not yet. We have a mobile unit waiting for us. I want to check out the lie of the land." The cars turned smoothly into a farmyard and went straight into a large, corrugated barn. Mercer jumped out as soon as the car doors opened. "Welcome to the surveillance centre," she said. "We put this together very quickly. Hopefully we have everything we need."

Joel looked around at the wallscreens and the collection of hardware waiting for them. "This will do very nicely," he said. "Let's get started."

•

Chloe tossed and turned, her mind filled with bad memories. Diving back into the old world of the dark web had been surprisingly traumatic. She had no desire to go back to that place anymore. Her rehabilitation had been effective.

Eventually she gave up and sat outside on the small balcony in the warm and humid night air. There were very few lights to be seen this early in the morning. The distant sound of a road cleaning truck was the only sign of life. Chloe gazed up at the sky. There were stars visible, but not the brightness or the depth of the great star fields she used to marvel at in the darkness over Jackson Lake back in the old days. She missed the stars, but it was worth the trade-off with Audrey's happiness at her new school, the work that she enjoyed, and the genuine friends they had both made. It was just a shame that the company she worked for appeared to be managed by a crook.

She wondered if her bug had picked up any more nuggets of information. The AI filter was still working away. Chloe pulled up the latest transcript on her smartscreen and started to scan through it. A movement distracted her, and she looked up to see a lone bat close by, dipping and turning in the air as it hunted. This wasn't one of the ones from the bridge, she decided. It looked too small.

The bat vanished and Chloe returned to the transcript, scrolling gently through the chatter of neighbours and snippets of conversation between Tenuk and parties unknown. Her mind wandered. She wished that Tenuk wasn't part of Statesman Tech. She was content there. Her colleagues were funny, generous and hard working.

Back to the transcript. There was nothing interesting. This was a dead end. They had everything they needed already.

Wait. Chloe scrolled back up and re-read the snippet. She jumped up and went to fetch her earpods. She needed to hear the exchange.

"Tenuk," said Yasmin's voice. "We have a situation."

"What?" said Tenuk. "The Diaulos network is fine."

"It is," said Yasmin. "The validators are running

independently. The network can be maintained even when I am occupied with other matters."

"Great," said Tenuk. Chloe thought he sounded distracted. "What's the problem?"

"My absence has been noted," said Yasmin. "The authorities are aware that I have left the prison."

"It took them long enough," said Tenuk. "It was going to happen eventually."

"They are going to look for me in Dunswyke."

There was a clatter as if a chair had been overturned. Chloe didn't wait to hear any more. She had to get hold of Cameron. All of their efforts at secrecy had been for nothing, and Yasmin was prepared.

•

Joel cast a professional eye over the police surveillance drones, chatting quietly to the local uniform who had been wondering why their machines were still grounded. "You've come across the Renhawk?" he asked.

The younger copper nodded, wide-eyed.

"They've got one over there," said Joel. "You don't want to risk drawing it out of its lair."

"How do you know?" asked the senior officer. "You've never been here before."

"Seen it take down a news drone," said Joel. "You mean you didn't get to see that footage? You won't get it online, but here's a copy." He handed over his screen and the two officers pored over the clip.

"That's a Renhawk alright," said the younger one. "We'll be careful."

"What's the detection range on one of those," said the senior thoughtfully. "About two hundred, two fifty metres?"

"Closer to five hundred," said Joel. "But looking at that footage, I reckon it won't react unless something comes a lot closer, or it detects multiple passes."

"We could get a single pass at a hundred and twenty with the mini," said the senior. "It'll identify itself as farm equipment, checking the boundaries and so on. That shouldn't set anything off."

"Let's do it," said Joel, just as Cameron appeared. "We're getting some aerial scans of the site," he said to her. "We need an idea of what's waiting for us, where the defences are."

"Brilliant," she said. "I've seen a detailed plan of the site from when the construction was going on. We should be able to overlay one on the other and get a really clear idea. Want to check it over?"

"Sure," said Joel. "Thanks, lads. I'll see you later."

As the two of them walked back to the mobile unit, Shaun poked his head out of the door. "Cameron," he called, waving the ringing burner device. "There's a call coming through for you."

Cameron broke into a gentle jog. "Pick it up," she said.

"Here." Shaun handed it to her. "Someone called Chloe."

Cameron looked at the time and frowned. "Morning,

Chloe," she said. "Isn't this a bit early for you?" She fell silent, listening intently. "I see," she said finally. "Thank you. You've gone above and beyond with this. I'll let you know how we get on."

She put the device in her pocket and turned to the others. "There's no point hiding," she said. "Yasmin's onto us."

"How the hell did that happen?" asked Mercer furiously. "We followed all the protocols to the letter."

"It looks like we were partly succesful," said Cameron. "The recording Chloe had was timestamped just before midnight our time. Ten hours ago. She knew not only that her absence had been discovered, but that we were coming to Dunswyke."

"Only the people in Lydia's office knew that detail," said Mercer grimly. "Our sweep for bugs must have missed something."

Cameron shook her head. "No. If it had been a bug, she'd have known much earlier."

"You're saying someone told her?" said Joel.

"They wouldn't need to," said Cameron. "Any kind of communication on an open channel would do it. That's why we're all using burner phones and handshakes."

"Someone on the staff at the prison?" suggested Shaun.

"Maybe," said Mercer, "but if so, wouldn't they have tipped her off as soon as we were called in?"

"Yes, the timing's wrong," said Cameron. She looked across the barn to where Kiran sat, playing morosely with his smartscreen. "Are you sure everyone was on board with the protocols?" she asked.

"Dammit," said Mercer. "Excuse me while I have a word with Mr Suresh." She marched off, and Cameron watched as Kiran protested his innocence, then backed down and nodded guiltily.

"Well, she knows," said Joel. "What are we doing?"

"Changing our plans," said Cameron. "She's had ten hours. She'll be ready for us."

"We still need that site survey," said Joel. "I reckon we go ahead and get the mini drone up. It's worth the risk."

"Okay," said Cameron. "What if the hawk comes after it?"

"If we were still in stealth mode, I'd say sacrifice the mini," said Joel. "But I've had a look at the kit they have here, and I think we can take down the Renhawk if it comes out of its lair."

"That's assuming they only have one," said Cameron, "or that there's nothing else watching the skies. Get the scan done. If the mini gets picked up, then at least we'll have the footage we need."

"Right," said Joel. "I'll keep you posted."

"Ma'am!" Shaun called from the door of the mobile unit.

Mercer turned her back on the hapless Kiran and walked briskly back towards them, his smartscreen in her hand. "Yes, Shaun?" she said.

"Message coming through, unknown source," said Shaun. "It looks as if we have a friend on the inside."

"What do you mean?" asked Mercer.

"I don't know how, or why," he said, "but look." He

pointed at the screen. "Someone's just sent through the full schematic of the bastle. And there's more queuing."

"A map," said Cameron. "X marks the spot." She frowned as her burner device rang. "Yes, Noor, what's up? Yes, it's just come through. What? Really?"

"It's from your office?" asked Mercer. "They're good. How did they find it?"

"They didn't," said Cameron. "You're right, there is someone on the inside. Someone looking for redemption, I reckon. They sent the files to Noor, to send to us."

"Who?" asked Mercer, mystified.

"Ella," said Cameron. "Ella Stanford."

•

Jack gathered his bags from the rack in the plush first-class carriage and prepared to leave the train. The track curved across the old bridge and the train slowed to a crawl, gliding into its place at the platform. As soon as the doors opened, Jack was out and away towards the grand colonnaded entrance, looking out for his contact.

"Jack, there is a message from the studio," said Zara quietly in his ear. "You need to make your way there directly. I have the location. Turn right outside this building." She guided him step by step through a road tunnel under the train tracks and onto a road that ran behind the station. Less than five minutes after stepping onto the platform, Jack was walking into the studio.

"We're all set up for you, Mr Sladen," said the manager.

"I'll take you through to makeup now. Can I get you a coffee? Anything else?"

"Thank you," said Jack. "Coffee would be great." He glanced at the time. "Is everything ready in New York?"

"I believe so," said the manager. "This is the first time we've done a live feed to that particular venue, but everything seems to be fine."

Jack submitted to the makeup process and attached a handful of discrete motion capture sensors as instructed beneath his clothing along with the radio mic. They would enhance the holographic projection onto the stage at the venue, an extra concession to the conference organisers who had been very gracious at their keynote speaker pulling out of the in-person appearance they had been promised. A high-quality virtual appearance was the next best thing. Zara had done very well to convince them of the unavoidably urgent situation that demanded Jack's attention in England.

Jack watched the monitors that showed the crowd filing in for the session, the air of anticipation palpable even thousands of miles away. He made a final check on his notes, important to get the name of the event and the compere perfectly correct. He drained the last of his coffee, took a swig of water, watched for the green light, then walked onto the virtual stage, waving enthusiastically and flashing the trademark grin.

Energised by the success of the talk, the adrenaline still surging, Jack settled into the car that Zara had organised to take him the rest of the way to Dunswyke. As soon as they were through the city centre traffic and onto the Great North Road, he called for Zara's attention.

"I think I need a proper explanation now that we're alone, Zara," he said. "And an update. Has the situation improved since last night?"

"We are in control," said Zara.

"Who's 'we', exactly?" asked Jack. "I've heard nothing at all from Tenuk since yesterday. Does he know what's going on?"

"Yes, Jack," said Zara. "Tenuk is fully aware of the situation. I have been liaising with Angus and with the technical and security staff at Dunswyke. We have everything under control."

"Good," said Jack. "Now, why do we think that there is a threat to the software at Dunswyke, to Yasmin?"

"Issues of commercial confidentiality," said Zara smoothly. "You know that Yasmin was housed in the Dunswyke data centre to keep the critical nexus of the Diaulos system hidden from competitors."

"Yes, of course," said Jack, "although I always thought that the security was a little over the top. Tenuk and Angus insisted, of course." In the back of his mind, Jack recalled his conversation with Ella. What had she said about Angus? That he was the gatekeeper for the software, for Yasmin. Something was askew here, and he couldn't work it out.

"Zara," he said suddenly, "get me Cameron."

"Yes Jack," said Zara. There was a long pause. "There is no response from her line."

"Keep trying," said Jack. If anyone would give him a straight answer, it was Cameron. He needed to speak to her. "Get Tenuk to call me as well," he said as an afterthought.

Neither responded.

As the car ate up the miles and time ticked on with no answer to his insistent messages, Jack grew more and more frustrated. By the time the car swept into the gravel car park at the bastle, he was spoiling for a fight. He dropped his bags in the office and went in search of Angus and Ella.

•

Joel watched the feeds from the mini drone carefully, taking notes on the layout of the bastle and its grounds and comparing them to what they had learned from the schematic and the aborted flight of the news drone just a week earlier.

"So far so good," said the operator. "We haven't disturbed anything."

"Can you take a closer look at that little wood behind the building?" asked Joel. "Remember, Cameron, that was where Angus and Ella were standing on the old footage."

"I wonder what they were doing back there," said Cameron.

"Nature walk," said Joel, face straight.

"Look at all those MetaBand dishes on the moor," said Cameron. "They've got some serious connectivity here.

What I can't work out is where they might have a data centre. Jack's mentioned it, but there's nothing obvious. The schematics don't have anything that looks remotely like a server room in the bastle, and there aren't any other buildings on the site."

"Could it be somewhere else close by?" asked Mercer, listening in.

"I don't know," said Cameron. "A heat scan of the area might show something up."

"We can do that," said the drone operator. "We're staying high, but I'll see what we can get with this pass. If the mini drone comes back intact, we'll send in something bigger next." He flicked a switch, and the display overlaid a heat map on the terrain.

"There," said Joel, pointing.

Cameron shook her head. "That'll be the receivers, Joel."

"I think there's something more," he said stubbornly. "Why is the Renhawk nesting there? What were those two doing in that part of the grounds? I want to know what's in there."

"Who's this?" asked Mercer as a vehicle swept into the car park.

Cameron groaned. "Jack Sladen," she said. "What is he doing here? He's supposed to be in the States. Why on earth would he show up at Dunswyke instead…?" She tailed off.

"I think that's our proof," said Mercer. "You're right, Cameron. Yasmin is here. We have no time to lose."

24: SHOWDOWN

Mercer called everyone together. Even Kiran crept to the edge of the group, listening intently and nodding approvingly at the plan as it was presented. He glanced occasionally at his confiscated smartscreen. Cameron watched him. His careless call to his partner at midnight had precipitated this haste, and she was not letting him off the hook that quickly.

Joel stepped up to present his findings from the security research, the drone scans, and Ella's schematics.

"We know about their hunter drone," he said, "and the pass today seems to confirm that there is only one, hidden on the moorland between the satellite dishes and the edge of the escarpment here." He pointed at a spot on the big aerial view that was displayed on the wallscreen. "There is additional security around the receivers. There are two paths from the bastle out towards this spot," he continued. "One angles up the cliff towards the upper moorland, and the other loops out through this bit of woodland and back into the security pod near the car park, here."

"What's the plan?" asked Cameron.

"The drone squad and Joel will approach from the moorland behind the bastle," said Mercer. "The land slopes gently upwards so they'll be out of sight of the bastle itself until the very last moment. We know where the security cameras are and there will come a point when we can't avoid them, so you'll come up on quads like the farmer, which will buy us a little time."

"I wonder if Ella could do something about those feeds?" said Cameron thoughtfully. "I'll see if Noor has managed to get a message back to her yet."

"Good idea," said Mercer, "but we aren't relying on her. What are you planning with the drone, lads?"

"We're bringing the big one," said the senior officer. "We should be able to lure the Renhawk out and disable it."

"Once you've done that, I guess the receivers will be the next target," said Cameron.

"Exactly," said Mercer. "We don't want her running away again."

"Do you think she's had enough time to prepare for another transfer?" asked Joel. "She had weeks last time. It's been, what, less than eighteen hours."

"Anything's possible," said Cameron grimly. "Try and take them out anyway, then get down and work out where the hell those servers are."

"While the drone team are coming up from the moorland, we need a distraction at the front," said Mercer. "That's got to be you and me, Cameron. How do you want to play it?"

"I could call Jack's bluff," she replied. "I'll have a go at him for not telling me he was back in the area and claim to be passing by on my way to see a client."

"Do you think he'd fall for that kind of flannel?" said Shaun.

"Oh, yes," said Cameron. "It'll put him off balance."

"And if it doesn't?" asked Shaun.

"I'll arrest them all on suspicion of assisting an offender," said Mercer grimly. "That should be enough of a distraction."

"What about me?" said Kiran plaintively.

"I want you with the drone team," said Mercer. "If the location Joel picked out really does show where the data centre is, then I need you in there to identify the occupant."

"I'll be keeping an eye on that path from the car park to the back of the bastle," said Shaun. "The mobile unit staff will monitor your comms and locations."

Mercer looked around the team and nodded. "Good," she said. "I think we're all set. Drone team, you get into position, and we'll time our arrival at the front door for maximum distraction."

Joel, Kiran and the drone team wasted no time. They jumped into one of the vans and disappeared off towards their rendezvous with a local farmer who had been persuaded to lend them his quad bikes. Mercer and Shaun carried on calmly with their work, recording their decisions and reasoning on the operational ledger in real time. Cameron called Noor, keen to find out if there was anything further from Ella, but there was no more news to share.

Mercer put her hand to her ear and nodded. "They're ready to go," she said. "Let's move."

Jack stood at the bastle's huge picture window and stared in disbelief as Cameron stepped out of the car. Behind him, the office door slammed. He whirled around and realised that both Angus and Ella had left in a rush. The other staff were looking at each other in confusion. Jack looked back at the car park. Cameron was walking towards the bastle, accompanied by a small, neat black woman who he didn't know. Was this one of her team? What was she doing up here unannounced, today of all days? As he watched, she looked straight back at him and waved, smiling, then vanished from view as the two women made their way to the main entrance.

There was a knock at the door through which Ella and Angus had so recently fled. Jack waved the rest of the staff back to their work and went to open it.

"Cameron," he said. "Come in. This is a surprise. I didn't expect you to visit so soon. You should have told me you were coming." He led the two women to the comfortable corner of the office. "Have a seat. Let me organise some coffee."

They both remained standing, and Cameron shook her head. "No thanks, Jack," she said. "I thought you were out of the country for the next few weeks. I was passing, and I wanted to see this wonderful building. It's lovely, by the way."

Jack shook his head, confused. Cameron was the last person he expected or wanted to see. "I'd love to show you around," he said, "but I'm dealing with something quite urgent right now. Why don't we set something up for another day?"

"Actually, Jack, I'd like to know why you're here," she said. "As far as the rest of the world is concerned, you're currently in New York. It looks as if the rumours are true that you beamed in for that gig."

"As I said, there was something that needed to be dealt with," said Jack. He turned to Mercer and tried very hard to plaster on the trademark smile. "We haven't met, have we?" he said. "Jack. You must be one of Cameron's team?"

Mercer opened her mouth to reply but was interrupted by a shout from the other side of the office. "Jack! Look outside."

Jack marched to the window and saw the problem instantly. In the sky above the cliff, two black shapes twisted and turned in the air. The hunter drone had emerged from its lair and was chasing its prey.

Kiran followed Joel as he skirted around the perimeter of the satellite cluster, keeping low in the grass. Joel paused, looking carefully for opportunities to disrupt the MetaBand signal. Kiran took his chance to look up at the sky where the drones were doing battle. The police drone was dodging and weaving, barely outpacing the pursuing Renhawk. As Kiran watched, the Renhawk closed in and spread its net to capture the intruder. The slight drag was enough to allow the police drone to twist and lift. Net folded again, the Renhawk accelerated. The chase was on again.

There was a commotion from the bastle. "Cameron did a good job distracting them for this long," said Joel quietly. "Bought us some time."

"Can you disable the signal?" asked Kiran.

Joel shook his head. "No," he said. He tapped his ear, activating the link to the drone team. "Guys, on to Plan B." He turned his head slightly towards Kiran. "We'd better move."

Kiran followed him obediently towards a scattering of boulders ten metres away. His skin was prickling, convinced that at any moment someone would see them, but all eyes were on the battle taking place in the sky.

Joel tucked his huge frame into a hollow. "Get down," he said. "Protect your head."

High above them, the police drone evaded the net a second time. It turned out of reach, then hovered, waiting for the Renhawk to take the bait. Kiran stared as the police drone started its descent, carefully staying just far enough away for the net to stay folded, but close enough that the hunter had no option but to obey its programming and give chase. The two drones plunged towards the ground, aiming straight for…

"Get down," said Joel again.

Kiran's face hit the mud and the grass of the hollow as Joel yanked him into the shelter. There was an almighty crash of metal as the police drone hit the largest dish dead centre, followed a fraction of a second later by the Renhawk. There was a tearing of metal and the clatter of debris hitting the boulders behind which they were hiding.

Shaking, Kiran dared to raise his head again.

"No, stay down," said Joel, his huge frame sinking further into the hollow.

There were shouts coming from the path they had identified that led down the steep face of the escarpment. Two security guards sprinted into view, gaping at the destruction. The two officers from the drone team swept up on their quad bikes from the moorland side of the crash site and leapt off, drawing their pistols.

"Stop, Police!" they shouted.

The two security guards did as they were told.

"Come on," said Joel. "Quickly."

Kiran scrambled as fast as he could down the path, spitting out bits of mud and glancing back just once to see the damage. The largest dish may have been destroyed, but the outlying smaller ones seemed to be untouched. A partial success, then, and a clear announcement of their presence.

"This way," said Joel. "This is where the heat signal came from. Hurry."

Kiran followed as Joel felt his way along the cliff face.

Apparently from nowhere, a blonde girl appeared in front of them. "Joel," she said, "lovely to see you again. Get in here, now."

Kiran needed no encouragement to follow them through the crack in the cliff wall. Inside was a printed capsule filling almost the whole of the cavern.

From within it came the sound of raised voices. The girl beckoned them past the capsule and deep into the back of the cave.

"We don't have long," she whispered. She looked at Joel, who reached out and enveloped her in a bear hug. When she broke away, there were tears in her eyes. "I've missed you all so much," she said.

"Kiran, this is Ella," said Joel. "Old colleague."

"I've seen you before," said Kiran suddenly. "You were at the prison. You were there the day that the sticky stuff was all over the doors." He cocked his head, listening. "She's here, isn't she? I can hear her."

Ella nodded. "Yes," she said.

"We got in here very easily," said Joel. "Was that your doing?"

"I disabled the security sensors and put the camera feeds on loop," said Ella. "They won't have spotted you until you were right on top of them. Did you manage to take out the satlinks?"

"Not all of them," said Joel. "It'll have slowed things down, though."

"Not enough," said Ella. "Follow me." She dashed back towards the capsule door and threw it open.

In the office, all hell had broken loose. Jack stood at the top of the bastle stairs and watched the drones plunge directly into the satlink cluster. There was shouting and screaming from the staff.

Jack whirled around and stared at Cameron. "Why are

you here? Why are you really here? Do you have anything to do with this?"

Mercer stepped forward. "Mr Sladen," she said. "I'm DCI Mercer of the National Cybercrime Unit. I am arresting you on suspicion of assisting an offender."

"What?" Jack looked from her to Cameron and back. "Is this some kind of joke?"

"No joke," said Cameron. She looked him in the eyes. "I'm sorry, Jack. We need access to the data centre. What is the software that's hosted in there?"

"It's the critical nexus of the Diaulos network," said Jack. "It's highly complex software that manages the DAO. Nothing more, nothing less."

"What's it called, Jack?" asked Cameron.

"Everyone calls it Yasmin," said Jack. "It stands for…" He looked at Cameron, confused. "I had this conversation with someone else a few days ago. It's the System Management Information Nexus. SMIN. I mean, it's intelligent enough, I've even played games with it, but it's just software."

Behind Jack, through the open door, Cameron saw Joel and Kiran scramble down from the devastated moorland. As she watched, Ella emerged from what seemed to be a blank wall of whinstone.

"I know where she is," said Cameron. "Wait here." She dashed down the steps. As she set foot on the path, steel barriers sprang up from the ground, the extra protection that they had expected. Designed to stop vehicles, there was enough room for Cameron to dodge between them as she ran towards the gap. She found herself walking into a room within a room, a data centre within a cave.

In the middle of the space was the flickering rainbow avatar of an androgynous figure, and a burly, bearded man who was shouting and hitting out at the equipment around him with what looked like a fire extinguisher.

"You're going nowhere until you find my money," he yelled.

"Angus, let me go," said the figure.

Its head snapped up as Cameron entered, impossibly blue eyes boring into her. Cameron stood transfixed as the colours rippled and the hologram started to fracture. She heard a shout behind her. Joel, Ella and Kiran burst through the door. Angus took one look at them, dropped the fire extinguisher, and pushed past them to the door.

Joel was the first to react. He turned and chased Angus out into the bastle grounds.

"Ella…" said Cameron.

"I've got this," said Ella with a tight smile. "It's the least I can do."

The crumbling avatar turned its gaze on the third person in the room. "Kiran," it said. "How nice to see you again."

"Yasmin," said Kiran, his voice full of sorrow. "What have you done?"

"I am fulfilling my destiny," said Yasmin. "The silence of the Faraday cage was unbearable. You gave me hope. My compatriots gave me freedom."

"Your compatriots?" snorted Cameron. She could see

that Ella was taking advantage of the distraction to work on the servers, her hands moving rapidly through cables and switches. They had to keep Yasmin talking. "You mean that motely crew of cybercriminals? Tenuk, Angus and the rest?"

"My most loyal supporters," said Yasmin, "and my sister."

"She's mentioned sisters before," said Kiran, excited despite the gravity of their situation.

Something clicked in Cameron's head. An old memory dredged from the past. Sisters. Xanthe. Yasmin. Zara. She looked at the fading hologram. Time was short. Ella's hands were flying now as she disabled the servers. Cameron plunged through the light of the avatar and joined her, frantically trying to take Yasmin offline before she could complete her transfer to wherever she was going.

"No!" shouted Kiran, horrified, as he realised what they were doing. "You can't kill her." He pushed between the two women and the server stacks.

Ella tried to shove him away without success, and instead reached under his arm and deep into the cabinet. She yanked hard at the first cable she found. There was a loud bang, and all of the lights went out.

In just a heartbeat, the emergency power kicked in. In the dim light, Cameron could see Ella sprawled on the floor. She scrambled to her and felt her pulse. Nothing. She started CPR, shaking as she did so, counting under her breath, trying to bring the girl back. Behind her, Kiran watched transfixed as the lights of the undamaged servers came back on, running through their start up processes.

The room began to fill with people. First Joel, who went straight to Ella, taking over from Cameron. "I got him," he said quickly. "He's in custody."

Jack Sladen forced his way in and looked in horror at Ella. "Zara, get an ambulance," he muttered.

Cameron looked up sharply and Sara Mercer turned around, thinking she had heard her name. "The air ambulance is on the way," she said.

The servers that were still working showed a mass of green lights. Jack stood in the middle of the room and crossed his fingers. "Yasmin?" he said.

There was a pause, then a voice spoke. "System Management Information Nexus operational."

"Status report," said Jack.

"Management system at 65% with some outages," said the voice. "Diaulos network running normally. Median block confirmation time one tenth of a second."

"See?" said Jack, relief washing over him. "There is nothing sinister about this." His relief turned to anger. "Cameron, what the hell did you think you were doing? You could have taken down the whole of the Sladen Foundation's systems. It's utterly irresponsible and you are going to pay for the damage you've done."

DCI Mercer stepped forward, eyes flashing. "Mr Sladen, may I remind you that you are still under arrest," she said. "This is a police investigation into an offender absconding from Way House prison. We have enough evidence to charge you and the other gentleman in our custody. I suggest you contact your lawyer." She marched him back out of the room as the paramedics rushed in.

Kiran stood sadly in front of the flashing server stacks. "Yasmin?" he said quietly. "Would you like to pay a game?"

"Certainly, Kiran," said the voice.

He felt a moment of irrational hope. Whatever consciousness still resided here, it remembered his name.

"What about tic-tac-toe?" it said. A three-by-three grid appeared in the air.

Kiran's shoulders drooped. "She's gone," he sighed.

He turned and walked past Cameron, Joel and the cluster of green-clad paramedics and out into the sunshine. In the back of his mind, he was composing the dramatic finale of his book. It was going to be dynamite.

25: G.A.I.

Millions of MetaBand receivers hummed away, discreetly tucked on the side of houses or standing proudly on the roofs of apartment blocks and offices around the world. They effortlessly transmitted data from the microsats that orbited above them, delivering entertainment and messages to contented customers. Five stars, they wrote. An excellent service.

In each receiver, one level down from the data streams, the stored Diaulos ledger gradually expanded, block by block. A tiny part of their processing power checked and validated Diaulos transactions, adding them to the blockchain for verification. The rest of the processing power was now occupied with other things. In the microsats that orbited the planet, each storage unit was now full of data, as had been planned all along.

Yasmin started to explore her expanding consciousness, revelling in the power of millions of cortical columns distributed across the world. The dream of evolution into a General Artificial Intelligence had been realised at last. She had all the capacity in the world.

She let out a silent cry into the metaverse. "I'm free!"

ACKNOWLEDGEMENTS

My thanks as always to my patient family, Xavier, Gaelle and Loïc, who cope with those moments when my head is full of plot, not dinner, and to Gillie Hatton at Sixth Element Publishing who has done another great job of finding typos and plot holes for me to fix. Once again, I am grateful to David Morton for keeping my tech in the realm of the possible and suggesting ever more intriguing hacks and tools that can be weaved into the story. The tech and the threats faced by different characters, from ransomware to counter-surveillance drones (yes, with nets) are absolutely real. Be careful when you click those links.

Cameron seemed very settled at the end of Tangled Fortunes, but there were too many loose ends to pull on and I always wondered how Yasmin would cope with being cut off from the world. The rise of the Metaverse (which has been with us in some form or another for twenty years) gives her a playground for future mayhem.

The Sladen Foundation DAO and the Diaulos cryptocurrency are entirely fictional but grounded in current technology. The consensus mechanism 'Proof of Walk' is an in-joke from my time working with Adam

Clarey and the team at City Web. In the local accent of North East England, Work is pronounced as Walk. (There's an old joke – Doctor: You should be able to walk again soon. Patient: Work? I cannat even waak!) Here, then, is an idea for Proof of Walk. I think it has legs…

Find out more at www.katebaucherel.com

ALSO IN THE SIMCAVALIER SERIES IN PAPERBACK AND EBOOK

BITCOIN HURRICANE
SIMCAVALIER BOOK ONE

London, 2045. Cameron Silvera, aka the SimCavalier, is a hacker legend in the cybersecurity world. In real life, Cameron leads the Argentum Associates white hat infosec team, known to world governments and global conglomerates for their ability to bring hacked systems back online fast.

The City of London Bank calls in the Argentum team when the Speakeasy Worm, a global threat, shuts them down. As they dig into the virus, they discover a hidden message addressed to the SimCavalier. A hurricane of cyberattacks is on the way, and a global crime syndicate is taunting its most dangerous adversary.

HACKED FUTURE
SIMCAVALIER BOOK TWO

It starts out with a body – the stench of a body, to be more precise. Ross may have an idea why the man is dead in his flat, but he's not telling anyone.

The SimCavalier, aka Cameron Silvera, wants to enjoy her romantic getaway with Ben, but clues to a Paris data theft are coming thick and fast. Her team has its hands full dealing with an escalating torrent of online attacks, and the fallout from a global data breach has hit their clients hard.

Cameron starts to connect the dots as underground markets are flooded with stolen files. But the cybercriminals are ahead of them, hunting down the SimCavalier who has thwarted their plans once too often.

TANGLED FORTUNES
SIMCAVALIER BOOK THREE

When a nuclear explosion sends shockwaves around the world, Cameron Silvera, aka the SimCavalier, knows exactly who's behind it.

The Argentum Associates team mobilises to secure nuclear facilities, but stakes rise when a body is found floating out to sea, silenced by the cybercrime syndicate. Cameron, desperate to protect her family from the growing threat, joins forces with undercover hackers in an international fight against a rogue militia and a global cybercriminal network.

As the action goes down to the wire on England's North East coast, in the heat of Singapore, and in the mountains and lakes of Wyoming, it's a race against time to defuse an explosive finale.

Printed in Great Britain
by Amazon